TOUCHED SERIES, BOOK 3

CENTAUR RIVALRY

NANCY STRAIGHT

Book design by Inkstain Interior Book Designing
Available electronically from all major bookstores.
Printed in paperback in 2013.

BOOKS BY NANCY STRAIGHT

MYTHOLOGY

TOUCHED SERIES

Blood Debt
Centaur Legacy
Centaur Rivalry
Centaur Redemption

Think Centaurs can't be sexy? Think Again!

PARANORMAL ROMANCE

DESTINY SERIES

Meeting Destiny
Destiny's Revenge
Destiny's Wrath

How many lifetimes are enough with your soul mate?

THRILLER/SUSPENSE

BREWER BROTHERS SERIES

His Frozen Heart
Fractured Karma
Shroud of Lies

Award-winning series!

CHAPTER 1

Camille – Deserted Motel in South Dakota

Bianca's eyes were huge as she stood frozen in the door frame. Her shrill voice could have shattered a vase if the cheap motel had one, "What the hell?!"

Gage took a step inside the doorway; his was a wordless reaction as he grabbed Bianca and yanked her behind him. They had just arrived in our remote hideaway in South Dakota, and from their reaction to seeing Drake, both had been unaware that he was no longer in human form. I wanted to shout, "Surprise," but no one would have appreciated the humor – especially Drake.

I eased myself in front of Drake, plastered a smile on my face, and made my expression as welcoming as possible. Though my voice was unsteady, I tried to at least control the tempo, so it wouldn't be too fast or too slow. "So, how was your trip?"

Gage's eyes glanced my way, but quickly returned to the towering Centaur standing behind me. Drake stood over seven feet tall; his bare chest was exposed – every muscle rigid. At his waist, the body of a brown horse now stood where his legs should have been. He was an imposing sight, and neither Bianca nor Gage had been prepared to see him like this. Both were too stunned to speak for an uncomfortable minute.

Drake's eyes went to the floor. He'd expected this reaction and told me we should have warned them ahead of time. Drake and Gage had been close friends growing up. If anyone would blindly accept his transformation, Drake hoped it would be Gage. Their reaction to seeing him as a true Centaur wounded him – he didn't need to say it out loud. I felt his pain.

Bianca peeked around Gage's tall shoulders. I'd missed her. Bianca reminded me of a living, breathing Barbie-doll. Her long blonde hair, bright blue eyes, and easy smile drew people to her. A quick flash of a memory sped through my mind.

She and I had been outside William's house shortly after I learned I was a Centauride. I was still learning about Centauride powers, and Bianca took it upon herself to teach me how to hide my thoughts from others. A smile emerged at the memory. The thoughts she was helping me to hide at the time were of Drake – *her* betrothed.

I shared this memory with her telepathically – when I did, her eyes lit up. She closed her eyes, and then pushed one of her memories to me. It was an image of Gage and her standing in the surf, exchanging their wedding vows. More than just an image, I felt the cool of the water on her feet, the heat from the sun beating down, and the smoothness of the sand between her toes. As her wedding day memory faded, she stepped away from her Centaur barrier, a.k.a Gage, and pulled me into a death grip of a hug.

The initial shock of seeing Drake had worn off, at least for Bianca. Gage and Drake both looked like they were ready to tackle the other if an aggressive move were made.

We had been through so much together in a short period of time – all four of us had. Bianca and I first met at my brother Bruce's wedding when she was engaged to Drake. Within days she decided Drake and I were destined for one another. She'd never told me why she believed it, but it probably had something to do with her being madly in love with Gage at the time. She didn't let the fact that she and Drake were already betrothed stop her from matchmaking.

Bianca had become my first friend after I found out I was a Centauride. I wanted to know everything that had happened since we separated after our escape from Zandra's house. What little glimpse she shared with me looked amazing, but it had been weeks since we saw each other. Bianca's voice answered in my head, "*I'll never be able to thank you enough.*"

I could have answered her telepathically, but Gage and Drake were still eyeing each other with concern. Speaking for Drake and me, "We're glad it worked out – for all of us."

Gage refused to take his eyes off of Drake.

Drake made it a habit of not moving around much in the cramped motel room. The less he moved, the less damage happened to the little room. Drake took a ginger step forward; one of his strides now was nearly the length of two of mine. This landed Drake squarely in front of Gage, towering nearly a foot over him.

Gage's mouth opened, but nothing came out. Bianca turned toward Gage, scolding him as if he were a child. "No more trying to catch snowflakes – we're inside. Close your mouth."

Drake slowly held out his hand to Gage. "Good to see you."

Gage's head bobbed in response, his cheeks flushed a deep red. He took Drake's extended hand, but no words escaped him.

I didn't want the awkwardness to grow, so I turned back to Bianca. "Tell me all about it. Don't leave out any details. You got married in the Caribbean?" I grabbed her forearm, motioning for her to sit beside me on the double bed closest to the door. "Start with when we dropped you at Gage's house."

Gage finally found his voice, "Bianca, dear, I think Camille may have more pressing things to share with us."

I played dumb because this was too good of a chance to waste. Looking up at Gage with the most perplexed expression I could find, I asked, "How do you mean? Oh, right, Zandra and I had a run in again, but she didn't throw me in her car's trunk this last time. I have a twin brother, Cameron. He seems okay, but I've only talked to him on the phone and he's at Zandra's estate – so I hope he's not locked up the way we were. It turns out I'm part of the Lost Herd, and Centaurs everywhere don't seem happy about it. Something else. . . what was it? I was sure I wanted to tell you. . . something."

Gage didn't appreciate my humor. "Funny, Camille! What happened to Drake?"

Drake's hoof did an involuntary stomp; the lamp closest to him, along with the window pane, rattled in fear. Drake's voice was quiet but clear, "Gage, ease up. I didn't know how to tell you when you called."

"A little warning would have been helpful. Something like, oh, by the way – I don't have feet anymore!"

"You were the one who wanted to come here. What was I supposed to say? I've put on a little weight; we're not sure if you'll want to hang out with us."

Gage shook his head in disbelief. Bianca and I watched the conversation between them. The last couple weeks as Drake told me of all the things he missed about his old life, not having Gage around had been the hardest for him. The two had been like brothers. The shock of seeing Drake's transformation without any warning ahead of time must have felt like some sort of a betrayal. Gage's voice was calmer when he asked, "How did this happen?"

Drake exhaled deeply, slicked his hand through his hair, gave a pained look in my direction, and answered, "Hercules' arrow."

"What?!" Gage's eyes darted between Drake's and mine. "You mean the stories of the Chirons having Hercules' arrow were true? How did it transform you into a Centaur?"

"From what I was told, Chiron put all his remaining magic in that arrow. He felt Cami was in danger, so this was his way of protecting his Centauride heir."

Disbelief echoed in Gage's voice, "From what you were told? Who told you that?"

Drake looked at me, trying to decide if he could trust Gage and Bianca with the truth. Finding out that he had had an actual conversation with Zeus would be hard for anyone to swallow. Drake's expression was torn. I used our telepathic connection and encouraged him, "*Tell them. I don't want to keep secrets from either of them. They can handle the truth.*"

Drake eased back from Gage, knocking the dresser that was behind him and rocking the television that was positioned on it. He let out a breath as his word hung in the air, "Zeus."

Gage grinned. "Zeus? Like the father of the gods? He talked to you?"

Drake nodded. "Yeah. After the arrow transformed me, I hoped it would somehow be able to change me back. I went to retrieve it from where I'd hidden it away, but Goddess Harmonia took it."

Confused, Gage asked, "Why did Goddess Harmonia want the arrow?"

"She said it never belonged to Chiron. It was Hercules' arrow and was too dangerous to remain on earth. She took it back to Hercules."

"I'm not following. When did you talk to Zeus?"

Drake's eyes fell on me. He'd never told me the whole story, so I hung on his words just as the others did. His hand slid along the smooth surface of the dresser beside him. "I was angry. Cami had just found me. I thought maybe the arrow. . . I thought I could get my life back."

Drake's gaze settled on Gage, "After Harmonia took it I got mad and cursed the gods."

"You what?!"

"I don't know what all I said, but I cursed them. When I did, Zeus reminded me of his Centaur tenet. I told him to strike me down because my life was over anyway." He dropped Gage's stare and looked at me. "I couldn't bear the thought of losing Cami, again."

"He didn't impose a death sentence? Your punishment for cursing the gods was to remain a Centaur Warrior?"

"No. Zeus let the curse go. He even offered to turn me back to human." The three of us stared at Drake for a second before he continued, "Zeus told me I wouldn't be strong enough to protect Cami if I were a human. He said he could turn me back, but the only way to protect her was to stay a warrior. He was right. A couple nights ago, a few hours before you called me, we had just been attacked by thirty Centaurs. There's no way we would have survived if I had been in human form."

Gage's eyes opened wide as surprise colored his voice, "You *chose* to stay like this?"

"I had to." Drake's voice was solemn as he confessed, "I couldn't protect Cami when I was in a human form. Remember Phineas?"

Gage nodded. How could any of us forget Phineas? While I was under house arrest at Zandra's estate, Phineas had been one of my guards. He was the one who helped me find Drake and Bianca, then helped us escape.

"Phineas is the leader of the Lost Herd. He and several other Centaurs kidnapped Cami and left me for dead when we first arrived in South Dakota."

"Wait! Why am I just now hearing about all of this?"

"You two were out of the country. We started out in Ireland, then Cami's great-uncle told us we needed to go to South Dakota to find her twin brother. Right after we arrived she was kidnapped by Phineas. Cami's family came to South Dakota to help me search for her. Even

Zandra was in on trying to find her, but Phineas was smarter than that and got her away from here before everyone arrived."

Bianca looked mortified when she interrupted, "How did you find her?"

Drake confessed, "I didn't. None of us found her. We searched for days and kept coming up empty." He dropped Bianca's gaze and looked at me when he finished, "She freed herself."

Bianca's confusion was evident, "So, tell me again. Why do you look like a horse?"

Drake crossed his arms; his biceps bulged and his expression turned rigid. "Don't you see? A few Centaurs took me by surprise and I almost lost her. Once word gets out that she's descended from the Lost Herd, it won't be just three or four Centaurs after her. I couldn't take the chance of losing her, again."

Bianca eyed him skeptically. Before she could ask him another question, I pushed the memory of the thirty Centaurs who had ambushed us at Cameron's house two nights before. Gage needed the same information even though I couldn't *show* him what had happened. Reiterating what Drake had already told them, "Thirty Centaurs attacked us two nights ago while we were hiding out at Cameron's house. The only reason we're still together is because Drake chose this form and was able to fight our way out."

After watching the memory of our escape, she answered me, "*Okay, I get why he did it, but what kind of a future do you two have?*"

Without an ounce of hesitation, I answered, "*Our future. We're together, that's all that matters.*" My hand clumsily reached for Drake's. His was warm and strong as it wrapped itself around mine.

Drake and Gage couldn't hear us, but both must have sensed Bianca and I were talking because neither said a word. She asked, "Will Zeus turn him back into a human when the danger has passed?"

My teeth sunk into my lip. "No. Zeus told Drake it was permanent." Although answering Bianca, I turned toward Drake and squeezed his hand that was still holding mine. "We've been through too much together. I chose him, and he chose this form to keep us alive. When it's safe, he'll be human again. I don't know how I know – I just know."

Bianca didn't look like she believed me. I would have been more concerned if she were a seer. The future didn't lay itself out in front of her the way it did for Gretchen, Lacey and me.

Just then a car pulled into the parking lot in front of the motel. Our room wasn't in a direct line of sight to the parking lot. The door to the little room we were all crammed in was still ajar. When Gage and Bianca arrived, they'd been too stunned to close it all the way, so all four of us heard the car pull up. No one moved. The motel was closed for the season and was remote. There wasn't a gas station or store around for miles; with the recent snow, it was nearly impossible to see it from the little mountain highway. I reached out with my mind, trying to identify who was here and what they wanted.

No, it couldn't be.

CHAPTER 2

Camille – Deserted Motel in South Dakota

Both Gage and Drake were peeking out the corner of the window to try to get a better view, before Bianca and I said in stereo, "What's Brent doing here?" We shared a giggle, then both of us said, "jinx ya'," again, in stereo. The giggles morphed into actual laughter.

Brent's voice shouted from the parking lot, "Drake! I want to see for myself! Show yourself!"

I looked over at Drake; he shrugged his shoulders, but made no move for the door.

Brent didn't relent. He stood in the middle of the parking lot, facing the abandoned motel and yelled so loudly that birds perched in the trees above took flight. "I know you're here. The car engine is still warm." I reached out with my mind and saw he was alone.

Gage pressed his lips together and raised his eyebrows as he mouthed the words, "I'm sorry." There was no reason for him to feel sorry for parking their car in front of the abandoned motel. We would have done the same if we had one.

Brent shouted again, still facing the little motel. "Dammit Drake! My brothers have picked on me my whole life. I just need to know if it's true or if they're screwing with me."

I let go of Drake's hand, put my hand on Drake's cheek and gave him a half-smile. "I'll talk to him. He already knows." As I grabbed the handle to go outside, Drake placed his hand lightly over the top of mine. His touch was soothing, a wordless gesture telling me it would be okay. He opened his mouth as if he had something to say, but held the door open for me instead. The bitter cold forced me to step back into the room, reach around him, and grab my coat off of the chair.

The little motel had a block of ten rooms that faced the parking lot and a second block of rooms directly behind the first building. The two little buildings were separated by a covered sidewalk. The night Drake and I had come here, we purposely chose one of the rooms that was next to impossible to see from the front, just in case someone happened by. Because the sidewalk between the two buildings was covered, there was no snow to give away our footprints leading into the room.

I sprinted down the sidewalk toward the parking lot. When I peered over my shoulder, Drake had left the door cracked. He could be at my side in the blink of an eye if I needed him. I rounded the corner to the parking lot and shouted, "Brent!" Once I had his attention, more quietly I chided, "Keep your voice down. What are you doing here?"

A Cheshire-cat grin spread over his face. "Looking for you and Drake."

"Okay, Inspector Gadget, you found us. In case Will didn't tell you – we're hiding out."

Brent stood up straight, still smirking, "Yeah, I heard." He looked around our desolate hideout, "Nice hiding place. The only ones that'll find you here are the elk and the rabbits." His eyes took in the decades-old structure. The front window sported a huge crack in the glass with thick gray duct tape holding it in place. The snow-covered sign barely showed the message that the motel would be closed until Memorial Day. Brent didn't say anything about its condition. Instead he asked, "Did you hear Beau married a Centauride from California?"

I couldn't help but smile. Lacey had chosen him, but I didn't know they had already married. "Lacey. Yeah, that was fast. Do you know where they took off to?"

Brent shook his head and jammed his exposed hands into his pockets. "To the winds. They flew into Charleston, packed up Beau's stuff, and said goodbye – then they were gone."

I placed my hand on Brent's shoulder. He flinched but didn't pull away. I wasn't sure that he was used to the idea of having a sister, and like most unbetrothed Centaurs, he shied away from the touch of any woman. Of my five brothers, Brent was the closest to my age – only a year older than I was. He was also the one who openly disapproved of me having grown up as a human. Brent was quick to judge and had no tolerance for any actions that were outside of acceptable Centaur traditions.

I wasn't sure how much he knew, so I stayed with a safe topic. "You were right, Brent. Remember when you showed me the rolled up family tapestry in your room? It was staring at us the whole time. You knew we were part of the Lost Herd."

Brent shook his head, "I didn't know for sure. When you showed up, I couldn't understand how I had a half-sister. Up until then, it was just a coincidence that our lineage happened to trace back to a Centaur named Rupert – I mean, there were probably lots of Ruperts, right?"

"But you knew as soon as I came to South Carolina?"

"Sure – I think we all did. I kept expecting guards from the Centaur Council to storm the house, especially when Dad introduced you to everyone at Bruce's wedding. The first Centaur tenet is pretty clear: A Centaur shall only claim one wife. There shall be no divorce, and death shall not break their bond."

"But Will didn't marry *my* mom, so, technically, he didn't break the first tenet."

Brent shook his head, "No, Zeus's tenet 'shall only claim one wife,' means no girlfriend on the side, either. These were rules set down by Zeus himself. Up until Zeus changed Centaurs to look like humans, it was common for a Centaur to have a bunch of wives. They were warriors and Centaurs had a pretty short life expectancy. Once we had to blend in with the humans, one wife was enough. For Dad to break a rule like that, he couldn't have been one of Zeus's Centaurs – he had to be of the Lost Herd."

I was skeptical of Brent's logic. "So, no Centaurs ever have affairs?"

Brent shook his head, "No. I remember hearing stories when I was a kid about Centaurs who had tried a long time ago. All were dealt with severely. The only way Dad could have had an affair and not been struck down was for him to be a member of the Lost Herd."

"But why?"

"When Zeus changed all Centaurs to human form, he gave them seven rules to live by. If any Centaur were to break one of the seven tenets, the penalty can be death. Breaking one of the tenets is like spitting in Zeus's face – he just knows."

"Death?"

"No one ever breaks the seven tenets."

Something had been bothering me, and Brent might have a theory on this one, too. "So how did the Lost Herd take a human form? If they were cast out before Zeus made Centaurs look human – shouldn't we all still have hooves?"

"I don't know, Cami – but we need to find out."

"So, technically, the Lost Herd doesn't need to abide by the seven tenets?"

"I guess not. Our ancestors had a death sentence put on their heads as soon as Zeus cast them out of the pasture of Thessaly. The fact that we're here proves that a god had to have gone against Zeus's wishes and helped hide us for all these years. Part of hiding us must have been to allow us to blend in with the humans like the other herds."

Brent's explanation made sense, sort of, but it brought a new question to the forefront. "Why would Will have introduced me at Bruce's wedding? Why wouldn't he have hidden me away? He had to know that others would realize."

"None of us knew what to think. Dad said he had a daughter, and we thought maybe he was trying to cover for another Centaur or something."

"So, you didn't believe I was really your sister?"

"Mom and Dad told me you were my sister. Maybe they had had you in secret somehow and then hid you away. Believe me, I had all kinds of scenarios in my head."

I shook my head at him. "You thought Gretchen and Will had me then hid me away? That's the dumbest thing I've ever heard."

My cheeks were getting numb from the cold, and I couldn't feel my toes. I stomped a couple times to try to encourage blood flow. Brent moved closer to me, almost whispering, "You have to understand, that was more palatable than the alternative. I never expected to hear we were of the Lost Herd and would soon be wearing a death sentence of our own."

I remembered a conversation I had had with my mother's spirit before she left for the pasture. Since we were sharing confessions, I looked away and decided to share what she had told me. "Will purposely seduced Mom. He even told her so after."

"What?! No way."

I wasn't sure how much Brent knew, but for some reason I needed to tell him. Will had gone out of his way to help Drake and me, but I still didn't trust him, and I needed Brent to know why. "It's true. She told me that before Will left to return to South Carolina he came clean.

He told her about Gretchen. He told her he'd been ordered to seduce her and father a set of Chiron twins."

Doubt was written all over Brent's face. "That makes no sense. Why would he do that?"

"I think it was the Lost Herd's way of announcing to Zeus that they weren't extinct. The leader was banking on the fact that no one would kill Cameron and me – since we were the last set of twins from Chiron's line."

"Who's the leader of the Lost Herd?"

"That's the kicker. He was one of my guards when I was at Zandra's house. His name's Phineas. He lives in Melbourne, Florida. I don't know his last name, but he helped us escape from Zandra's."

Brent stiffened, "Wait. Phineas? Phineas is the leader of the Lost Herd?"

"You know him?" I felt my eyebrows raise, "Beau had never heard of him."

"Phineas and Dad are related, I think. I met him once. Dad flew me to Disney World for my birthday when I was like eight. It was just the two of us. We were in line for the log ride when a huge Centaur named Phineas introduced himself to me. He told me he was my uncle. After Phineas left, Dad said not to mention it to anyone – Mom didn't like him. None of my brothers were with us on that trip."

Brent scanned the abandoned parking lot. "Where's Drake?"

"He's inside." Trying desperately not to sound like a jerk, I asked, "What're you doing here?"

"Camille, didn't you hear me? Our whole family has disappeared. They're gone."

"You mean they've gone into hiding, right?"

Brent's gaze shifted to the iced over asphalt. "Dad gave me cash, an account in the Caymans, a passport, a birth certificate with a new name, and told me to leave." Brent rubbed one of his eyes as if some dust were in it. I leaned over to give him a hug, but he pulled away. "I want to see Drake."

My teeth sank hard into my lower lip. The fewer Centaurs who saw Drake, the safer we were. "It might be better if you didn't."

"So it's true? Beau told me before he and Lacey left. I didn't believe him. I wanted to see for myself."

I nodded. "How'd you find us?"

"Beau said you two were still in South Dakota. I didn't have anywhere else to go, so I came here. I saw Gage and Bianca when they arrived at the airport, so I followed them. I couldn't think of any other reason that they would be here. I tried to hang back so they wouldn't know I was following them, but I lost them near the base of the mountain. I was just getting ready to turn around when I saw a set of tire tracks in the snow on the highway's off ramp and took a chance that the tire tracks were from their car. They're here, too, right?"

If Brent really did know about Drake's transformation, it wouldn't be nearly the shock that Gage and Bianca had. He and Drake had spent an afternoon on Will's yacht with Bianca and me – they were friends, too. "What exactly did Beau tell you?"

Brent lowered his voice, not that there was anyone here to hear us. "Beau says he's a real Centaur. He's like eight feet tall and even faster than before."

"He's over seven feet tall and, yes, he's beyond fast."

An unfamiliar voice shouted at us from the tree line. "Whatcha doin' here? Got car trouble?"

We both froze, but it had nothing to do with the temperature.

CHAPTER 3

Camille – Deserted Motel in South Dakota

What was this, Grand Central Station? A young woman wearing a white ski parka and matching snow pants emerged from the tree line. Bright red hair fell around her face from under her jacket's hood. It wasn't curly, but it wasn't straight, either. She wore half a grimace; I couldn't tell if she was angry or if it was an expression against the cold. Her rounded face and big eyes were attractive, but not in a beauty queen way. She wore no make-up, and her skin was nearly as white as the snow.

I mentally reached out to her the same way Bianca had taught me months ago. It only took seconds to know she wasn't a Centauride, and I breathed a sigh of relief. I didn't detect anyone else near her.

Brent was the first to recover from our unexpected visitor. "We got lost and were looking for a map."

Her voice sounded skeptical, "Lookin' for a map, outside your cars?" Brent's car was pulled in right beside Bianca and Gage's.

Where had this woman come from? People don't just appear out of the woods, not in temperatures like this. I looked behind her to confirm she was alone. Her question hung in the air a few seconds too long.

She eyed us suspiciously. "If yer up here snoopin' for the Henderson brothers, ya can tell 'em the same thing I already told 'em – it's not fer sale."

Brent snapped back, "We weren't snooping."

Her tone said more than her words as she looked at the uncovered portion of the sidewalk. "There are an awful lot of footprints here for jus' the two of ya."

Panic grabbed me when I looked around the property. My mind flashed to the other night when we'd been surrounded by Centaurs at Cameron's house. I looked around and saw the only footprints belonged to Gage, Bianca, Brent and me. I let out a breath and answered, "Sorry, we aren't from around here. My friend and her husband looked around back to see if a map was posted somewhere."

"Uh huh, where are yer friends?"

"Good question." Hoping they were paying attention to our unexpected visitor, I yelled, "Gage? Bianca? Hey, where'd you two go?"

Bianca was the first to come around the corner. She answered, "Right here. There's no map around back." Bianca could have been an actress when she looked at the red-headed human and looked almost startled. "Oh, hi." She held out her hand to the stranger and gave the woman her best southern belle impersonation, "Shame on me for my manners. I'm Bianca Richardson." She held out her hand, gesturing to Gage trailing her, "And this is my husband, Gage. It's so very nice to make your acquaintance."

I hadn't heard anyone talk like that the whole time I was down south. She sounded just like the ladies in the movie *Steel Magnolias*, and it took every bit of control I had not to giggle. The woman accepted Bianca's hand, but looked stunned. Bianca didn't ease back on the southern charm for even a half a second. "I see you've met Cami and Brent Strayer already."

"Uh, yeah."

Bianca gestured to the snow-covered forests surrounding the little motel, "This place is just gorgeous. Do you come here often?"

The woman sounded skeptical, but answered. "Lived here my whole life. It's only gorgeous if yer inside looking at it through a window. So, where you guys from?"

Bianca had been larger than life for as long as I had known her. She had a way of quickly becoming the center of attention – which was exactly what we needed. "Charleston. Charleston, South Carolina, and I'm afraid none of us see snow very often. We couldn't help but do some exploring. I hope we weren't any trouble?"

The stranger shook her head. "No. No trouble at all. This place is pretty remote. I wanted ta make sure no one was tryin' ta break inta the motel."

"Oh, I'm sure the owner appreciates a conscientious caretaker like yourself. Do you live nearby?"

"I *am* the owner. My place is jus' through the tree line." She gestured over her shoulder, but I couldn't make out anything beyond the thick evergreens. "Now, do ya need some directions back ta town or somethin'?"

"You're the owner? Well, isn't that something!" Charm still oozed from each of Bianca's words.

The red-haired woman grinned, "I won it in a card game a few years ago over in Deadwood."

Brent had been oblivious up until this point, but her last comment caught his attention. He looked impressed, "A card game? You won a motel? What was your ante?"

"None of yer business!" She shot him a glare and Brent immediately looked away.

He mumbled more to himself than to anyone else, "Must have been a hell of a hand."

She had heard his mumble and responded full of pride, “It was a bluff, but it worked.”

Bianca was still all smiles, “Well, thank you for the warning. I’ll make sure to keep Gage away from Deadwood. It sounds like it might be teaming with card sharks.”

A little more at ease with the four of us, “Naw. It’s jus’ for the locals. Tourists don’t ever get invited inta those games.”

Brent was quick to add. “I’ve played poker a time or two. Any chance my tourist status could be overlooked?”

The woman rolled her eyes, “I’m sure yer wife wouldn’t appreciate me takin’ ya into town and takin’ all yer money.”

“My wife?!” Brent’s eyes grew to the size of quarters. “She’s not my wife.” He raised an accusatory finger in my direction, “She’s my sister. I’m not married.”

The woman blushed then looked at me. I confirmed my status with a short nod. She looked Brent over in a not so subtle way. “Maybe. I can call inta town ta see if the regulars are getting’ together. But it’s high stakes. Migh’ be a little rich for yer blood.”

Brent was beyond excited. Bianca cut him off before he could answer, “I’m sorry, I didn’t catch your name?”

“Katherine. Katherine Newton.”

“Katherine, I know your place is closed down for the season, but we absolutely adore it. Is there any chance you’d consider renting a few rooms? Just for a few days? We promise not to be any trouble.”

Katherine looked at the four of us, and I felt a big fat “no” coming on. She shook her head, “Ya can’t get up and down the mountain pass withou’ chains, doncha know?” Katherine looked at the two cars in her motel’s parking lot and added, “At least not mos’ days. The only way around up here this time a year is with snowmobiles and ATVs. There’s nothing ta eat and nowhere ta cook excep’ the office kitchen. Sorry.”

Gage spoke up for the first time. "Bianca and I are newlyweds. It would only be for a few days. I'm sure we could run into town and find some supplies today while the road is clear."

Katherine shook her head, "You're not listening. Today is a nice day. I'm gonna make a trip inta town for groceries, but the weather changes aroun' here quick. If I let you stay, I'd have ta feed ya, too. There's a good chance ya wouldn't even be able to make it down the mountain a few days from now."

Gage gave her a winning smile. "I think we can make it worth your while." He pulled a wad of cash out of his pocket. "Bianca loves it here. Is there a place nearby where we could rent snowmobiles or ATVs?"

Katherine looked at the wad of cash in Gage's hand. "Did ya guys rob a bank or somethin'? Who carries that kind of cash aroun' with 'em?"

We all laughed. Thinking we were felons on the run was preferable to the truth. Bianca cut in, "I promise, we won't be any trouble at all. I'm a great cook. Point me to the kitchen."

Katherine shook her head as if she intended to say "no," but kept her eyes trained on Gage, "How long would ja want ta stay?"

Bianca answered, "A week, tops. Please say yes." Her blue eyes sparkled and her blonde curls bounced around her face. It was impossible to tell her no.

"All right. I guess it wouldn't be bad ta have some company for a few days." She looked at Brent when she added, "It gets pretty lonely aroun' here."

From all my conversations with Brent, I don't know what I expected, but seeing his complexion blush a deep red was not anything I anticipated. Katherine didn't let up, as her eyes remained trained on Brent's, "So, does one of ya want to ride along ta town and help me pick up supplies?"

Gage recognized the invitation for Brent. Bianca attempted to take a step forward, but Gage held her in place and answered, "Brent, why don't you accompany Katherine? Bianca and I will go into town and see if we can trade our rental car for something with four-wheel drive."

Katherine's eyes darted to me. "You can come along, too, if ya want." Although it was a gracious offer, I liked the idea of Brent blushing.

"If it's okay with you, I'll just stay here. Maybe catch a nap or something."

Katherine looked skeptical but not enough to press it. "All righ'. Come on." Katherine walked toward the office and motioned for me to follow. She unlocked the front door, walked behind the counter and pulled the keys out for rooms one, two and three. "Clean sheets are in the top drawers of the dressers. We should be back in a couple hours." She paused for a minute before returning to the others. Her eyes were bright green. She asked, "Ya said he's yer brother?"

"Yes. Brent's a year older than I am."

Katherine cocked her head to the side, "What's his story?"

I knew little about her, but I liked that she was blunt. Just what Brent needed in his life: a human who spoke her mind. My smile grew. She had no idea that he might be the toughest nut to crack on the planet. "Twenty-four, college degree in finance, no girlfriend, a little on the arrogant side – overall a nice guy."

She looked at the floor. I waited for a question that apparently she decided not to ask. Instead she answered, "All right. We'll see."

I wasn't sure what to make of her comment, but she handed me the key to room one and I followed her out of the office. Bianca and Gage waved excitedly as they drove away. Brent stood next to me on the curb as Katherine pulled up in a huge Ford pickup. I gestured to Katherine's passenger side door as Brent looked almost panicked. His voice was low and his words fast, "You have to come, Cami. I can't be alone with a woman. What if a Centauride saw us?"

"Relax, Brent. Centaurides are the least of your worries right now. Besides, it would be good for you to be around humans for a while.

You're going to have to blend in soon. Think of Katherine as a crash course in being a human."

Brent gave an annoyed huff, "I've been around humans. I went to public school."

"Yeah, now you're actually going to have to talk to one. She's fine. It's good practice."

Brent rolled his eyes. "Fine, but if she comes on to me, what am I supposed to do?"

"Don't flatter yourself. She's taking you along to help carry groceries." I scribbled Drake's cell on a piece of paper I found in my pocket. "Call me if you need us. I'll see you when you get back." Brent climbed into Katherine's truck, and they pulled away. Once they were completely out of sight, I went back to the room where we'd left Drake.

I slid the cracked door open. As long as we had been out front, I half expected him to have run for the cover of the woods. He stood just inside the door where we had left him. His eyes were full of worry, his voice solemn as he asked, "What was going on?"

"We met the motel's owner. Gage and Bianca convinced her to open the place up for us for a week."

His eyelids were heavy. I didn't know if he'd gotten any sleep at all the last two days. My hand instinctively went to his face. I wished that I could ease some of his worry. His eyes snapped open at my touch, and he stammered, "Okay, I won't be far."

"Wait, what do you mean you won't be far? Where are you going?"

"I can't stay here. What if the owner sees me?"

"It's fine. She gave me the key to a room at the front of the motel. She doesn't know we've been using this room."

"We can't risk it. I'll keep an eye on you from the tree line." Drake leaned in and gently pressed his lips to my forehead.

It didn't sound like my voice that answered; it was too weak – fragile. "Don't leave me. Stay."

Drake gathered me in his arms, "I'll be close. I promise."

He was right. It was risky for him to stay here, but no riskier than anything else we'd done. I loved the feeling of his warmth. Since his transformation, Drake had kept a distance from me. He remained close enough to protect me, but not close enough to stave off the loneliness. So much had happened. Katherine's words "*It gets lonely around here,*" rang true for me, too.

I gripped him tightly, refusing to let him leave. I didn't need to argue with him; he heard my silent message. Drake rested his chin on the top of my head. "Okay. I'll stay until the others return."

I didn't like the idea of him by himself in the woods, but arguing the point now would accomplish nothing. I caressed his shoulder, "You're tired. Why don't you get some rest? I'll stay awake so you can sleep."

Drake shook his head, but I cut him off before he could speak. "You haven't slept in almost two days. How are you going to protect me if you pass out on your feet?"

His hands glided from my shoulders to my elbows. "I'm fine, Love."

I walked over to the head of both beds and threw all the pillows onto the floor. I motioned to the space on the floor between the two beds. "If you won't sleep, will you hold me?"

Drake's expression was pained. His chest spread wide as he inhaled deeply. "Cami, I. . ."

I cut him off before he could argue. "I miss how close we were in Ireland, waking up each morning to your eyes looking back at mine. Your arms around me. . . I just miss it."

Drake eased over to where I stood. His hand rose to cup my jaw. His thumb lightly caressed my chin while his eyes fell from mine. "We need to think practically. Ireland was a long time ago."

My voice was quiet, but I kept it from shaking. "Not so long."

The sorrow in his eyes dug deeper, "It was a lifetime ago."

"Only if we let it be a lifetime ago. I know *this*," I let my hand run along the horse part of his body, "is only temporary. Don't let it come between us."

"Cami. . . it's who I am now."

I had held it together since the first moment I saw him in the moonlight. The joy of finding him alive outweighed the pain of discovering his transformation. I hadn't shed a single tear that night or any of the nights after. I hadn't considered turning my back on him. But more than his body had changed that night –he no longer saw me as *his Centauride;* he saw me as his responsibility. I wanted him to look at me the way he did before –like I was his whole life – like the world would stop spinning if I weren't in it.

My voice barely more than a whisper, "You're still you." My chest tightened and my eyes threatened to let loose.

"Open your eyes, Cami. Things have changed."

The first tear streaked down my cheek without any warning. A second and a third rolled free. I turned my back to him, burying my face in my hands. I wouldn't have been able to see Drake through my tears anyway, and my voice wouldn't work enough to argue. I wanted to escape, to find a dark corner and hide – to give myself over to the loneliness. I bolted toward the door, but Drake grabbed me before I could turn the handle.

He pulled me tight against him, my back tucked snug to his chest, his arms anchoring me in place. Drake's chin rested on the top of my head as he whispered, "I'm here, Love. I'm right here."

I tried to pull away, but his arms wouldn't budge. I didn't want to hear things had changed or everything we'd gone through had been for nothing. I'd lost Mom, my family had to go into hiding because of me, I had a twin brother I might never meet, and I would be hunted every day for the rest of my life. Even if Drake stayed with me, I would live out the rest of my life alone. All of this was my reality, and for the first time in my life, I wasn't strong enough to accept it.

His words tried to soothe me. "Shhhh, I'm not going anywhere. I'll be here as long as you need me. Don't cry." They had the opposite effect, and I cried harder. I had held everything in for too long. I tried to remember the last time I'd cried – it had been when Zandra told me Drake was dead. The idea that I had lost him nearly destroyed me. As I stood in this motel room, maybe I had lost him after all.

The life I saw for the two of us – was it really gone? He couldn't stay like this forever. I choked out between the sobs, "It's only temporary. It's not forever. Say it's only temporary." He couldn't have understood my pleas through the sobs.

His arms gripped me harder; I felt his lips on my ear. His gentle kiss warmed me. If I closed my eyes, I could pretend things were normal: Drake holding me tight – the plans for our future.

After several minutes, my own private implosion began to subside. I wiped my cheeks dry but couldn't turn around. If there were pity in his eyes, it would break me, and I would never recover.

I needed him and, whether he knew it or not, he needed me, too. Drake tugged my shoulders to turn me to face him, but I refused to move. He lifted me off my feet and cradled me in his arms. I buried my face in his chest as he eased me onto the awaiting pile of pillows on the floor. I wound my arms around his neck while I felt his breath against mine.

I finally found my voice, "Say it. Say it's only temporary."

A heavy sigh escaped Drake, but no words. I pulled my face away from his chest. My eyes were swollen and his face was blurry, but I stared into his eyes, forcing him to hear me. "It's only temporary. You won't be like this forever. We have a future."

For the first time in weeks, the smolder in his eyes was back. He had the same desire burning through that first made my knees buckle. When

Drake found his voice, it was clear and confident, "I'll take any future I'm given, so long as you're in it. No regrets."

Drake's lips found mine; not the tentative kisses we'd shared since his transformation – a kiss that screamed of his love for me. His lips crushed hard against mine. His fingers wove into my hair as my body's raw desire responded to his touch. We lay on the floor wrapped up in each other's arms, both reminding the other of the love that would trade anything, be anything, endure any amount of pain for the love of the other.

CHAPTER 4

Camille – Small Town in South Dakota

The bar had a brick front with two small blacked-out windows. It was nothing special to look at sandwiched in between Murray's Grocery Store and Vic's Laundromat. From the outside it looked dark and empty inside. A few people passed by it on the street without even giving it a second look. I questioned whether Katherine had sent us on a wild goose chase when she'd told us to meet her here. She had mentioned Deadwood earlier, but that was forty miles away. Had she mixed up the address?

I sat in the truck, teetering on the edge of returning to the motel. This was the first time I'd been away from Drake since we'd decided to meet at Cameron's house almost three weeks ago. My whole life, I'd never felt like I needed protection from anything or anyone, but here, now, with just Brent, I couldn't help the uneasy feeling.

Two nights ago, when the Centaurs had stormed Cameron's house, was the first time it had sunk in that we were in real danger. That was at least ten towns from here, but what if those Centaurs were searching for us? I still didn't know who they were, who had sent them, or what they wanted.

Brent was oblivious to the fear I felt, his voice brimming with excitement, "Look, there's Katherine's truck. She must already be inside. Let's go." My gaze followed his extended finger. Her truck was parked one side-street over on the far side of the little grocery store. As I sat in the cab of the truck, I couldn't shake my uneasy feeling.

When Brent came back from his shopping trip with Katherine, he was much more relaxed around her. After dinner, Brent and Katherine were rarin' to go to town for an impromptu poker game. I wasn't all that interested in going, but we couldn't let Brent go with just Katherine. If anything happened to him, I'd never forgive myself.

After Katherine's warning earlier, Gage and Bianca decided not to take any unnecessary chances if we needed a fast escape, so they traded in their compact car for a full-sized four-wheel drive pick-up. They insisted Brent and I take their truck into town tonight, which left them with Brent's rental car at the motel.

Bianca and Gage opted to stay at the motel. Gage handed the truck keys to me for the trip into town, and I thought Drake was going to have a melt-down. Despite Drake's protest, Brent reasoned that if we didn't go, Katherine would be suspicious. We googled the sleepy little town on Bianca's phone; its population was fewer than a thousand people: two bars, a restaurant, a bank, three churches, and two gas stations – not exactly a thriving metropolis.

Drake's words to me as I walked out the door, "I can't lose you again," were on a constant replay in my mind. The look in his ice blue eyes as I closed the motel room door haunted me. I was tempted to turn around and go back to the motel, but Brent was already waiting outside the passenger side door of the truck where we had parked on the quiet street. I took a breath and murmured to myself, "Hopefully he loses quickly."

When I volunteered to go with Brent, it was because Gage and Bianca wanted to plan a strategy with Drake for our trip to Africa. I was even a little excited because this would give me some quality time with Brent. When I'd first arrived in South Carolina, Brent was the brother who was closest to my age, met me at the airport, and spent the most time with me.

I'd grown very close to Beau in the short time we'd spent together in South Dakota. His absence left a hole in me. Having Brent here was like having a small piece of home. Home. What was that, anyway? All those years I'd grown up with just Mom. After her death, I was lucky enough to learn about the rest of my family: Will, Beau, Bart, Ben, Bruce, Brent, even Gretchen. Given everything that had happened since finding them – I wondered just how lucky I was.

The last couple months had felt like a runaway roller coaster. I had just barely gotten to know my brothers when Zandra yanked me away from everyone and held me hostage. Phineas helped Drake and me escape Zandra's house, and Will helped us get to Ireland. It took us a week to find my great-uncle Zethus, only to find out that the whole trip was for nothing because he didn't have Hercules' arrow, and he sent us empty-handed to South Dakota. I got kidnapped a second time – strangely enough by Phineas, the one who had helped me escape Zandra. I was able to free myself only to come back and to find Drake was a Centaur. For added fun, the father of gods, Zeus, reiterated a millenniums' old death decree on my family.

The odds had been stacked against me from the moment I made that first phone call to Will. I needed a break – to catch my breath. Brent was waving his hand in front of the windshield where I sat, "Hello, earth to Cami." It worked – he'd popped me out of my own little pity party. A night out with Brent could be just what I needed. I reached for the door handle and froze.

Across the street, the door to the little bar where Katherine had told us to meet her opened. Light flooded out from the bar illuminating his face. He was on the sidewalk holding the door handle. I couldn't help myself. I would know that face anywhere. Scrambling to open the door, I yanked the handle hard and threw all my weight at the door when I screamed, "Daniel!"

He stopped and looked behind him, but we were a block away, and he didn't see me. He must have decided he'd been hearing things because he went inside the bar, allowing the door to shut behind him. Brent was in mid-sentence, but I didn't care. I jumped out of the truck, sprinted the block to the bar, threw open the door and searched the faces in the smoky room. His back was to me, but I recognized his silhouette immediately.

Creeping up behind him, I wrapped my arms around him and buried my head against his shoulder blades. The words were out before I even gave a thought to them, "I worried I'd never see you again."

His body turned stiff under my touch. Daniel didn't move, but his voice questioned, "Cami? Cami?!" I squeezed him tighter from behind. Daniel whipped around and drew me in a tight bear hug. When I was ready to beg for air, he lifted me up off the floor then brought me back hard into his chest. I might as well have been a rag doll. It was Daniel. He was here. In the middle of this frozen tundra, he had appeared just when I needed him the most.

My Centauride senses kicked in as the hairs on my arms stood on end. There was a Centaur here. . . wait, not a Centaur . . . a Centauride.

Behind the bar stood the tallest Centauride I'd ever seen. She might have been an Amazon – she was well over six feet tall. Her hair was platinum blonde – the color you can only get from a box. Her make-up was meticulously applied with dark smoky blues on her eyes and a rich red on her lips.

Every Centauride I'd met had a conservative, almost demure look about them – this Centauride looked nothing like the Centaurides I'd seen before. She had a "celebrity-look" about her as if she were on loan from Hollywood.

Brent was oblivious to the tall blonde Centauride behind the bar; he was too focused on the man with his arms around me. The Centauride was watching me carefully, and Daniel. . . well, Daniel kept squeezing the air out of me.

Katherine emerged from a wall of people surrounding a billiard table. She, too, was paying closer attention to me. That nervous feeling started cinching tight on my stomach. I could count on Daniel and Brent if it came to it, but after my second kidnapping, I caught myself being much more aware of my surroundings. A Centauride tending bar for humans was unexpected and set off warning bells in my head.

Katherine's curiosity got the better of her, "Ya know Daniel?"

Her question caught me off-guard. How did Katherine know Daniel? What was he doing here? Why hadn't he gone back to California when Beau left?

I was exposed. Drake had a knack for knowing exactly what was going on in my head. In the few weeks we'd been together, I'd grown accustomed to our *non-verbal* conversations. I felt vulnerable because neither Brent nor Daniel could hear my thoughts. How would I tell them I had a bad feeling about this place? If I said it aloud, would we be overheard? My eyes darted between the two men, and they were oblivious to my worry, still sizing each other up.

Katherine was the first to speak, "Daniel, either ya already know Cami or yer a magnet for women."

The smile on Daniel's face stretched from one ear to the other, "What? Cami, who? I thought you brought me that stripper you promised me! You know I won fair and square." Without missing a beat, my hand swatted at his head as he ducked and my hand whizzed past just missing his ear.

Katherine beamed, "Can't hide anything from ya!" Katherine, Daniel, the Amazon-looking bartender, and I laughed; Brent scowled.

I thought for sure Daniel and Brent had met before, but the way both eyed each other – I wasn't so sure. Daniel eased up on his grip, but kept one arm wrapped around my waist while he held out his hand to greet Brent. "Name's Daniel. Which brother are you?"

Brent's voice was less than welcoming, but he extended his hand and answered, "Brent." Despite the introduction, his glare at Daniel didn't diminish.

I was proud of Daniel for ignoring Brent's reaction. He must have realized Brent was less than thrilled to see him, so in typical Daniel fashion he jumped right into conversation as if they were old pals. "How's Beau doin'? Haven't heard from him since he and Lacey boarded a plane bound for South Carolina."

Brent shook his head, "I don't know. They didn't stay long. He packed up his things and both were gone a few hours after they showed up." Daniel's question about Beau seemed to calm Brent a little. I guessed that Brent was still not comfortable with a male touching a Centauride who wasn't betrothed to him, but at least he stopped glaring. His stare fixated on Daniel's arm still wrapped around me, but he didn't look like he was ready to tackle him – it was an improvement.

I was baffled as to why Daniel was still here. I was sure he had gone back to California when Beau and Lacey left for South Carolina. Why would Daniel be in this bar? Why tonight? Was he supposed to stay a part of my life, even after I'd turned my back on my *human* existence? Apprehensively, I asked, "So, you were sick of the beach or what? You didn't go home?"

"Naw. Wasn't anything for me there. Pops and I have been on the outs for a while. I got fired when I took my unannounced, extended vacation here to look for you. I didn't have anyone to go back to, and some card shark took me for everything I had my first night here."

Daniel shot a teasing look toward Katherine as she oozed pride over her obvious exploits. I cringed when he said he'd been fired. Katherine didn't comment when he said he'd been here looking for me. I hoped she'd let it go without any questions.

When he said there was nothing for him in California – that was a lie; at least the part about not having anyone to go back to. Daniel had always had any number of women who were as close as a smile or a wink away. From the two women looking at me, his charms weren't left in California. Katherine playfully punched Daniel, "A card shark? You can't hold me responsible for yer lack of skills."

"Katherine, no woman has ever accused me of being short on skills."

She cocked her head to the side as a sly smile emerged, "There's a first for everything. Let me know if ya want ta sign up for some tutoring."

The Amazon-sized Centauride behind the bar watched their exchange. She'd wiped the same spot on the bar at least a dozen times. Her eyes caught mine, and it looked like she tried to cover up her interest, "Nice reunion. What're you drinking?" She gave a condescending look, "I know, Sweetheart, you'll have a pop." She looked at Brent, "Escorts drink these days?"

Brent's mouth opened, his pupils dilated and quickly dwarfed the whites of his eyes, while his Adam's apple slid down his throat as he swallowed. "Eagle-eyes" Brent realized in that moment that our bartender was a Centauride. He was speechless.

The bartender looked at me, "What? You don't let him talk? Okay, fine, *you* tell me what he's drinking."

I snickered when I looked over at Brent who still hadn't recovered. Centaurides were revered. Few if any had jobs, and none would stoop to serving humans. At least that was the world Brent was from. Amused at Brent's inability to regain his speech, I ordered. "We'll both have whatever light beer you've got on draft."

She reached into a freezer and pulled out two frozen mugs. As she was pouring, Brent leaned into my ear and whispered, "She's a Centauride."

I smiled, but before I could respond, she'd put both glasses on the bar a little harder than was necessary. Beer spilled up over the lip of the mugs and slid down the side. She looked straight at Brent and with a menacing tone said, "And *she* expects her tip to be representative of the fabulous service you just received. That'll be six dollars." Either she had dog-hearing, or she was psychic. What did I know – maybe she belonged to a herd that had both.

Brent 's hand dove deep into his jeans pocket, pulled out a twenty, and wordlessly handed it over to the bartender. She smiled a dazzling smile, winked at him, and said, "I'm keeping the change, stud."

Brent nodded. It was almost too funny to watch. I wondered if he'd ever recover.

Katherine had quietly watched the exchange between Brent and the bartender. She shook her head, addressing the bartender in a no-nonsense way, "Jessica, give Brent his change."

Brent's voice actually cracked when he looked from Katherine back to Jessica, "No. Keep it." Jessica blew Brent a kiss, and I thought he was going to melt into a puddle of goo where he stood. Katherine's face flushed a bright red. It wasn't the cute kind of blush where she'd heard something that embarrassed her; it was the aggravated blush of a woman swallowing her words.

Daniel leaned up on the bar with his arm still loosely hooked around me. "Jessica. Now that's a beautiful name. Seems my good friend Brent forgot to order my drink. I'll have a Seven and Seven."

Katherine walked away from the bar, motioning for me to follow her. She walked in the direction of the billiard table but then pointed to a door along the back wall of the bar. A sign hung on the door in clear block letters that read: Authorized Personnel Only. Katherine looked at me as she opened the door, "Well, it'll be a few days before either of 'em figure out they don' have a shot in hell with her. Until then, I bet neither is worth a crap at cards."

The little room hidden behind the door was small. There was only the one way in and no other exits. Katherine watched me as I took in the room. It was odd. With most humans I could hear the questions in their heads before they spoke, but Katherine's mind was silent – eerily silent.

CHAPTER 5

Camille – Small Town in South Dakota

She pulled out a chair, dusted off the seat and eased down with the grace of a swan. "So, what's yer story?"

I shouldn't have been surprised by her forwardness. This had been her demeanor since the moment we met this morning. I didn't like the idea of her thinking we were felons, but there wasn't much of an alternative to give her without lying. "No story, just on vacation with friends."

Suspicion clouded her face, "Uh huh. Yer friends brought you and yer brother on their honeymoon?"

Okay, when she put it like that, we did look suspicious. "Extended honeymoon. I think it was officially over last week."

Her eyes pierced mine. She wasn't buying it. "Whatcha doin' here? No one comes ta South Dakota this time of year ta see the monuments, and it's too cold for a bike rally." One of the largest motorcycle rallies happens in Sturgis, South Dakota each summer – I remembered seeing faded billboards from last summer along the highway into town. Even if we had been here during the right time of year, none of us had motorcycles with us.

Drake and I had spent so much time trying to hide, it never occurred to me to develop some sort of cover story. Maybe coloring a lie in truth would make her less skeptical. "My other brother used to live here. I was between jobs, and he said I could stay at his house."

"Yet, yer staying at my motel?"

My heart started speeding up. Why wasn't I at Cameron's house? I couldn't tell her it was because thirty rogue Centaurs stormed the place, busting every door and window during their assault and were no doubt hunting for me right now. "Infestation. The place was crawling with undesirable creatures."

Katherine cocked her head. She didn't call me an outright liar, but she didn't believe me. "This time of year?"

"The view is better from your mountain, and we haven't seen any . . . creatures since we arrived to scare us away."

"Fine. You don't have ta tell me what you're runnin' from, but don't try ta bullshit me. If it's the law lookin' for ya, you picked the right town ta hide in."

What did she mean by that? Was the town full of criminals? Did they not have any law enforcement? I should have asked her, but asking would only cement in her mind that we were on the run from the law. Katherine picked up a deck of cards off of the green felt-covered table and started shuffling.

Absent any other story I could give her, I let her believe we were criminals. She shuffled the cards the way a Vegas dealer does, laying them out flat, expertly folding them together, cutting them, reshuffling and cutting again. Her hands moved so fast I could hardly keep my eyes on them.

I'd been mesmerized by her hands, endlessly shuffling the deck. She looked up at me, not even glancing at the table, and flipped the top card – an Ace of Spades. The second card she flipped was the King of Spades, the third was the Queen, two more cards appeared until she had dealt a royal flush.

"Impressive. How many casinos have you been barred from?"

For the first time since we entered the room, a sly smile crept across her face, "None. At least, Katherine Newton hasn't been barred from any. I don't ever gamble under my real name. If I did, I'd hafta pay taxes on my winnings."

Okay, so Katherine was a criminal. Tax evasion was a federal offense, and she seemed not to be the least worried about me knowing. I cleared my throat, "So, who owns the motel we're staying in?"

Katherine sounded defensive, "That was a legit win. I don't do any sharking here. Jessica doesn't allow it."

I didn't forget the worrisome feeling I had when we arrived. The more I knew, the better our chances for not getting caught by surprise. "Jessica's the morality police?"

"Uh, no. Jessica owns the bar. She was twenty-one when she inherited this place from her grandparents. No one gives her any trouble. She doesn't like cheats, so no one cheats here."

"Every game's on the up and up?" Daniel's words echoed in my head: *some card shark took me for everything I had my first night here.* "Daniel said you took him for everything he had."

Her sly smile from minutes ago re-emerged. "Jessica takes a night off every now and again."

I felt my eyes narrowing on reflex, "Daniel's my best friend in the world. I'd hate to think you stole from him."

She put on an innocent expression, "Stole . . . that's a strong accusation."

Her eyes weren't the least bit angry at my insinuation, so I pressed again. "But, no denial?"

"I said that's a strong accusation. I didn't say I didn't cheat him."

I could hardly believe my ears, "You're pretty brazen about it."

Katherine looked at me with a cross between admiration and frustration, "You've got that same look about ya that Jessica does. I don't ever try ta tell her a half-truth because somehow she always knows which half is a lie."

My whole body tensed. Katherine was undeniably human. I didn't sense even a drop of Centauride blood in her veins. How could she so easily know that Jessica and I were the same? I began searching through her thoughts trying to figure out *exactly* what she knew. It was like trying to see through a stone wall. I couldn't get anything from her.

Katherine tapped the deck of cards on the table a few times, "That other friend of yers, Bianca, she's the same, too, right?"

A lump formed in my throat. I stammered, "I. . . don't. . . I don't have any. . . what do you. . ." Before I could win a bumbling idiot award, the door swung open with Jessica leading Brent and Daniel into the room. Jessica's lips spread in a thin smile.

Jessica was looking straight at me when I telepathically asked her, "*What does Katherine know? How does she know we're both Centaurides if she's human?*"

Her smile morphed into a grimace. "*Eerie, isn't it? It's like she can sense it or something. Centaurides are easier for her. Centaurs come through every now and again, and she doesn't hone in on them as easily unless she's really trying.*"

Katherine's voice cut off my mind-versation with Jessica. "Daniel, I didn't expect ta see ya back here."

Without taking his eyes off of Jessica, Daniel answered, "The company in this bar is worth the monetary setbacks."

Everyone took a seat around the table. Brent and Daniel sat on either side of me, Jessica sat on the other side of Brent. Katherine started dealing when Jessica announced, "Deal me out."

Daniel was still watching her from across the table, and when he spoke it was as if no one else were in the room, "No. If someone's going to take the shirt off my back, I want it to be you."

This comment infuriated Brent. I'd wager a bet that Brent had spent almost no time with Centaurides other than Gretchen and our sister-in-law, Hannah. He had this way about him of putting Centaurides up on a pedestal. Daniel's thinly veiled innuendos were like an accelerant poured on an open flame.

Ignoring Brent's obvious frustration with Daniel, Jessica answered, "I like a good view as well. You could hand it over now and save Katherine the effort of taking it from you."

Katherine watched the two men ogling over her friend. She didn't like it. I'd spent enough time around Daniel and the women who were sweet on him; I recognized the pangs of jealousy that shot out of her eyes like laser beams. Brent pulled out a wad of cash and set it on the table in front of him. Daniel, not wanting to be outdone, reached in his pocket and pulled out a set of keys.

I picked up the keys, "What are these to?"

Daniel answered me, but his eyes were still locked on Jessica. "My cabin. I hate to think I could leave here homeless tonight. I wonder if anyone would take me in?"

Jessica's face flushed. After having seen Katherine's demonstration before the other three arrived, I wasn't about to let either *donate* their antes. Instead, I offered, "How about if we play a friendly game tonight?"

Katherine answered, "No one's leaving homeless. Max ante will be twenty dollars. We'll keep track on paper, losers have forty-eight hours ta pay. Fair enough?"

I shook my head. "Not with those cards, Katherine." Ignoring her offended look, I turned to Jessica, "Do you have a new deck around here?"

Jessica smiled at me. "Of course." She reached into a drawer on the table and took out a freshly wrapped pack of cards and handed it over to Katherine. The deck of cards Katherine had been using was carefully tucked into her back pocket.

Conversation was sparse as the four of us played and Jessica watched. Everyone won a hand or two, but Katherine had a real knack for playing. I kept hearing that old Kenny Roger's country song in my head about knowing when to hold 'em and knowing when to fold 'em.

As the hours ticked by, I began to wonder about Drake. He was probably a nervous wreck. We'd been gone for over four hours. If there was trouble, he'd be able to contact me telepathically through our betrothal connection, but he'd remained silent since we left the motel. I closed my eyes and sent him a message, "*Drake, can you hear me?*"

The answer was immediate. "*Yes, Love. Are you okay?*"

"Just missing you."

"I wish I could be there with you."

"Me, too. Daniel's here."

Drake hesitated, *"Daniel's with you?"*

"Yeah. He didn't go back to San Diego after Beau and Lacey left."

"That's good news."

"Really? I thought you two didn't hit it off."

"I'm not looking for someone to watch a game with. We could use him. Invite him back to the motel."

Use him for what? Daniel needed to keep his distance – he didn't stand a chance if we were attacked again. "What did you three decide?"

"We've planned out the route. I think you'll like Bianca's travel plans. You're still sure about going to Centauride, South Africa to address the Centaur Council, right?"

"Among other things." I pushed an image of me wrapped up in his arms with my head buried in his chest.

"*How long until you get back?*"

"*Soon. Very soon.*"

It was Drake's turn to push an image to me. His lips were on my collar bone, lightly making their way up my neck, his breath was heavy at my ear when the words reverberated in my head, "*Not soon enough.*" He broke our conversation as waves of heat spread through me.

When I looked up, all eyes in the room were on me – it must have been my turn. I mumbled, "Sorry, daydreaming." Oblivious to the game, I tapped the table and said, "I call."

Katherine rolled her eyes, "You can't call. Are ya staying?" Crap, this was a fresh hand. I looked at it and I'd been dealt a royal flush! "I'm staying." Brent took two cards, Katherine took one.

Daniel upped the bet by ten dollars, I raised another ten, Brent anted, and the bet was to Katherine. Jessica, who had been very quiet throughout the night said, "It's about time for last call, I need to go home and *fold* laundry tonight."

Katherine made a frustrated face and tossed her cards on the table. I'm not sure if it was because I'd just finished chatting with Drake or what, but I remembered the few phrases I'd heard Jessica utter while we played: "Remind me to hook *up* a fresh keg before we leave tonight." "I need to have the juke box looked at, see if they can set the volume *up*, you can hardly hear it from in here." "There are towels in the dryer I need to *fold* before closing tonight."

Nice. Not only was she a Centauride who tended bar, she helped her friend cheat at cards! Katherine's comment earlier about Jessica not allowing sharking in her bar must have been a joke. Jessica would be able to hear my message loud and clear. My eyes narrowed at her as I telepathically scolded her, "*Stop it now. No more cheating.*"

Jessica's laughter interrupted the quiet of the game. Brent, Daniel and Katherine all looked at her as if she'd grown a third eye. Katherine's voice sounded concerned, "Ya okay, Jess?"

"Never better." Her eyes remained locked on mine. "*What are you three running from?*"

"*If you don't already know, I'd like to keep it that way.*"

Jessica's eyes narrowed. "*Part of that Lost Herd nonsense?*"

Nonsense? Maybe she didn't care there was a death warrant on our heads. "*You could say that.*"

She nodded slightly, not enough for the others at the table to notice. "*I thought so. Why are you traveling with a half-breed?*"

"*Don't call him that! Daniel isn't traveling with us. We just happened in on him here. I thought he'd gone back to California weeks ago.*"

"*Hate to break it to you, but he* is *a half-breed.*"

"*He's my friend. My very good friend.*"

Jessica's features took on a knowing look. "*Oh, I see. You're from the Lost Herd. They're the only ones who can mate outside of wedlock.*"

I nearly lost my temper and shouted out loud, but caught myself just before I could make a fool of myself. I scowled at Jessica, "*Not that kind of very good friend!*"

Katherine's voice was frustrated from across the table. "Earth ta Cami, are ya in or what?" I wasn't sure why she asked, Katherine had already folded her hand.

Trying to keep up with Jessica's mind-versation and the card game was hard. "I call. Hey, this is my last hand. Deal me out on the next one. I'll help Jessica fold those towels."

My royal flush won. With Jessica and me out of the room, Daniel and Brent had half a chance against Katherine. I stood up and motioned for the door. Jessica followed me out, but it seemed our conversation was over. Once we were out of the room, she made a beeline for the bar. She ducked through an opening under the bar, grabbed a dishrag, and began scrubbing the counter.

As I looked around, there were five people still inside the place, not including the mousey-looking man who had tended the bar in Jessica's absence. She turned to the man, "I've got it, Brandon. Go ahead and head home."

Brandon had long stringy dark hair, and even in the dimly lit bar his yellowing teeth were gross. I gave him plenty of room as he ducked under the opening and headed toward the door. As he was zipping up his jacket, he asked, "Fine. Tomorrow night?"

Jessica hesitated, "Can you open for me tomorrow morning?"

Brandon answered, "Sure. Going to be late tonight?"

"Katherine's in the back playing cards, so, yeah, I think so."

Brandon shook his head. He didn't say anything specific, but I got the impression he didn't care for Katherine. Jessica reached up to a large brass bell over her shoulder. She rang it loudly as the clang reverberated off of every surface. "Last call! You've got five minutes! No camping out tonight, folks. Stanley wants us shut down by two – no excuses."

Jessica continued scrubbing the bar without looking back at me. I wanted to get Jessica talking again and decided the best way would be to ask a few benign questions first. "Who's Stanley, the owner?"

When her eyes met mine, the look was close to a glare. "I already told you, this is my bar. Stanley's the town cop. He gets pretty pissy when we close late."

"But you just told Brandon it'd be a late night."

"Sometimes it takes Katherine longer to take the other players for everything they've got. I stop serving before two, but I let her stay as long as it takes."

I chuckled at her, "Even without you telling her what to do with her cards?"

A wide smile erupted on Jessica's lips, "We don't get many Centaurides in here. I could have made it a quick night for everyone, but I was trying to be stealthy."

"Newsflash. You suck at stealth."

Her smile didn't diminish, "Oh, on the contrary, it wasn't until you got flustered that you even had a clue."

She had a point. I hadn't suspected anything until after I spoke with Drake. "Most of the Centaurides I've met don't use their gifts for gambling."

"Gifts? You mean curse! I can't help that I can see what I see. Believe me, there's a lot in this world I wish I'd never seen."

"Like what?"

"You see that guy over there?" She pointed at a heavyset man across the room from us. His eyes were half closed, he wore a bright red and black checkered winter hat, stubble covered his face and wrinkles nearly enveloped his eyes. "He stays until closing three nights a week because his wife left with their kids. He's trying to figure out if his life is worth living – from the shoebox, rat-infested apartment he's going back to – I'm not sure it is."

"Jessica! If you know he's hurting, why don't you offer to help him?"

She kept scrubbing the bar, not even looking in my direction. "Not my business. Even if it were, how do I approach a guy who's never said more to me than his drink order?"

"You go up and start a conversation. Where's your compassion?"

"It's long gone. Or that guy over there." Jessica nodded toward a rail thin man slowly peeling the label off of his bottle of beer. "He's a convicted rapist. He did his time and he's out, so I guess he's paid his debt to society, but the thoughts in his head are awful. He may be out, but he's not rehabilitated."

I didn't want to stare but felt my eyes lingering on the skinny stranger too long. "So tune out his thoughts and go help the guy with the hat."

"I told you. Not my business."

I huffed out a breath, straightened my blouse and walked over to the man who had been contemplating suicide. I reached his table and extended my hand, "Hi, I'm Cami. Mind if I sit?"

He gestured to the seat across from him. Now that I was here, I had no idea what to say. "So, I couldn't help but notice you were sitting here by yourself. Are you going to be okay to drive home?"

"What? No. I just live a few blocks from here. I'll walk it."

"You've been sitting here by yourself. Is everything okay?" His mind was numb. I couldn't make out many coherent thoughts, but I smirked when I realized he thought I was trying to pick him up. Then some other fuzzy thoughts flew by, and he decided I must be a prostitute.

Jessica must have been listening in because a glass dropped behind the bar. I looked in her direction, and she was covering her mouth to keep the laugh in.

"Fine. Everything's fine."

"I recognize the look on your face. You're lonely. My mom had that same look most of her life." I listened to my words as they came out and cringed. I wasn't doing much to dispel the conclusion he'd drawn.

His speech was slurred, and he was much more interested in his near-empty glass than he was in me. "You don't say."

"I know something that might make you less lonely if you want to give it a try."

He leaned across the table, a smile crept on his face, and he took my hand. "I'm all for it, sweetheart, but I don't have much money."

Repulsed that he would actually voice his thoughts, I was still careful not to rip my hand from his grasp and offend him. "Do something nice for someone – for no reason. When you get home, shovel someone's sidewalk, or put salt down on your neighbor's steps, or take a pot of chili to a neighbor tomorrow. Doing something for someone who hasn't asked for help will make you not so lonely."

He eased his hand away from mine, "I'm not that kind of lonely, sweetheart."

"Everyone is that kind of lonely. How we react to the loneliness is what defines us. Doing something nice for a friend or a stranger will make you feel better – I promise."

His eyebrows pursed together, "What's your angle?"

"No angle. You're not alone, even if it feels like you are. Connect with someone."

The door to the bar opened, Jessica's voice shouted in my head, "*Cami, get in the back room, now!*" My body froze on instinct. I should have bolted. I should have listened without question. I didn't.

As I glanced toward her frame behind the bar, her warning screamed in my head, "*Don't look this way. In the back. Now!*"

Heavy feet stomped snow on the welcome mat just inside the door, as her voice greeted the newcomer. "Hi, Roscoe. We've already had last call. You know how Stanley gets after two a.m."

"Awe, Jess. You can spare a thimble of something to warm me up. I've been searching through the snow fer two straight days." Roscoe wasn't a common name. One of the Centaurs who had assaulted Cameron's house two nights ago was named Roscoe. My whole body tensed as I stood up from the table and left the man in the checkered hat without another word.

Jessica's voice sounded apologetic. "Sorry, Roscoe. Can't do it. I've got some liquor at the house. Go help yourself."

His frustrated voice ignored her offer, "Is Katherine around tonight?" I felt sweat peppering my brow. If I went in the back room and Roscoe followed me in, what would happen to Daniel, Brent and Katherine? I searched the near empty bar for a dark corner to escape into. Nothing.

Jessica's voice didn't waiver. She sounded like she was talking to someone she'd known her whole life – trying to convince him to walk out the way he'd come. "Yeah, she's got some tourists in the back. I'll be home soon. She's just about cleaned them out."

I couldn't stay where I was – in the open. If he looked this way he'd see me for sure. I was a few strides from the door to the back room when it hit me. If I went inside, there was no other exit. We'd all be trapped. I didn't know if Roscoe was by himself, and I didn't want to take the chance and put the others in danger.

Jessica called out to the bar. "Okay, folks: two a.m. – time to go."

The man I'd just talked to at the table stood up. He put some cash under his empty glass and zipped up his coat. Could I make it out with him? Did Roscoe know what I looked like?

Jessica's words sounded in my mind. "*Don't do it. Go in the back room. I'll get rid of him. Stay with Katherine.*"

I had no reason to trust her. As my heartbeat picked up speed, I wanted to make a run for it. Roscoe was a Centaur – I felt it. He didn't realize I was here. If I made a break for it, I could make it to the truck. He wouldn't know anything about Brent or Daniel. They'd be safe.

Jessica's voice was loud in my mind, "*You're going to get me punished. Don't you dare make a run for it. Get in back.*"

Roscoe was staring at Jessica. "Joo see something, Jess? Joo got a premonition fer me?" He reached over and tugged her sleeve. Who was Roscoe to Jessica? Would she allow a Centaur to touch her if she weren't betrothed? Was she betrothed to Roscoe? When we arrived, Katherine had said neither Daniel nor Brent had a chance with her. My stomach cinched tight as my heart raced out of control.

Jessica never took her eyes off of Roscoe, but her words were unmistakable in my mind, "*Hide before he sees you. Katherine's been drinking and she won't be able to protect us both.*"

Katherine can't protect us? What was she talking about? Did she have a gun on her or something? I wanted to ask for clarification, but the fear of Roscoe finding us was too much of a possibility. I gave in. I couldn't hear what Jessica said to Roscoe, and I hoped my gut was right to trust her. I casually walked to the back room, hoping not to draw any attention to myself. As I closed the door behind me to the little room where Katherine, Daniel and Brent were still playing, I closed my eyes and took a deep breath. If I told Drake there was danger, he would be here in minutes. I couldn't risk anything happening to him either. I called out to Bianca instead. "*Bianca, can you hear me?*"

"Cami, what are you three doing? You've been gone for hours."

"Drake's with you, right?"

"Yes, he and Gage are still working transportation details to Africa."

"Good. Don't say anything to either of them. One of the Centaurs who stormed my brother Cameron's house just walked into the bar where we're at."

"What?!"

"I don't think he recognized me, but I may need your help. Be listening for me, okay?"

"Cami, Gage and Drake can be there in minutes."

"I know. I'm counting on it. But don't warn them yet. I need to see if he'll go away on his own."

"I don't like this, Cami."

"I don't like it, either. I just wanted you to know, in case I need you."

I opened my eyes and saw a huge pile of chips in front of Brent while Katherine wore an unhappy face. Daniel looked at his hand and grimaced, "Hey, where's my good-luck charm?"

I didn't understand what he was asking, but could tell from the way he angled his body around he was talking to me. "Good-luck charm?"

"You two said you were going to close up the bar or fold towels or whatever. If it's closed, where's Jessica?"

"She's getting the last couple customers out. You guys about done?"

Katherine and Daniel nodded, Brent answered, "No. We could do this for a while yet. Can you call Gage and Bianca and let them know we'll be late?"

"Already did. One of the stragglers seems to be a friend of Jessica's. His name's Roscoe."

Daniel pursed his eyebrows together wondering what my comment meant. Katherine put her cards down and looked me square in the eye. "Did he see you?"

I shook my head that he hadn't. She set her cards on the table, left her chips where they lay, and walked to a lighted Coke machine in the back corner of the room. It must have been on wheels because it slid easily away from the wall. Her voice was urgent, but not panicked, "In here, all of ya, now."

CHAPTER 6

Camille – Small Town in South Dakota

Brent and Daniel were confused – I didn't know what to think, either. The three of us didn't move, Katherine peeked around from the side of the Coke machine, "For the love of Zeus, get over here."

I reached down to the table and messed up the cards so it didn't look like there was an unfinished game. The three of us grabbed our coats and cautiously crept over to the soda machine where Katherine stood. When I looked at the wall behind it, a small door led to a rickety old ladder. The ladder fed into a black hole under the building. Brent was the first to speak, "What're you doing?"

Katherine didn't mince words, "If Roscoe's in the bar, yer all in danger. Down, now."

Brent asked, "Who's Roscoe?"

"The lead enforcer for the Centaur Council in the area, that's who. He's rounding up all the members of the Lost Herd."

My jaw slacked as my mouth fell open. Katherine knew who we were. "You knew. But how did you. . . I mean. . . did we say. . . "

She cut me off, "In the tunnel, before he comes in here."

I recouped my senses, "Jessica told him you were back here taking money from tourists."

"Shit. I'll go down, too. It'd be better if he thought I'd slipped out without Jessica noticing if he comes looking for me."

"You can't put yourself in danger for our sake. We should stay put. If he comes through the door, there are three of us."

Katherine shook her head in disbelief, "Cami, I'm not in any danger. Yer jus' as naive as everyone said you were." She paused for a minute as if she had to offer a better explanation for helping us. "I don't need the hassle of Centaurs patrolling my mountain. A girl likes her privacy. Now get down there before he comes back here."

My feet planted – something still didn't feel right. "So, you knew who we were the whole time?"

"Not right away. Every Centaur in this region is looking for Camille Chiron. I suspected, but I couldn't be sure."

"But, *you're* not a Centauride."

Katherine rolled her eyes, "What gave ya the first clue?"

I thought of the Centaurs who had attacked Drake and me at Cameron's house. We didn't sense their danger until they were right on top of us. It was a well-rehearsed attack, carried out with military precision – they came through all the doors and windows at once. Had Drake's transformation not surprised them, we may not have made it out alive. I wanted to warn her what she was getting herself into, "Katherine, these Centaurs are dangerous."

Her worried look gave way to a smirk, "Yer protected by the dangerous one."

Brent and Daniel stood watching our exchange. Neither made any effort to interrupt until Katherine's last comment. Daniel leaned toward me, "What's she talking about, Cami?"

I couldn't lie to Daniel, but I didn't feel right telling him about Drake's transformation. "Drake and I were attacked a couple nights ago at my brother's house." Daniel immediately turned to Brent who looked completely oblivious. I clarified, "Not Brent. We were hiding out at my twin brother's house."

Daniel shook his head, "Cameron? But he took off to Florida. I saw him get on a plane myself."

"He did, but I called and asked if we could lay low at his house. It was fine until a couple nights ago when thirty Centaurs showed up and stormed the place."

Katherine's expression seemed more urgent and her voice layered in frustration, "Look, I get there are some things you'll need to fill us in on, but here, with Roscoe jus' on the other side of that wall, isn't the right place. Get down inta the tunnel." She shoved me through the door and onto the ladder.

I'd never been afraid of the dark, but the ladder seemed to be stretching into nothing but pitch black. The old wooden steps didn't seem strong enough to support my weight, let alone the weight of four of us climbing down at once. Katherine was at the top of the ladder while Brent, Drake and I were making our way down. She shut the little door, so the only stream of light came through a small circular hole cut in the middle of the hidden door. She pulled a rope from inside the tunnel and what little light there had been completely disappeared. The soda machine had to have been attached to the rope, securing it in place to hide our departure.

My foot stepped onto solid ground as a wave of relief settled over me. My second foot felt the uneven earth below, and my hands immediately started groping at the vast expanse, trying to feel the wall. I couldn't estimate how far down we were, but it felt like we'd climbed down a three story building. The tunnel was cool, not the bone-chilling cold of the outside temperatures, but cool and damp. It smelled of stale water and sulfur.

My hands found the wall of jagged rock. I'd never feared the dark, but every Scooby Doo cartoon I'd watched as a kid started flashing through my mind as my head ducked down in fear of imaginary bats. I couldn't imagine how we would find our way out of this place. There was no illumination, no shadows, nothing but damp air.

I felt Daniel's hands on my shoulder. I couldn't be sure how I knew they belonged to him, but I did. In the silence of the tunnel, his touch was a comfort, momentarily easing my fear of the bats, rats and snakes I was sure were waiting to attack us. I turned toward Daniel in the dark and grabbed onto him for comfort. His embrace was strong, making me believe we'd be okay.

When Katherine reached the bottom of the ladder, her footsteps sounded off to the right. Her hands scrambled in search of something along the walls. An audible "click" sounded, and a string of light bulbs stretched out through the cavernous passageway, several were burned out. We were standing in an old mine shaft. Railroad tracks stretched out as far as my eye could see in both directions. Huge wooden support beams lined the walls and held the ceiling in place.

Handwritten signs hung on the wall with arrows pointing to the left or right: Hotel 2 miles, Stable 2.5 miles, Doctor 3 miles, and Train Station 2.5 miles. One arrow pointed up the ladder we had just climbed down with the word "Tavern," indicating the bar was just overhead.

I turned to Katherine, "Your hotel is only two miles from here?"

"Uh, no. Those signs are over a hundred years old. The old hotel was torn down before I was born and a Wal-Mart sets on the old site. That opening was sealed a long time ago."

"So, how do we get back to the motel?"

"We go ta the old stables. The barn's gone, but the access door is still there. Yer friends can pick us up there."

We were out of other options. Katherine knew way more about our society and about us specifically than she had let on. We began walking as hundreds of questions were swimming in my mind. Who was she? How did she know about Centaurs? Why wasn't she in any danger for helping us? How did she know about this tunnel? Had Jessica told her about us? If Centaurs were really looking for us, what would they do to her if they found us?

Despite all the questions in my head, I only asked one. "I'll get a hold of Bianca. Where do I tell her to meet us?"

"Just off of mile marker 78 on the highway that leads inta town, there's a turnoff. Under a billboard fer Bio-Diesel is the access panel. Have 'em meet us by the billboard."

I called out to Bianca, "*I think we're safe. Can you and Gage come pick us up?*"

"*You think you're safe? Where are you?*"

"*We're on our way to the old horse stables outside of town. It'll take us about 25 minutes to get there. We're underground – in a mine shaft.*" I gave Bianca the pick-up location that Katherine had described, then added, "*Tell Drake what's going on, but tell him to stay at the motel. I'll contact him if it looks like there's trouble.*"

"*I'll tell him, but don't count on him letting you out of his sight after this.*"

I kept one foot in front of the other and walked in the direction Katherine led us. I couldn't think of any good reason that she would stick her neck out for us, but I didn't want to question her gesture in front of Brent and Daniel until we were safely out of the tunnel.

The mine shaft showed no evidence of recent use. The lights gave off just enough illumination to keep from tripping over the old railroad ties. It was cool and damp, but not cold. With every step I became more desensitized to the sulfur smell I'd first noticed. Every few steps my fingers brushed against the wall. Jagged rock and hard packed clay lined the shaft.

Brent must have been wondering some of the same things because while I stayed silent, he quietly asked Katherine, "So, you said you weren't in any danger from Centaurs. How are you so sure?"

Even without seeing her face, I knew she'd rolled her eyes at him. "Any Centaur who so much as looked at me cross-eyed would be punished severely. Yer lucky I le' you win tonight."

Punished severely? Was she some sort of deity? I had a clear view of Brent: he looked confused. "Let me win? Oh, no, you were the big talker. I beat you."

Katherine's playful tone shot back, "Ya did no such thing. I was lulling ya inta a false sense a security. The next hand was mine and so were all the winnings."

Brent shrugged his shoulders good-naturedly, "I guess we'll never know."

"You're right, Centaur." The way Katherine said it, "Centaur" was not some mystical race she revered. It was as if we were beneath her or something. Jessica's words, "*Hide before he sees you. Katherine can't protect us both,*" echoed in my mind.

What had Jessica meant by "Katherine can't protect us"? All my senses told me she was human. How could a human protect a Centauride? Especially from a Centaur who was following orders from Zeus? I hated trying to put puzzles together while I was missing pieces.

Daniel, whose mouth was always moving at full-speed, remained suspiciously quiet. I didn't want to listen to Katherine and Brent argue over who was the poker master. I hadn't had a chance to catch up with him, and we had some time on our hands. "So, why didn't you go back to California? Why stay here?"

Daniel wrapped his arm around me as we walked. His familiar touch felt like home. Given everything that had happened so quickly, I should have been a nervous wreck – I wasn't. It felt good to be with Daniel again – like a huge piece of me had been missing and I'd just found it again.

"Pops was pretty pissed when Beau and I took his plane. He's never been your biggest fan," Daniel wrinkled his nose and gave me a smirk, "and he didn't want me mixed up in any of it."

His relationship with his dad had always been stiff, but I hated that I was the reason he didn't go home. "I'm sorry, Daniel."

"Don't be. I like it here. More solitude, things are slower. The only traffic jams are caused by tractors on the highway, not ten thousand cars all going to the same place."

"So that's it? You've defected?"

Daniel laughed one of his hearty laughs that I hadn't heard in months. He stopped walking and wrapped both his arms around me. I hugged him back, ignoring the angry stare from Brent. When I let go, we were walking quite a ways behind Katherine and Brent. Daniel asked in a low voice, "I'm not staying for long. So, I take it you found lover boy?"

I tried to keep the frustration out of my voice, "Drake, his name is Drake. Yes, I found him a couple weeks ago."

Daniel's arm was still draped over my shoulder. He squeezed my shoulder and asked, "So why is Brent your escort tonight?"

What could I say? Could I tell him the truth? If there were anyone on the planet who knew me, really knew me, it was Daniel. I'd never kept any secrets from him my whole life. "Drake. . . wasn't feeling up to it."

Daniel's arm still stretched across my back, his hand glided to my waist, "You know he's not good enough for you, right?"

"He's good enough. There's a lot you don't know about Drake."

"And I'll probably never know. That crap he tried to pull after you'd been kidnapped – I'm still pissed."

"There were circumstances he didn't share with you."

"Really? Circumstances, like what?" Daniel's gaze was accusatory, but it wasn't my place to tell him about Drake's transformation. He'd chosen to become half a horse to protect me. After the attack at Cameron's house, his choice was the only reason we were still together and alive.

If I told Daniel, he'd try to find an angle on why Drake would do it, never accepting that he did it out of love for me. Daniel had been my best friend for as long as I had known what a best friend was, but this was too much, even for him.

"It's not up to me to tell. You'll have to ask him yourself, but it was the most selfless action I've ever known."

We were still walking about twenty paces behind Katherine and Brent. Daniel leaned over and awkwardly kissed my temple, "You're blind, Cami."

My voice came out stiff, "You don't have all the facts, Daniel."

"Look. I don't wanna argue. I get that you've claimed him – it doesn't mean I have to like it."

"No. But it'd be nice if you could be happy for me."

"Yeah? That's not going to happen. Not unless you dump him. If you do, I'll throw you a party – then I'll be happy for you."

I was readying my sharp response to Daniel when Katherine raised her voice to Brent. "Be mindful of yer laws. There are only seven; it shouldn't be that hard ta remember 'em!" They were far enough in front of us that I couldn't see what had just happened.

Brent's voice went low, but we heard him clearly, "Do not touch me. You are but a woman, and I am a Centaur." Damn, Brent! Who talks like that? *That* human was our only shot at making it out safely, and he had to start antagonizing her.

I jogged up between the two of them with Daniel on my heels. "Katherine, don't mind Brent. None of the tenets require Centaurs to have manners – so he left his in South Carolina."

Brent's eyes were fierce when he snapped at me, "Stay out of this."

Equal contempt shot back at him when I answered, "Stop being a jerk. Katherine has been extremely accommodating. You forget, Bianca and Gage are coming to pick us up and Katherine's helping us to safety. Don't be rude."

"Rude? She tried to accost me."

Daniel snickered behind me, and I did everything in my power to hold a straight face. Katherine's shoulder-length fire red hair swung around clipping me in the eye, "I did no such thing!"

Brent shouted, "You did! You touched my arm and asked why I'd not yet been chosen. Just because you are aware of our ways, does not give you the right to mock them."

"I wasn't mocking anything. Some Centaurs may have considered my words a compliment."

"On what planet? And what makes you think I haven't been chosen?"

All three of us stood, mouths agape. Had Brent been chosen? Why wouldn't Brent have told us the minute he arrived? Having been chosen by a Centauride would explain his reaction to Katherine. It might even explain his reaction to Daniel around Jessica.

I was the first to recover, "Brent, wow. Congratulations. Why didn't you tell us?"

His words were nearly inaudible, "I'm not sure. . . I mean. . . never mind. You wouldn't understand."

"You were chosen, but she changed her mind?" I questioned.

"No!" Brent's angry stare cooled as his eyes darted to the floor, "Maybe."

"You don't know if you're betrothed?"

Brent pursed his lips together tightly and shook his head.

Confused, I could only manage, "I don't understand." I eased over toward Brent, but he put his back to me.

I was surprised when it was Daniel who took two steps forward, laid his hand on Brent's shoulder, and said, "Because of the Lost Herd?"

Brent's eyes went glossy, as he nodded. Daniel reached his arm around Brent's neck, and brought their heads together in a hard head-butt, "It'll work out."

Brent shoved his hands in his pockets. His gaze went to the floor as the words started flowing out of him. "Cassie's father called and talked to Mom. Dad wasn't home. It wasn't like Bruce and Hannah, I mean, Cassie chose me, no money was exchanged. She's beautiful, and smart, and she chose *me*." Brent's voice cracked and he stopped.

Brent had been chosen by a Centauride, but after word spread about my family being part of the Lost Herd, he had to go into hiding. Maybe she hadn't backed out. Maybe she just didn't know how to reach him. Why hadn't he just called her?

Daniel had a way of always saying exactly the right thing when it was most important, and now was no exception. "Humans are seriously underrated. If your Centauride backs out, I've got a list of girls you can start weeding through."

Katherine walked away. I wasn't sure if she was offended by Daniel trivializing women or if she was just anxious to get out of the tunnel. Daniel let go of Brent as the three of us trailed her. Within ten minutes we found ourselves directly under another ladder. An arrow pointed up that read, "Stable." Katherine turned around, looking only at me, "Tell yer friends we're in position and can come up as soon as they're ready for us."

"*Bianca, we're right under the access panel from the tunnel. Are you ready for us to come up?*"

Her response was immediate, "*No. Don't come up. We're dealing with a situation. Stay put.*"

I opened my eyes as three sets of eyes looked back at me. Bewildered, I shook my head, "She said not now."

Daniel's voice was loud, "Why not?"

All three of us shushed him, "She didn't say. All she said is they're dealing with a situation and to stay put."

I glanced at my watch: it was approaching two-thirty a.m. What situation could be going on this time of night? Katherine had said the stables were remote. Were there some high school students having a kegger in the middle of nowhere? No, it was too cold for something like that.

Katherine showed concern for the first time, "Ask if we shud meet 'em at a different access point."

I nodded and quickly asked Bianca, "*Do you want us to meet you somewhere else?*" Nothing. Not a single thought or image came in response. "*Bianca? Bianca, can you hear me?*" Concern began to ebb into my consciousness. Why wouldn't she respond? Had something happened to her? I counted to ten, slowly, and tried again. "*Bianca, it's me. What's going on?*"

When she didn't respond again, I snapped my eyes open wide, "Something's wrong. I don't know what happened, but she's not answering now."

Brent reached for the ladder and started climbing. Katherine reached up and caught his pant leg, then cursed under her breath. Brent got the hint and stopped climbing. She turned to me, "Ask Jessica if she knows what's going on." My eyes closed again. I'd spent less time with Jessica, but it should have been enough time to zero in on her thoughts. I visualized the tall Centauride, her platinum-colored hair, her easy smile and her rough demeanor. "*Jessica, can you hear me?*"

"*Now isn't the best time, Cami. Are you still with Katherine?*"

"*Yes. She's right here.*"

"*Wherever you are, they can't find you. Stay there.*"

"*Who can't find us?*"

I got the same response I'd gotten from Bianca. It was as if they both severed their connection with me. My palms began to sweat. My eyes fell on Katherine. How could she help us? Why did Jessica want us to stay with her? What was going on?

CHAPTER 7

Camille – Abandoned Mining Tunnel in South Dakota

Before I allowed full-blown panic to overtake me, I tried one more conversation. "*Drake, can you hear me?*"

His response was immediate, "*What's taking you guys so long?*"

I breathed a sigh of relief and wiped my palms on my jeans. "*I'm not sure. Daniel, Brent, Katherine and I are fine, but Jessica and Bianca both severed their connection with me without much explanation.*"

Worry clouded his voice, "*Severed it? Bianca tuned you out? Who's Jessica?*"

"*She's a Centauride who owns the bar Katherine took us to tonight. Neither one will answer me.*"

"*It's probably just a precaution.*" His words were meant to calm me, but I felt his tension. "*Where are you? I can come to you.*"

I waffled about whether to tell him Roscoe had been at the bar before Katherine shoved us down the tunnel. If I did, Drake would come running no matter what I said after. Bianca had told me to stay put. If she thought I needed Drake charging in here, she would have told me. "*No, we're fine.*"

"*Say the word and I'll be there.*"

I felt the corners of my mouth curl up. I could count on Drake. "*I know. We're safe here. I'll let you know if anything changes.*"

"*I'll be here. I'm ready to run now.*" Drake could run faster than any car drove; he could be here in minutes if I needed him. Brent was almost as fast, and despite his foul mood, there's nothing he wouldn't do to protect me, either. Daniel wasn't like Drake or Brent, but I'd pity anyone who tried to get past him – whether they had mythological powers or not.

"*Okay. If anything changes, I promise I'll let you know.*" My nervousness was back under control. I marveled at the soothing effect of Drake's voice. We were going to be fine.

I opened my eyes; Daniel, Brent and Katherine were staring at me, concern set deep in their eyes. "Jessica couldn't communicate with me either. I'm not sure why they would both just cut their connection with me." I purposely left out that I had contacted Drake. There was no sense getting Daniel worked up by mentioning him.

Katherine blew out a sigh of frustration. "Yer related to Zandra Chiron, aren't cha?"

I answered through gritted teeth. "Only by blood." Zandra was my grandmother. After everything I'd gone through, I still didn't know what to think of her. There were times when the only emotion I had for the woman was hate.

She'd kidnapped me, put a horrible device around my neck that passed itself off as jewelry to the naked eye – but was the equivalent of a shock collar for a dog. She'd lied to me and told me she'd murdered Bianca and Drake, in an effort to trick me into marrying Gage.

When I was at my lowest moment searching for Drake by myself in South Dakota – Zandra knew he had transformed into a Centaur, yet her only concern was getting the Chiron arrow back. Zandra fed me a story about trying to protect me from my destiny – but I didn't believe it. Mom hid from Zandra her whole adult life – regardless of her intentions, Zandra was evil.

Katherine clenched her fists, "There aren't many powerful Centaurides in the world, and Zandra's the only one I've seen in the area."

I grabbed Katherine's shoulder, "Wait, you've seen Zandra in the area? Recently?"

Katherine looked at my hand on her shoulder. I let go but stood in front of her so she couldn't dodge my question. "She was here a couple days ago and had Roscoe all in a tizzy. She left, but maybe she came back. It would make sense."

"What would make sense? Bianca and Jessica would stop communicating with me if Zandra were nearby?"

Katherine chuckled, "You're so clueless. How did ya make it this long?"

I shrugged my shoulders, trying to follow my earlier advice to Brent: to be respectful and to remember she's helping us.

When I didn't try to defend myself, Katherine continued, "Yer blood is like a homing beacon for Zandra, so as long as she's within fifty miles, maybe a hundred, she'll always be able to find ja. She's the chairman of the Centaur Council – that's not a job ya get because of congeniality. Bianca and Jessica are smart enough to know she's looking for ya and ta mute their conversations with ya if she's close."

"So, it's just a matter of time." I looked among the three of them, wondering if they'd come to the same conclusion I had. "She's close, and if I don't get out of here, she's going to find all of us?"

Katherine shook her head, "Yer with me. She may know yer close, but she won't be able to find ja."

What did she mean? "With you? But you're a human."

Katherine crossed her arms defiantly, "Think of me as a cloaking device."

Incredulously, I stammered, "A what?"

"Zandra could be ten feet away from us, and she couldn't find ja if I'm close."

"How is that possible?"

"Cami, I'm human, but I have a special ancestry, too."

Brent's eyes went wide, and he was suddenly standing in between Katherine and me. He'd moved so fast I hadn't even seen him flinch, yet all I could see was the back of him. His tone was accusatory, "Wait, are you telling us you're a Lapith? But . . . Lapiths are extinct?!"

Cockiness seeped into her voice, "You're right. Lapiths are extinct . . . just like the Lost Herd of Centaurs."

I shook my head, "What's a Lapith?"

Brent stood tall, still blocking me from Katherine, and answered my question without so much as a glance in my direction. "The only natural enemy of the Centaur."

Blood iced in my veins. If she was our enemy, had we been dragged down here to our deaths? Had other Lapiths taken Jessica, Bianca and Gage hostage? I took a few steps away from her.

She shook her head, "If I wanted ja dead, I'd have let Roscoe take ya at Jessica's bar. Get closer to me before she figures out where ya are."

I wanted to believe Katherine, but if I'd learned anything from Phineas, trust had to be earned, not given freely. Instead of moving closer to her, I angled myself around the side of Brent so I could see her. "So when you first saw us at the motel, you knew who we were?"

"No. I thought it was strange you were all drawn ta my motel. I didn't learn who ya were until I went inta town with Brent."

Brent's eyes went wide, "Hey, I never said a word!" His eyes danced between Katherine and me.

Katherine smirked as she held up her index finger, "You tol' me ya couldn't go home." Her middle finger sprang to attention, "You tol' me you'd followed yer friends up from South Carolina." Katherine's ring finger joined the other two, “You said yer sister has a different mother. It’s not rocket science, Einstein.”

Brent blushed. Had Katherine been who we all thought her to be – a normal human girl, none of those tidbits of information would have caused alarm with anyone. Since she had some insight into our world, it was easy for her to know who we were. “So who are we hiding from? Zandra?”

“That’s the only Centauride Bianca and Jessica would be worried about. Neither of them have anything to do with the Lost Herd round-up going on all over the place, so there would be no reason for them ta be detained. It’s got to be Zandra.”

“You think they’re being detained?”

A regretful expression spread on her face, “That’s a stronger word than I shoulda used.” She was trying to pacify me, “Jessica is Roscoe’s sister. No way is she being interrogated without any proof she broke one of the Centaur tenets. Bianca is from out of town, and her story about honeymooning with Gage is pretty believable.”

“So what do you think is going on?”

Katherine looked to Brent and Daniel, as if she were worried something she was about to say shouldn’t be said in front of them. She wasn’t a Centauride, so I couldn’t have a telepathic conversation. Her face flushed and she answered conspiratorially, “There are rumors that yer being protected by a Centaur.”

Daniel threw up his hands, “Who is, once again, nowhere in sight when she needs him.”

Katherine ignored Daniel’s outburst and asked me, “It’s true? Yer protected by a Centaur warrior?”

I looked at Daniel who was seconds away from losing his cool. I nodded, “Yeah. His name’s Drake. He’s back at the motel. He’s my betrothed.”

Katherine looked astonished, as if searching my eyes for a morsel of doubt. "A true Centaur warrior?"

I nodded again. Brent, who had said remarkably little to Katherine since the "accosting" incident, belligerently asked, "Why Lapith? Do you intend to murder him?"

Katherine's glare was hard, her voice low and full of authority, "Watch yer tongue, Centaur."

Daniel all but ignored the insults flying between Katherine and Brent. "Her true," using his fingers for quotation marks in the air, "Centaur warrior, you're referring to, why are there rumors floating around about that? Wouldn't it be more of a scandal if a human were protecting her?"

I felt a blush, hoping Daniel was just speaking hypothetically and not volunteering for the job.

I watched Katherine's teeth sink into her lip. She didn't know how much Brent and Daniel knew. I was sick of the secrets, because half of them I didn't understand anyway. Rather than try to keep them, I started rattling off everything that was potentially important, "Okay, just so we're all on the same page. Brent and I have the same Centaur father but two different Centauride mothers. The Lost Herd is the only bloodline who is capable of procreation out of wedlock." So far none of the three looked surprised by this revelation.

I looked directly at Brent; his back straightened as if bracing for the worst. "I'm sorry you're in limbo. I'm excited for you for having been chosen, and I think it sucks that you don't know if the betrothal is still on. When we get out of here, we'll figure out how to call her without giving away our location. If we can't get her on the phone, I'll figure out how to contact your Centauride telepathically to see if she still chooses you." Brent pressed his lips together; in that brief second he shared the turmoil in his thoughts with me and nodded a silent "thank you."

I gestured to Daniel with my hand, "Daniel is three-quarters Centaur. His father is pure-blooded and his mother is half-Centaur. I'm not sure what the big whoopy-do is, because everyone keeps calling him a half-breed when he's obviously more than that." Daniel grinned but didn't move to interrupt me.

"Drake is my Centaur. I chose him. He doesn't care that I'm from the Lost Herd, and yes, currently he doesn't look human." Daniel was the only one with a confused expression, but he let me continue.

"That's everything I know. Now, why in the heck do Lapiths not like Centaurs?"

Katherine snickered, "It's nice to have a Centauride who doesn't mind laying her cards on the table." Katherine gestured to herself, "Lapiths are the humans who inhabited the pasture of Thessaly before Kentauros decided ta procreate with our mares. The first Centaurs born on the pasture of Thessaly were Lapith property."

Brent's reaction was loud and laced with anger, "My ancestors were not property! They were children of a god and protected from harsh treatment at the hands of the Lapith, by the very god who fathered them."

Katherine's volume matched Brent's, "Right. Protected? If that's what cha want ta call it. You were creatures loathed by the gods. Zeus couldn't stand ta look at you, so he re-created you in his image and gave you seven simple rules to follow."

"That's not true!"

I jumped in between Katherine and Brent, "STOP! Would you two give it a rest? Decisions made by gods thousands of years ago seem less pressing than the fact that we have Zandra and a pile of Centaurs looking for us right now."

I took a breath, exhaled slowly and did my best to sound calm. "Brent is known to be of the Lost Herd, so he needs a wing-man. Daniel – that's your job. Katherine, use your cloaking powers or whatever they are to keep us hidden. We wait fifteen minutes, and I'll try contacting Bianca and Jessica again. Until then, we keep our voices low and hang tight."

Ten minutes later, Jessica's voice was in my head, "*Come back to the bar. They've got patrols all over the place in the woods.*" I breathed a sigh of relief.

Relief looked back at me from three sets of eyes when I announced, "Jessica wants us to go back to the bar."

Katherine was quick to answer, "Wait, ask her what her favorite ice cream flavor is."

I didn't understand what Katherine was up to. "What?"

"Just do it."

"*Jessica, Katherine wants to know what your favorite ice cream flavor is.*"

"*Oh, right. Tell her, Lamborghini.*"

"*Seriously? Lamborghini?*"

"*Just tell her. Hurry up and get back here.*"

I cleared my throat, wondering if I'd heard her wrong. "She said Lamborghini, and to hurry up and get back to the bar."

Katherine was visibly relieved. "Okay, coast is clear. Let's go."

I didn't understand the little code between the two and wanted clarification before we took a single step. "What are you two – spies?"

"No, just cautious."

Still suspicious, "Lamborghini flavored ice cream? I don't remember seeing that at the grocery store. Is that a South Dakota thing?"

"That was Jessica's idea." Katherine wrapped her fingers around my forearm and squeezed hard, "Always ask that question if she tells ya to meet her somewhere. If she's being coerced in any way, she'll answer with an ice cream flavor – chocolate, vanilla, rainbow sherbet, something. Don't let on that ya know it's a trap, and stay as far away from where yer supposed to meet as possible."

I couldn't understand how they would have put together a code system like this one. "When did she tell you that?"

Katherine looked off into the distance of the tunnel. At first I didn't think she would answer my question, but when she did, her voice was shaky. "She and I used ta have a friend -- Gayle. She died because Jessica couldn't warn her she was being led into a trap. After Gayle was buried, we came up with the code thing."

We had a long walk ahead of us, back to the bar through the tunnel. I wasn't sure if we could trust them. For all I knew the code meant something else entirely. There was likely a bounty on my head, maybe Brent's, too. I began walking, but kept my pace slow while I pressed for more information. "A trap?"

Katherine's gaze was far off in front of us, remaining focused on the dimly lit tunnel ahead. I couldn't be sure what special powers a Lapith might possess. From Brent's reaction to her identity, I needed to be cautious. She must have sensed my apprehension because words began pouring out of her.

"We grew up together. Gayle, Jessica, and I grew up right here – in this town. We met in kindergarten, and everyone, even our teachers, called us the three amigas."

I expected to see images playing in Katherine's mind while she spoke. When people talked about the past, life-like images played in their head. As Katherine spoke, hers was blank. The absence of the images was eerie.

"When we were little we played tetherball together on the playground, hopscotch on the sidewalk in the sunshine. I can't tell ya how many notebooks I went through in junior high, passing notes to 'em in the hallway at school. We were inseparable."

She paused looking at each of us. Her brows pulled together and her complexion lost some of its color. She was wrestling with how much to share. When she found her voice, it was steady, maybe a little distant, as if she were trying to barricade her emotions up – away from us.

"There aren't many Centaur families in this part of the country – only a handful. I had always known my ancestry, and so on instinct alone

– I knew theirs. We gave up the playgrounds and recesses as we got older. I remember endless Saturday afternoons at movie theaters, window shopping at malls for fancy dresses we'd never wear, sharing chicken nuggets in the food court long after the stores closed, studying together for classes none of us cared about, and even ice skating on Gayle's pond, praying the ice would hold the three of us. We were natural enemies and here I was looking at 'em like we were sisters."

The strength in her expression seemed to diminish. "Lying to them about who I was started eatin' me up from the inside. We were supposed to be enemies. . . but . . . I loved them both." Katherine's voice lowered to barely more than a whisper, "They *were* my sisters, or at least the sisters I had always wanted."

She finally settled her gaze on me. "Centaurides can't detect a Lapith – to them I was a human. I worried they would abandon me, ridicule me, maybe even send their family after me if they found out. But, I couldn't keep lying to 'em." A thin smile formed on Katherine's lips, "We were playing a game of truth-or-dare one weekend at Gayle's house. We were fourteen, and I blurted out that I was a Lapith."

"How did they take it?"

Katherine muffled a laugh against the back of her hand, "Gayle offered ta give me a blood transfusion." She smiled at the memory and shook her head, "Can ya imagine?"

My eyes widened, "What would that have done?"

"Nothing. But it was sweet of her to think she could dilute my Lapith blood with her Centauride blood. Gayle tried ta convince Jessica that they should look for a doctor to do the transfusion, and they could each give me a couple pints. She reasoned that if they put more Centauride blood in me than Lapith, they could change who I was, or make me a hybrid. It sounds silly now, but we all wanted ta be sisters."

"So, did they?"

"No, but they would have if I let them. They cared about me whether or not I was their sworn enemy. The two of them agreed never ta tell a soul."

Katherine's bright green eyes went misty, she wiped them hard with the palms of her hands, and her voice began to shake again. "Centaurides don't date, or they're not supposed to. Gayle got asked ta some stupid high school dance by the star football player. He was gorgeous, built like a brick house, and completely wrapped around Gayle's little finger." She shook her head at the memory, as if she were still frustrated with it. "Gayle agreed to be his date."

"The football player killed her?"

"No." Katherine took a breath to steady herself, "Jessica's brother did."

My heart stopped, then began beating like crazy. "Wait. Jessica's brother, Roscoe, killed Gayle?" She nodded, "But why?"

"Gayle's parents were furious with her for agreeing to go on a date with a human. It was our junior year. Her father didn't want ta take a chance on her getting involved with a human, so he arranged a marriage to Roscoe. At first Gayle said she'd go along with it. She chose Roscoe. Gayle said it was her duty, and this way she and Jessica could really be sisters – at least by marriage."

Katherine began trembling. She wrapped her arms around herself and bowed her head. What little color she had drained completely out of her face. "The football player wouldn't let it go. He brought her flowers. He gave her his jersey. He walked her ta class – anything to be close to her. He didn't understand she'd already been promised to Roscoe, and Gayle couldn't tell him about Centaur traditions. None of it would have mattered ta him anyway – he was head-over-heels for Gayle."

"The football player convinced her to break the betrothal?"

Katherine's voice was hollow. "Jessica didn't know Roscoe intended to seek a Blood Debt that day. She found out just before Gayle arrived."

Katherine stood in the middle of the three of us. Her eyes met mine, and I wanted to comfort her. None of us made a sound, waiting for her to continue, but unwilling to prod her. When she spoke, there was a rhythm to her words, as if she were forcing herself to tell us. "Jessica's mother told her she would know if Jessica tried ta warn Gayle. Her mother threatened a betrothal to a Centaur who would make Jessica regret the day she was born if she betrayed her brother and warned Gayle."

Tears streamed down Katherine's cheeks, but she kept talking. "Instead, Jessica pled with Roscoe – begging him not ta kill Gayle. Jessica promised she could make Gayle change her mind and marry Roscoe. In the end, Gayle showed up at Jessica's house, and Roscoe took his Blood Debt right in front of Jessica." It was hard to understand Katherine through the sobs, but she couldn't keep the story in, "Roscoe told her that killing Gayle may end their blood line, but it would be ended with honor."

The barbarism – the thought that my life could have been sacrificed for Mom running away all those years ago sent shivers down my spine. I remembered the desperation I felt when I was told I might have to pay a Blood Debt. The debt for me would have been far better than the debt paid by Gayle. I would have been forced to marry Gage – no one planned to kill me. Tears flowed freely down Katherine's face, and the only response I could force out was, "I'm so sorry."

Katherine must have been holding this story inside since it happened because her words didn't stop. "Jessica didn't attend Gayle's funeral. Gayle's family said she died from the flu – but she hadn't been sick. It was weeks before Jessica could bring herself ta tell me the truth. She wouldn't talk ta me at school or answer my calls or. . ." Katherine trailed off, her voice choked from her own sobs. A full minute passed before she resumed. "Ever since, she's been lying low, biding her time until she can get out of here. When she goes – I'm going, too."

I could hear the truth in her words, and I saw the pain in her face. I believed her, but knew I had to be cautious. "That's why you're helping us? You two are getting back at Roscoe, by keeping us safe?"

CHAPTER 8

Katherine Newton – Deserted Mining Tunnel in South Dakota

Why was I helping them? They didn't have a clue what they were up against. If they did, they wouldn't have wandered around the countryside waiting for the Council's enforcers to find 'em.

Jessica was the only person outside my family that I cared about. Her family was a bunch of fanatics. I didn't know how long she had left. Her parents could arrange a marriage tomorrow, and her only future would be being tied ta some freak like her brother or death if she backed out. I couldn't lose Jess the way we lost Gayle.

Our only chance was helping these five get outta here. I kept a suitcase packed for Jessica at my house. It'd been there for two years – waiting for our escape. Right after Gayle was murdered, Jess and I talked about running away all the time. As the weeks turned inta months, our window of freedom grew slimmer. Jess was twenty-three now. She was the oldest unbetrothed Centauride in the area. This was it. This was our last chance.

Cami wants ta know if we're trying to get back at Roscoe. Roscoe is just the tip of the iceberg. Her eyes are fixed on mine. How can I make her understand? "No. I don't want revenge. Nothing will bring Gayle back. But I can't lose Jessica, too."

Cami's eyes were soft. I didn't want her pity. Jessica and I were sticking our necks out already; they owed us. "When we heard about your betrothed kickin' the crap outta Roscoe and the thirty Centaurs sent by the Centaur Council to kill ya, we thought things might be changing. We'll help ya, but you hafta help me get Jessica away from here."

Daniel and Brent hadn't said a word the whole time. Tears were still streaking down my cheeks. I hated that they saw me cry, but I couldn't help it. Every time I thought about Gayle, I either flew into a rage or bawled like a baby – it didn't matter that it happened six years ago. As much as I hated sharing it with 'em, I needed 'em to know about Gayle. I needed 'em to know why we had to get Jessica far away from her family.

Daniel seemed ta be the ring-leader. Cami trusted him. It wasn't normal for a Centauride to be so close to a human, even if the human was a half-breed. If I could just get Daniel to agree ta help us escape, everyone else would follow suit.

I stood there starin' at Daniel, tryin' to put the urgency into words, but none would come out. My eyes silently pleaded with him to understand – this couldn't be up for discussion. Daniel looked like he was going to ask me a question when Brent, who had been at least ten feet away, strode up to me and said, "I'm sorry for your loss. I never heard of a Lapith befriending a Centauride before."

I used every ounce of what was left of my strength to answer, "We weren't friends because she and Jessica were Centaurides – we were friends in spite of it."

Brent nodded. He closed the distance to me, wrapped both his arms around me and pulled me forcefully into his chest. I was surprised. . . stunned. . . shocked. I froze, not sure how ta react. Less than an hour ago, I had barely touched him, and he had about lost his mind. I stood stiffly against him, trying to make the tears stop, wanting to break free of his hold while my body only wanted to accept his warm embrace.

My lungs sucked in as much air as they could hold. I had to convince Daniel to help us. Brent's sudden willingness not only to touch me, but to try to ease my pain didn't make sense, and we didn't have the time to waste.

His strong hands held me close. His chest rose and fell under my head as he breathed. It was as hard as granite under my face. No matter how hard I tried, I couldn't hold it together. The tears that had streamed down my cheeks gave way to heavy sobs again, and I let 'em loose against his chest.

He whispered in my ear, "We'll get you out of here. We'll get you both out. You have my word." His gentle hands ran up and down my back, squeezing ever-so-gently every few seconds. He kept talkin', but I couldn't hear his whispers over my own sobs. I didn't need to hear his words: he was telling me he'd help us escape. . . both of us.

Brent's posture and his movements were so stiff. It seemed like he wasn't accustomed to being affectionate, to comfort someone with anything more than words, but he was trying his best. I could have shut off the tears if I hadn't been affected by how badly he wanted to make me feel better. The more he tried to comfort me, the more my emotions sailed outta control.

Instead of just leaning against him, my arms snaked around him, holding on to him for dear life. He gently kissed the top of my head and gave me one final squeeze. He didn't let go of me; he just loosened his grip so that if I wanted to pull away, I was no longer held in place. I didn't move. It took me a couple minutes, but I got my sobs under control, took a deep breath, and told them, "Jess is waiting for us. We need to go."

Brent didn't let go of me, at least not all the way. His arm hung over my shoulder as we started back down the dark tunnel. The warmth of his body walking next to mine was therapeutic and toxic rolled together. I'd been raised never to trust a Centaur – never to allow one to learn who I was or I would risk being killed on the spot. But, here, now, I more than wanted Brent's comfort. I craved it – which got me worried for a whole different reason. I silently prayed that I had not just felt the spark – Lily's spark.

Less than an hour ago he'd accused me of trying to accost him when nothing could have been further from reality. I understood why we were discouraged from any interaction with Centaurs, but for the first time since Gayle's death, I felt like things were going to be okay.

Daniel and Cami gave us some space. I could hear their footsteps behind us, but neither was talking.

Brent must have wanted ta explain his sudden change of heart. His eyes remained fixed on the tunnel in front of us. His voice was quiet, only loud enough for me to hear it. "I saw a Blood Debt paid when I was young; I was maybe eight. Even now the image is so clear it feels like it happened yesterday. I didn't know the Centauride who'd been murdered, but from that moment, no matter who wronged me, I knew I'd never collect one."

I hadn't seen what happened ta Gayle, but I'd imagined it ever since I heard how Roscoe had killed her. Gayle's Blood Debt had been an intimate affair – only Roscoe's family was present. The Centaur who had been wronged had the option to collect his debt in private or on a public display. The Centauride's family had the responsibility not only of claiming the body when it was over, but the added humiliation of disposing of the body, dealing with the human authorities, even having an autopsy faked.

Brent looked over his shoulder, maybe to make sure Daniel and Cami couldn't hear him. I wasn't sure. "When we thought Cami might owe a Blood Debt for her mother, my brothers and I agreed one of us would pay it for her. Dad was sure he could make it right to the Richardsons in cash, but we weren't willing to take the chance. Bruce was betrothed, so the four of us decided one of us would pay it before we let it be collected against her."

"One of you?"

"Yeah, Beau, Bart, Ben and I all agreed. No one would collect on Cami."

"I can't imagine that kind of sacrifice. Ya must be close."

Brent chuckled, "That's the funny thing. None of us knew her that well, but there's something about Cami. She's special."

"The last Chiron Centauride, right?"

"Well, yeah, but that's not what I mean. She's different. It's like, because she grew up as a human, she's doesn't just conform. She looks at our traditions and isn't afraid to say, 'Hey, that's dumb, and I'll do it my way.' Don't get me wrong, it drives me crazy, but we were all immediately drawn to her because of it."

Brent's description of Cami's take on the Centaur world made me laugh. Truthfully, I didn't know much about her other than she was Chiron's last female heir and was also from the Lost Herd. Hearing Brent describe her made me want to know her better. It reminded me of how Gayle basically did the same thing – she was willing to throw everything away for a human. It wasn't even someone she was madly in love with – Gayle was just a free spirit.

I may have misjudged Brent. He was different. A brother who would willingly pay a Blood Debt for his sister? Gayle had two brothers. Had they known Roscoe would collect a Blood Debt that day, would they have paid it for her? It didn't seem likely.

"I can't imagine Roscoe's willingness to collect his Blood Debt." Brent's comment hung in the air for a minute before he added, "If he knew how much Gayle meant to his sister, I mean, I just can't imagine. I could never hurt Cami the way Roscoe hurt Jessica, and we didn't even grow up together."

Could he be that selfless? The few Centaurs I'd met in Jessica and Gayle's families weren't like Brent – at all. They weren't the beasts my grandma had described to me in her freaky bedtime stories, but they were distanced – almost absent human emotions. Sure they had pride and courage, but none of the Centaurs in their families displayed even a morsel of empathy or sorrow.

We walked quietly for a few more minutes. Brent didn't remove his arm from my shoulder, and to let him know I appreciated his kindness, I reached up and took his hand that lay over my bicep. I had thought Brent was just like every other Centaur I'd known. I wasn't sure what to make of his thaw toward me. He may not be my friend, but after his promise, I no longer saw him as an adversary, either.

I thought about his touch and what it meant for a Centaur to touch a woman once he was betrothed. Brent must have believed that Cami and Daniel would never betray him to his fiancé. Or maybe he believed his betrothed had already changed her mind. Maybe he needed to tell someone that even if he had the choice, he wouldn't seek a Blood Debt. Whatever his reason, I was grateful for his comfort.

We found ourselves back underneath the bar. I looked up at the ladder that led to the secret entry behind the pop machine and wished we could stay here in the tunnel – just a few minutes more. I wanted to escape with Jessica, but I wanted to absorb the kindness Brent freely gave me, too.

Cami and Daniel caught up to us and peered up the ladder we had escaped down nearly an hour ago. I gave her an exhausted smile. We were close – we were seriously close to freedom. It lay just on the other side of the pop machine. "Cami, do yer thing. Ask Jessica if the coast is clear."

CHAPTER 9

Camille – Deserted Motel in South Dakota

I had the strangest sensation. Normally, when I called out to someone telepathically, I would visualize their face and feel a static-like connection establish – a little like making eye-contact where I could see the other's eyes, but not necessarily the dilation of their pupils. As I attempted to establish the connection with Jessica, it felt like it was already live. "*We're below. Is it safe to come up?*"

"*Yes, hurry. They'll be back any minute!*" If Jessica had felt anything strange in our connection, she didn't let on.

My eyes flashed open to the three sets staring back at me. "She says to go up, but they could be back any time."

Daniel immediately grabbed the ladder and shimmied up. Brent motioned for me to go next. I looked below me on the ladder and saw Katherine beneath me. When I followed Daniel through the access panel behind the soda machine, Jessica was waiting for us. Katherine was just a few feet away from the top when the "Click" of the light switch sounded below. My neck careened back through the hole; I moved out of the way so Katherine could climb through. I looked back down into the abyss and saw nothing but black.

My stomach tightened. I looked at my watch; mere seconds had passed, but the tunnel was so dark, and I couldn't hear Brent's feet on the ladder. Had someone followed us? Had they taken him? The fine hairs on my arm stood tall, as goose bumps peppered my arms. Where was he? What was taking him so long? I leaned back through the opening and shouted into the emptiness, "Brent!"

Brent's face came into view from the darkness with a determined scowl on his face. "Trying to knock me off, or what? Geeze."

Jessica's speech was rapid. "They know you're in the area. Roscoe is convinced you're in some human's house here in town. No one has even considered the motel because it's closed down for the season and it's almost impossible to get to. Get out of here quick before they find you." Jessica grabbed my forearm in a vice grip, "Your grandmother is here looking for you, too."

My eyes fixed on Katherine; she was right. That had to be why Bianca and Jessica had both tuned me out. Katherine placed both her hands on Jessica's shoulders from behind. It was an odd sight because she was so much shorter than Jessica. She leaned her head against Jessica's shoulder blades, "We're going with them, now, tonight."

Jessica's posture straightened while she searched our faces. Her expression was a mixture of fear, adrenaline, and relief, all rolled into one. I didn't want a repeat of Katherine's turmoil in the tunnel, so I telepathically answered Jessica's questioning look, "*Katherine told us about Gayle. We'll get you out of here. We'll tuck you away where no one can find you.*"

Jessica's eyes widened for a moment then returned to normal when she answered, "*You'll never be able to hide us from my family. My mother will find us.*"

Katherine's hands still lay on Jessica's shoulders. Jessica rested her hands over the top of Katherine's while the two women let it soak in that they would try to escape.

The two were such an odd couple. Katherine with her red hair, porcelain complexion and petite frame: even without her abrasive personality – she wasn't someone to blend in. Jessica was tall and slender, her features delicate, her platinum blonde locks fell over her shoulder, and she had this mischievous vibe about her. Neither were wallflowers, but I never would have pegged the two personalities to be so close to one another, either.

"*She told us about being a Lapith. As long as you two stick together, you can stay hidden for as long as you like. We'll get you somewhere safe.*"

Jessica patted Katherine's hands and then wordlessly walked over to me. I couldn't read her expression or her emotions until she pulled me into a tight hug. It felt strange because she was so much taller than I was, too. Her hair smelled like stale cigarette smoke from spending so much of her time in the bar. The others must have understood we were having a telepathic conversation because no one's eyebrows rose by our embrace or her, "Thank you."

I gave Jessica a short nod as an answer, then asked, "Everyone ready?" The four of them agreed, but I looked around, suddenly hit with the question: how were we going to get out of here? I held up a single finger, "Hold on just a second."

If we tried to make a run for it and were seen, we could be putting Jessica and Katherine in danger. No one was suspicious of either of them. As far as anyone knew, they hadn't seen us. I looked at Daniel. He wasn't a pure-blooded Centaur, and although I'd always told him he ran like a gazelle, his speed was not in the same league with Brent's. Daniel would need to go with Katherine and Jessica.

I looked at Brent, my brother who had already been through so much. If he were found, could he fight his way free from Centaur enforcers? No. I couldn't ask Jessica or Katherine to drive him because he and I already carried a death sentence. I didn't know what the punishment would be for anyone caught with either of us, but I wasn't willing to risk their lives.

I closed my eyes and called to Drake, "*We are on our way back to the motel. I'm with Brent. We'll be there soon.*"

There was no delay in his response, "*What?!*"

I tried to keep the fear from seeping into my voice, "*This place is crawling with Centaur enforcers, and Zandra is here. It'll be faster if Brent carries me through the woods.*"

"*Stay there. If you're going on foot I want to be there.*"

My heart swelled. There was no place safer than in Drake's arms, but if Jessica was right and the woods were full of Centaur enforcers, coming for me would put him at risk and that was unacceptable. "*No. Brent's ready to go. We'll be there in no time.*"

"*Bianca and Gage are already back from town. He said Centaur enforcers are looking for us. It's not safe for Brent to run and to try to stave off an attack. Show me where you are. I don't want you two by yourselves.*"

The tightness in my stomach increased. The image of Drake fighting off thirty enforcers played through my mind. He was right. We would be safer with Drake, but Drake and I had the element of surprise on our side the last time. That advantage was gone now. The enforcers were not only ready for us, they were looking for us.

Jessica, Katherine, Daniel and Brent looked nervous. I was wasting valuable time. "*Okay. You're right.*" I pushed an image of the bar to Drake. "*We won't be able to stay at the motel long, but we should be safe there until morning. We found a Lapith to help cloak us.*"

"*A Lapith? To cloak you? But they're extinct.*"

"*That's funny. That's what she said about the Lost Herd.*"

"*Give me a few minutes.*" Still connected to Drake, I could see the trees zooming past his head as he was already out of the motel and galloping through the forest.

I turned back to the others waiting in the back room of the bar. "Okay, Drake's coming. Katherine, you and Jessica take your truck back; it'll look suspicious if it's still on the street overnight. Daniel, no one thinks of you as a Centaur, so you take Gage's rental truck and follow them back. Brent, when Drake comes, he'll carry me, and you two can run back to the motel."

Brent looked at Katherine as if he wasn't in favor of my plan. He put his back to her and took a step in my direction, "Drake won't be able to run as fast carrying you. You and I should leave now and meet him outside of town."

I shook my head, "You haven't seen Drake yet. Carrying me won't slow him down." I motioned to Jessica, Katherine and Daniel, "You three, go. Brent and I'll wait by the back door for Drake."

Jessica started to protest, but before she could argue, I sent an image of Drake in his new form to her. She gave me an understanding nod, "Okay, we'll be there within thirty minutes. We'll meet at Katherine's house instead of the motel. You may even beat us there. Katherine, Daniel – let's go."

The door shut behind them. Jessica locked the front door from the outside. Brent stood beside me in the empty bar, the only illumination from beer signs hanging along the wall. The only sound was our breathing. I wasn't purposely trying to read his thoughts, but couldn't help seeing images of Jessica and Katherine, his worry for them obvious. I shook my head, "They'll be fine. None of them have ties to us. If the enforcers see them, they won't give them a second thought."

Brent shook his head. "Daniel has ties to you."

"Centaurs are too pompous to see the tie as anything more than a coincidence. Not one of them would give him any consideration. They'll be okay."

I could feel Drake outside the back door. I didn't need to hear his voice, his breath, or a knock on the door – I could feel his presence. His thoughts were laced with worry, not for himself, but the fear of running through the forest unprotected, carrying me. I opened the back door and there he stood, the size of a quarter-horse, well over seven feet tall – over nine hundred pounds of rage for any who tried to stop us.

The last few weeks of seeing Drake like this, I'd grown accustomed to his new physique – Brent, on the other hand, got an eyeful. He took a step in front of me on sheer instinct, and his easy flowing words from the tunnel were replaced with stammers as Drake stood directly in front of him. "Drake. . . you're. . . I mean, you have. . . are you able. . ."

I cut him off for fear that he'd never get a single coherent thought out. "I told you that you hadn't seen him in a while. You knew this happened: don't look so surprised. You ready?"

Brent's jaw hung open. He was able to control himself enough to send the signal to his brain and nod his head, but made no attempt to speak.

I looked into Drake's ice blue eyes. They were narrowed from the cold and likely close to being frozen that way. I'd experienced his speed two nights ago, when we escaped the Centaur assault at Cameron's house, but it was still hard to wrap my mind around the idea that he probably came close to breaking the sound barrier getting here.

Drake motioned for me to come closer. Brent didn't move out of my way, but he didn't try to stop me from going to Drake either. Brent stood motionless, frozen in place. Drake brought his hands to either side of my face. Despite the sub-zero temperatures, his hands were warm – almost hot to the touch. Drake's voice was soft, "I'm glad you're okay." His hands gently cradled my face, and he leaned down, brushing a whisper of a kiss across my lips.

His hands slid down from my face and gathered me in his arms with about as much effort as reaching down and picking up a toddler. He turned his attention to Brent. "Do your best to keep up. I'll try not to leave you behind, but we need to run as fast as possible through town. Watch your step out there. Centaur lookouts are strategically positioned throughout the forest. I found a riding trail where it looks like humans have been on their snowmobiles and ATVs. If you keep your feet light on the ground, the trails should camouflage our prints."

Brent finally spoke, "You're a Centaur."

Drake gave Brent a forced smile. I thought Brent had been prepared to see Drake. He came to South Dakota after Beau had told him about the transformation. Brent's eyes were fixed on Drake. In an eerie way, it bothered me that his eyes refused to blink.

Drake turned around to face the stunned Brent, his forced smile still on his lips, "Let's catch up back at the motel. I'll get us to the trail, then you set the pace. Don't worry about your speed; we'll be able to keep up."

Brent nodded, and the next thing I saw was the blur of the deserted street, evergreens and naked maples whizzing past us. I buried my face into Drake's bare chest and concentrated on the rhythm of his heart beat. There wasn't a safer place anywhere, or a place I wanted to be more than cradled in his arms – even if we were dodging Centaurs sent to kill us.

This close to Drake, his thoughts flowed easily to me. Every few seconds an image of Daniel flashed through his mind, followed by me and an image of Drake's now transformed body. His transformation hadn't tarnished his feelings for me, but it was obvious he was thinking about the possibility of Daniel and me ending up together. Drake loved me, but he no longer thought of us as the same species.

I don't know how many times over the last couple weeks I had told him this was temporary, that he wouldn't remain in this form forever. His mind was so focused on the dangers of the forest that his thoughts were nearly unguarded. I saw the truth of his thoughts for the first time

– Drake didn't believe me that this was temporary. Because he chose to remain this way after he was given the option to change back to being a human – in his mind, his transformation was a life sentence. I couldn't see his future, but when I thought of our long term plans, it was always with him in human form.

Drake's voice reverberated in my head, "*Almost there, Love. About one more minute.*"

I raised my head up enough to feel a branch slap me on the shoulder. The force of the branch because of Drake's speed could have sliced my face open, so I tucked back in close, to be sure I wouldn't have an enormous gash on my face when we stopped. His arms gripped me tighter as he smashed me against his chest, "*I said, 'almost,' I didn't say that we were there yet.*"

He was right, a few seconds later I could hear the earth under his feet. Drake and Brent were slowing down. As I peeked up, the lights of Katherine's house were ahead of us. Drake barely sounded winded, "Where to?"

"Katherine's house. It's right behind the motel's tree line. The others should arrive soon. They left a few minutes before you showed up."

Drake set me on my feet and took both my hands in his. The sight of him was still magnificent. The moonlight reflected off of his bare skin, his muscles somehow more defined in the darkness. I stood there mesmerized, forgetting the fear from seeing Roscoe, and the worry of the severed communications with Jessica and Bianca. I was safe with Drake, and for now that was enough.

Brent stood awkwardly next to us. His face was beet red, but he didn't seem to be out of breath. How could the two cover so much distance that quickly and act as if it had been no more than a stroll in the park?

I looked up at the rustic house standing before us. It looked like it had been carved out of the hardwoods it was nestled in. The front of the house was exposed wood, but it wasn't like the pre-fabricated mountain cabins that were so popular for second homes. The roof was covered in snow and the windows were steamed so badly they looked like frosted panes of glass. A path to the front door was well worn with Katherine's footprints.

Drake had been worrying since I first contacted him, but he hadn't wasted time asking questions before. As the three of us stood outside Katherine's house, he asked, "Who is this Lapith you said you found?"

"It's Katherine."

Drake's muscles flexed, his eyes widened as he looked at me, then at the house, then at the motel we had been staying in. "Katherine? The human who owns the motel?"

"Yes."

Thoughts swirled in Drake's mind, but he chose to keep most of them to himself. When he finally spoke, his tone was reserved, "A Lapith's nature is to war with Centaurs. At least, in the stories my father told, they were humans with extraordinary powers – powers used to attack Centaurs at will."

Brent answered Drake's indirect accusation, "She's okay. I heard the same stories growing up. Katherine's not like that. We found a pure-blooded Centauride at the bar tonight – Jessica. The two of them are tight."

Drake's eyebrow arched as he looked between Brent and me, "They're tight?"

I agreed, "Like best friends. They're with Daniel, on their way here now."

"How did you find Daniel?" Drake's muscles still refused to relax as I watched steam rise off of his exposed flesh. My stomach started cinching up as I remembered my earlier conversation with Daniel in the tunnel. Daniel didn't have any love for Drake, either.

I tried to sound oblivious to his contempt for Daniel. "He walked into the bar right before we did. Isn't it great?"

Drake muttered under his breath, "Yeah, fantastic."

We made our way to Katherine's house to wait for the others, careful to walk inside as many footprints and snowmobile tracks as we could find to try to hide all the extra footprints. She had left the door unlocked. Brent went in first, then Drake and I followed. Drake hit his head on the light hanging in the entryway, but steadied it with his hand before it could swing back and hit him a second time.

Drake rumbled, "Great, low ceilings."

I patted his arm, "I don't think we're staying long." I could feel Bianca was close. She had to be in the motel with Gage. "*Bianca, can you two come over to Katherine's house?*"

I could hear the joy in her response as I chastised myself for not cluing her in sooner, "*You're back? We've been looking for the truck to pull up out front.*"

"*Minor change of plans. We're at Katherine's house.*"

Less than three minutes passed before the door to the entryway burst open. Bianca navigated her way around Drake and threw her arms around me. "You're safe! OHMYGOODNESS, I froze when I saw Zandra tonight."

"Did she talk to you two?"

"No, not a word. She pretended she didn't even see us. We were parked right outside the access door to the tunnel like you told us. She came out of the woods with like seven Council enforcers."

I thought about what Katherine had told me about being close to her. Could we have been close enough that Bianca was cloaked, too? I asked cautiously, "So, she didn't see you?"

"She had to have seen us, we were right there in front of her! I didn't want to risk it by communicating with you. After they disappeared back into the woods, I was worried it was a trap, so we left."

"Did they follow you?"

"No, seriously, Cami. It was like they were pretending they couldn't see us! You don't think Zandra's helping hide you, do you?"

If Bianca and Gage were directly over the access, their position had to be at least forty feet from where we were standing below. I wondered if Katherine was even more powerful than she knew. Car doors slammed shut outside. Jessica, Katherine and Daniel had made it. I heard my own sigh of relief – we'd all made it.

Bianca was waiting for my answer. "No. Zandra's not here to help us."

None of us had moved past the entryway, so when Katherine opened the door, she must have been a little surprised to see us all wedged in there. The vulnerability in her voice from the tunnel was gone. She was frustrated, "For Pete's sake, Drake, there's no danger here. Change back." Katherine, Jessica and Daniel squeezed into the already packed entryway as she slammed the door shut. Daniel's eyes were enormous as he took in Drake's body.

You could have heard a pin drop in the cramped room. After the silence had gone about four seconds too long, I said, "He can't change back, Katherine."

"Well, of course, he can! Drake, I think it's great you're worried about Cami, but this is my house – change back to your human form or you're going outside. This may not be the Ritz, but I don't allow livestock inside."

I wanted to pull her off to the side and tell her privately this was a sacrifice Drake had made for me, but it was more than just Katherine who needed to hear it. I cleared my throat and looked Drake in the eyes as I shared with our little posse of friends. "When I'd been kidnapped, Drake thought the only way to get me back to safety was to find Chiron's arrow. Somehow he found my twin brother, and when he couldn't convince him to give it up, Drake took the arrow then went after me. There must have been some magic still in the arrow because Chiron turned him into a Centaur to protect me."

Drake's hands reached out and took mine in his tentatively. He squeezed my hand, letting me know it was okay to tell them the rest of the story. I looked around at all the eyes staring back at me, "Drake spoke with Zeus and was given the chance to return to his human form. Zeus knew that if he went back to being human, he wouldn't be able to protect me, so Drake chose to stay a Centaur."

I let my words hang in the air. Daniel was the one standing closest to the door. Drake had his back to him when Daniel reached over and swatted him on the hindquarter – hard. "You did this for Cami?"

Drake angled around and looked Daniel square in the eye. "I did."

Daniel didn't sound impressed. "It never occurred to you that you could have stayed human and just asked for help?"

Drake shook his head, "I know how you feel about Cami, but she's my responsibility. I made the right choice. Zeus knew what was coming. Two nights ago we were ambushed by thirty Centaurs," he clarified, "Centaurs with only two legs. It wouldn't have mattered if you, Beau and Bart had stayed back to help, there were too many of them. Cami and I escaped with our lives because of this." Drake gestured to his body.

Katherine sighed loudly, "Just like I thought. Chiron did this, not Zeus."

Drake hadn't met Katherine, but he turned around to face her, and in doing so shoved Gage and Bianca into the wall. "That's right. I will fight to the death for Cami." I couldn't be sure, but his tone sounded like a challenge of some sort, as if Katherine were the enemy.

Not at all impressed with Drake's words, Katherine answered, "Okay, fine. But while she's under my roof, she has *my* protection." She looked at the startled Gage and Bianca, who had stepped a little further inside the house and away from Drake. Katherine refused to back down when she demanded, again, "Change back before ya trample any more of my guests!"

Drake's normally calm demeanor disappeared, "You're not listening. I. Can't. Change. Back."

"You're not listening ta me, Centaur. Chiron changed you to protect his last Centauride heir, eh?"

Drake and I both nodded that that was what had happened. Katherine continued, "It's not so hard to figure out. Think abou' it. He wouldn't have done that if it meant she was miserable. Ya think he intended for you ta stay half a man? How would that carry on his bloodline?"

"Chiron decided her life was more important than carrying on his blood line. Zeus said it was permanent."

"And you believed him?"

A collective intake of breath sounded around the room. I hadn't spent my whole life as a Centauride, but I knew none of them ever said anything negative about the gods. Nor did they question any message delivered from a god. Did she realize she was questioning the father of the gods? She couldn't.

"I have no reason to doubt his words."

Katherine bowed her head and threw her hands in the air. "That's what I thought! You've never even tried ta change back, have ya?"

I froze. All those times, no less than a hundred, I'd told Drake it was temporary. Did he have the power to change back the entire time? How would he do it? Would he need to touch the arrow? It was gone – long gone. Could he summon Chiron to ask? Chiron hadn't spoken with Drake or me; *Zeus* told him it was forever, but I hadn't believed it, not really.

No one spoke, but thoughts buzzed all over the room, many echoing the same questions I had. Other than the thoughts whizzing by in all directions, the room itself remained silent as Drake and Katherine stared at each other. No one moved.

His nostrils flared, his eyebrows furrowed, and, if he would have had the ability to shoot her with lasers through his pupils, he would have. Drake's voice was forceful, "You're asking if I questioned Zeus?"

"I'm pointing out that you aren't looking at this change from Chiron's perspective. He didn't do it as a punishment. Zeus doesn't know Chiron's mind."

Everyone's voices were still absent, but their thoughts came crashing in on me. It felt like a tidal wave of doubt. Could Zeus have been wrong? Could he have been purposely deceptive? Why would he be? Daniel stared at me, and it was his thoughts that stood out compared to the others. "*Cami deserves to be happy. I can't stand Drake, but that's who she wants. I wonder. . .*"

Daniel winked at me, then turned toward Drake and cleared his throat. His tone was smug, borderline condescending, "Drake's right. He'll never be more than half a man. Cami, I think this is a sign from your great-grandaddy himself – I'm all yours."

Shocked faces around the room looked among Daniel, Drake and me. If Daniel meant it as a joke, no one was laughing.

I shook my head in a warning, "Daniel, stop."

Drake's hoof stomped and the light overhead swung slightly. Every person in the compact room tensed, silently begging Daniel not to antagonize Drake in the close quarters. Daniel didn't stop. He turned his back on Drake, so he stood facing me, as if daring Drake to stop him. His voice turned silky smooth, "Drake already gave you to me. He knew he could never be the man you needed. He already stepped aside for me. Ask him."

I couldn't believe my ears. Who was this guy? Certainly not the best friend I'd had since grade school. It was hard enough to convince Drake to stay with me; I didn't need Daniel antagonizing him into leaving. My voice shook as the first bits of anger escaped me, "He only did that because he thought I couldn't accept him. I hadn't found him yet when that happened. He thought I needed a man."

Daniel's voice was still full of confidence, "Oh, Cami, you *do* need a man. I've been waiting in the wings for you long enough. Don't worry, you'll get used to someone who can wrap their arms *and* legs around you when it's cold." Daniel wound his arms around me and kissed me, close mouthed while I struggled to get out of his grasp.

Everyone crammed into the little entryway tried to melt into the paint on the wall to give Drake whatever space they could.

I could feel Drake's fury. His rage was oozing from every pore on his body, and his thoughts were clouded in a red haze. Daniel was oblivious to Drake's anger and moved one of his hands down my side and slid it under the back of my shirt. Shock registered in everyone's thoughts as they helplessly watched Daniel's actions. My body remained strained, rigid against him. No matter how I struggled, I couldn't get away from Daniel. How had I never noticed how strong he was?

When Daniel eased his lips away from me, he added one final insult, "It's okay, Cami. We've got plenty of time to get re-acquainted – all night if you need it, as many nights as you want. I'm sure Katherine can spare a room."

Drake's body started shaking. Gage, Bianca, Brent and Jessica all inconspicuously began backing out of the entryway and into the adjacent room. Katherine stayed in the entryway but moved away from Drake. His whole body flushed. A powerful glare was aimed directly at the back of Daniel's head, then a shout so loud the walls shook, "She's mine!"

I tried to catch Drake's attention while struggling to wrench free of Daniel. "*Drake calm down. I chose you. Calm down. He doesn't know what he's saying. It's not like that between Daniel and me.*" Other incoherent fragments of thoughts were tossed in there, too. None seemed to have any effect on Drake's thoughts; the red tint to his thoughts only grew in intensity.

Daniel acted as if Drake's declaration had been no more than a whisper, "Yours, huh? Prove it. Prove you can be the man she needs you to be. If not, I'll take her off your hands." Daniel spun me around so I was standing with my back to him, facing Drake.

Drake didn't speak; his body was still trembling. Daniel's voice egged him on one last time, "That's what I thought. You're like every other Centaur I've ever met. Go ahead and be the tough guy saving the day, and I'll be the evening entertainment – keeping her warm."

Drake let out a guttural growl from deep within. Everyone froze. Tremors erupted on his flesh, spots of light danced on Drake's skin. The little spots of light grew, then intensified. Looking at Drake was like staring into Xenon headlights. I had to look away when the light enveloped his whole body.

It felt like his skin had caught fire as heat radiated off of him. I stood motionless, unsure what to do or how to help. The light's intensity grew so bright that everyone moved away and shielded their eyes. Daniel whipped me around, put his back to Drake's light-storm, and pulled me into his chest.

I tried to listen into Drake's thoughts, but it was a mixture of rage and heartbreak. I couldn't make out any of his thoughts clearly, and Daniel's body kept me from getting a look at what was going on. Daniel's grip on me eased as he brought his mouth to my ear and whispered, "You owe me big time for that. You better make sure he doesn't kick the crap out of me tonight."

I was confused, "What?"

The brightness in the room diminished. My eyes were trained on Daniel's wide smile as gasps sounded all around the room. I peeked over Daniel's shoulder and couldn't believe my eyes. Drake stood in the center of the entryway – not the Centaur who loved me and willingly sacrificed everything for my safety – but the man. The man who held my heart in his hand stood in the center of the room, bitterness glaring through his eyes.

Daniel's hands went slack around me. I scrambled around Daniel and threw myself into Drake. The realization hit me that Daniel had just risked his own life to give me Drake back. My eyes took in Drake, standing in the middle of the room, naked and bubbling with rage.

Tears stung as they formed in my eyes – I reached for Drake. Drake didn't even notice that my arms clung to him; his glare for Daniel told me he didn't understand what Daniel had just done. Daniel stood behind me, his voice full of humor, "Now would be a good time to let him in on what I was doing, Cami. Like now – before I get bloody."

Daniel's nervous laugh echoed behind me as smiles erupted throughout the little entryway.

I smoothed my hands on either side of Drake's face until his ice blue eyes finally focused on mine. "It's you. It's really you." The tears that had formed in my eyes rushed down my face as his arms pulled me tight against his body – his human body.

Daniel still stood behind me as he said, "Yes, it's all of him all right. Katherine, can you give him a towel or something? I don't know how much I can see before I'm blinded."

Snickers burst out in the room around us. I heard it, but my heart was already beating in rhythm with Drake's – strong and fast. I wanted the others to disappear – to leave us.

Bianca cleared her throat, "Um, Katherine, I think we should give them a minute. We should all go inside." I wanted to thank her, but I couldn't peel my eyes away from Drake's.

Jessica, Katherine, Bianca, Gage, Brent, and Daniel all walked through the entryway into the kitchen. Katherine popped back through the doorway and tossed a towel at Drake. He let it fall to the floor, making no effort to pick it up.

There was so much I wanted to say, but my words wouldn't come out. A look of horror stared back at me as he mumbled, "I can't protect you like this."

"You don't have to. We're safe with Katherine."

He shook his head, "For tonight. But what about tomorrow? And the day after that?" He reached down and picked up the towel from the floor, wrapping it around himself. His feet stayed planted and his expression didn't change.

I didn't care about tomorrow. Or next week. Or even three days ago. Drake was here with me right now. "We'll worry about tomorrow when it comes. Drake – you're you again."

"What if the Council's enforcers come again? What then?"

Self-preservation should have kicked in. It didn't. My mind refused to play the "what if" game. Drake was a human. We were safe right now. I wanted to shake him. If he could change into a human, he could change back to a Centaur Warrior. It wasn't all or nothing. This wasn't a punishment from Zeus – this was a gift from Chiron.

"If they find us, you change back."

His hollow words hung in the air, "I don't know how."

"You'll figure it out."

Both his hands gripped my arms, "You don't understand. I don't know how. What if I can't control it?"

I couldn't bring myself to say the words out loud because I knew my voice would betray me. "*I never asked for your protection. I didn't ask for you to give up your life for me. Is it so wrong to just be grateful that you're normal again?*"

Drake grimaced. "Your life is more important than my happiness. Don't you see? If something happens to you, I won't be able to stop it."

Hurt registered and I didn't try to hide it. I preferred the jealous, rage-induced warrior – the one who wanted me so badly he forced his body to change rather than risking someone else having me. Had I fooled myself into believing that's how he felt?

Maybe I had misjudged Drake? Maybe he didn't want me – at least not the way I wanted him. My knees began to buckle. I should have blocked what I was feeling: the anguish, the utter loneliness I'd been carrying with me for weeks. I didn't. I let Drake feel the rejection swelling inside me.

His expression changed as he took a tighter grip on my arms. Just as I'd allowed him to feel the hurt from his rejection, he opened up his emotions to me. Drake was ashamed that he'd lost control because of Daniel. He was scared that we'd be discovered and killed because of it. He was angry at himself for letting his guard down. But the emotion that chiseled away at all the other competing emotions was the desire he felt for me. His voice left no room for doubt, "I do want you the same way."

Confusion took control. No matter what he said about our safety – he did feel it. His desire boiled just under the surface, threatening to spill over. Still holding my arms, he leaned in to me. Drake's whisper was hot and slow in my ear, "You're mine." His hands drifted under the back of my shirt as sparks rained on my skin where his fingers greedily stroked me. Hungry lips found my neck as his words vibrated against my skin as he repeated, "You're mine."

CHAPTER 10

Camille – Katherine Newton's Home in South Dakota

In a fluid motion Drake opened a door along the wall I hadn't noticed before. He pulled me into the dark room and shut it behind us. My eyes hadn't adjusted to the dark, and it felt about thirty degrees colder. The floor was made of cement – we were in the garage.

His hand returned to the tender skin of my lower back while his other cupped my jaw. Drake's voice was slow, "I missed you."

His lips were on mine, soft and gentle – not matching my own building fire. Drake's touch fed off my hunger; his fingers dug hard into my back, pulling me fully to his body. I could feel him, all of him, as we stood wrapped together in the frigid garage. His voice sent shivers all the way to my toes, "I want you." His body guided me up against the metal door we had just walked through, as his other hand went to my face.

Drake's lips refused to let mine go. My heart beat erratically, the sound so loud I could hear the beating of it in my ears. I couldn't get the words out, so I answered him in thought, "*You can have me. Here. Now.*" I laced my hands around the towel gathered at his waist, my fingers sliding just under the rim. His skin was smooth, warm – inviting my touch.

A moan escaped his lips as he pressed his body fully into mine while his answer echoed in my mind. "*You feel incredible.*"

I didn't care that the door my back was pressed against felt like ice through my clothes. I didn't care that the room was so dark we could have been in a cave. I only cared that Drake's body was hot against mine, just as warm as it had been the night I found him shirtless in the woods before a blizzard. His lips were soft and his muscles rigid.

A soft tap on the other side of the door reminded us that we weren't alone in the house. When I opened my eyes, they had adjusted to the darkness, and I could make out Drake's face in front of mine. It was his angry growl that answered the knock, "Not now."

Katherine was on the other side of the door. "When you can untangle yourselves from each other, I've left some clothes out here for you on the table. We're in the kitchen waiting on you two."

"Give us a minute." Drake's lips were back on my neck sending more shivers through my body. His lips caressed their way up to my ear, as his teeth grazed the tender skin of my ear lobe. His breath was hot in my ear as he spoke the words in a heavy whisper, "Not now, but soon. *Very* soon." Drake thrust his body one more time against mine. A combination of heat and tingles erupted inside me. His hands slid down both my arms, as he took both my hands in his. He brought my hands to his lips. "No one, anywhere, will ever love you the way I do."

His eyes smoldered in the dark. I was speechless – a hot mess. I didn't care about the others in the kitchen, the Lost Herd, my grandmother, the Centaurs looking for us. Nothing mattered in this moment except Drake, and a promise of very soon wasn't good enough. My hands grabbed his exposed flesh while I crushed my lips hard against his. The waves of desire came crashing as I pushed myself away from the door and leaned hard into him.

Another deep moan escaped his lips, sending a fresh wave of shivers through my body. I wrapped my arms over his shoulders and hiked my legs around his waist.

If Drake was surprised, he didn't show it. His arms wound around me, holding me in place as he stood. I buried my face into his neck as my words came out, "I don't want to go in there. Stay here with me. Don't let me go."

"Never. I'll never let you go."

His arms held me in a steel grip. Any other circumstance and it would have bothered me that I couldn't breathe, but in this moment I didn't need air.

Drake whispered in my ear as he eased me back against the cold metal door. "We'd better get in there before they come looking for us."

I couldn't hide my disappointment if I tried. His lips were soft against my ear, "You've got me for eternity, I promise. We'll meet with the others, then it'll be us – just us."

Drake eased my legs back onto the floor and reached for the door handle. When the door opened to the entryway, light poured into the cavernous garage, nearly blinding us both.

The smell of popcorn permeated the entryway, and laughter echoed in from the kitchen. Stepping into the entryway felt like being wrapped in a warm blanket – but given the choice, I'd take the cold darkness of the garage with Drake as my only heat source. Drake put his back to me as he slid his legs into the sweat pants Katherine had left for him on the table. The brief glimpse of his perfectly sculpted body caught me in mid-breath. Drake dressed quickly then angled around to face me.

The pile of clothes Katherine had been able to scrounge up were two sizes too small for Drake – I didn't mind the view. He stood before me in tattered gray sweatpants that fell just below his knees and a white t-shirt that stretched tight against his chest. Little imagination was required to see his body through the material of either. Thank you, Katherine.

Drake saw me staring and smiled wide. "If you don't stop looking at me like that, I'm taking you back to the garage."

"Newsflash, you suck at threats."

Drake took a step toward me, his arms hanging at his sides. I moved to wrap my arms around him, but he leaned away and shook his head. "I want to show you something."

Confused by his statement, I stood motionless in front of him. His voice was deep but quiet. "Close your eyes." I did as I was told. On instinct I reached out with my mind to see if I could feel any Centaurs in the surrounding forest or anything out of the ordinary. No danger was near the little house. The laughter was still going in the kitchen; Brent and Gage were ribbing Daniel for the way he'd helped Drake to transform. Everyone's thoughts in the house were relaxed – openly happy.

Drake's mouth was right by my ear, his gravelly voice reminded me, "Don't open your eyes." His fingers slid into my hair, smoothing it to the side exposing my neck. Drake kissed me lightly from my collar bone to just below my ear lobe. His voice throaty in my ear, "Do you see it?"

In that moment Drake pushed an image of the two of us stretched out on hot white sand in front of a turquoise ocean. Waves gently rolled up on the shore. We were alone, not another person for miles. A seagull cried out overhead and palm trees swayed in the breeze behind us. My answer was breathless, "It's beautiful."

"That's where we're going. We're getting married, tomorrow."

My eyes snapped open. "Was that a proposal?"

"No, Love. It was a promise." Drake leaned down and softly kissed me, again.

Daniel's voice was loud as he shouted from the kitchen, "Katherine, maybe you can get some ice water for those two. If you don't break them up, we'll all still be sitting here when the sun comes up in a couple hours."

Drake's eyes opened in narrow slits, glaring at the wall that Daniel sat on the other side of. Saying it more to himself than to me, "I can't stand him."

I nuzzled Drake's neck, "If it weren't for Daniel, you'd still have hooves. Play nice."

I took a step in the direction of the kitchen; Drake grabbed my hand and pulled me back to him – hard. "It doesn't mean I have to like him." A wide smile spread on his face while the blue of Drake's eyes bore straight to my soul.

"You don't have to like him. He'll always be my best friend, so find a way to tolerate him." I tugged Drake's hand, and he followed me into the kitchen where everyone was waiting.

All six of our friends broke out in applause as we walked through the doorway. It was Daniel we could hear above everyone else. He slapped the table and laughed, "Look, it's Cami and Burly-Barbie." I took a closer look at the clothes Drake wore that were stretched so tight on him – Daniel was right, they were women's clothes.

Katherine flushed a bright red, "It was the best I could do. I don't keep clothes lyin' around for naked men."

Gage joined in the jeering, "No, it's a good look. We're flying commercial tomorrow. Wear that to the airport. Maybe there'll be a female ticket agent, and you can get us free upgrades."

Drake didn't look the least bit self-conscious, "Hey, you're just jealous. I make this look good."

Daniel sneered, "I can see why Cami's so into you. She hasn't had a boyfriend she could share clothes with before."

The laughter died out as Drake strode toward Daniel. Gage and Brent were on their feet ready to breakup whatever was about to happen. Drake and Daniel stared at each other. I was about to try to diffuse them when Drake said, "You can't stand me. I get why. If our roles were reversed, I'd feel the same way. You didn't do it for me, but thanks all the same." Drake offered his hand to Daniel.

Daniel looked at Drake's hand for a few seconds longer than was comfortable. Gage and Brent's eyes kept darting between the two. Daniel took Drake's hand, "There's nothing I won't do for her – ever. Even if it means pissing off a frickin' Clydesdale."

Smirks appeared all around the kitchen. Drake gave Daniel a genuine smile, "I wouldn't have it any other way, but I'd like to think I'm more of a thoroughbred."

Daniel laughed, "When you started shaking all over out there, I figured you'd either change into yourself or stomp me flat. Either way it meant I'd be out of this cold in less than a day."

I slapped Daniel's arm, "So, it wasn't a chivalrous ploy on your part? You just wanted out of the snow."

Daniel smirked, "The snow's not so bad, but the cold here sucks. I always thought of twenty degrees below zero as more of a theoretical temperature in science class. Who knew people actually lived in this?"

Jessica smoothed her long platinum blonde hair back behind her ear, "You just haven't been here long enough to learn how to keep warm."

Without missing a beat, Daniel responded, "I'm a slow-learner. Maybe you could suggest a good tutor to school me on the finer points of staying warm in these parts."

Brent's face looked like he was about to come unglued. Did Brent have a thing for Jessica? After seeing the way Brent had responded to Katherine in the tunnel, I assumed he might have some sort of a crush on her. He scowled openly at Daniel. Was it because of Centaur traditions? Maybe he just didn't like joking like that? He was still young by Centaur standards; maybe he thought Jessica was a possibility for him if his betrothal fell through.

Before a second situation had the potential to turn into a brawl, Gage cleared his throat and said, "All right. It's been a seriously long day.

Katherine has graciously offered to let us all stay here at her house. With her here, we should all be safe for tonight. Tomorrow morning, once it's warm enough to drive down the mountain, we're piling in the two trucks and going to Omaha, Nebraska. It should take us about eight hours to get there. That's far enough away that the Centaurs and Centaurides looking for us up here shouldn't be able to find us."

I'd been absent from all the planning sessions, so other than Drake's proposal in the entryway, I didn't have a clue what the plan was. "Then what?"

"Everyone has tonight to decide. Bianca and I are accompanying you and Drake to Centauride, South Africa next week. We're going to Cancun until it's time for the Council meeting. Brent, Daniel, Jessica and Katherine – you need to decide where you want to go from Omaha. Money isn't an issue, so figure out where you're going before we get to the airport. We'll leave here just before noon."

Katherine found sleeping bags, comforters, pillows and blankets, and then started sending everyone to their assigned sleeping quarters. There was a guest room for Gage and Bianca. Brent was on the couch in the living room; Daniel took the floor. Drake and I were on an air mattress on the floor in the dining room. Jessica stayed with Katherine in her room.

CHAPTER 11

Cameron – Camille's twin brother, His House in South Dakota

We pulled up outside my house. It looked like a war zone. Curtains swung in the breeze through broken windows, footprints stamped in the snow circled the yard, tire tracks snaked in all directions. I unclipped my seatbelt, flung open my car door, and ran to the gaping hole that used to be my front door.

The door was gone. The hinges were ripped from the doorway and hung mangled to the side. The front porch served as a mud room and the entryway to the kitchen. The kitchen door lay on the floor in front of the stove. Snow had blown onto the floor from the shattered picture window on the other side of the kitchen.

My whole life was in this house. I walked into the living room only to find more destruction. A picture of me trick or treating as a cowboy lay under the shattered glass of its frame on the floor. Pictures of Roger and me were tossed in a pile by the bookcase. Papers from my closet lay charred in the fireplace. I couldn't believe my own eyes, "What the hell happened?"

I hadn't meant for it to be a question, and I didn't know Grandma was right behind me. She placed a gentle hand on my shoulder, "I'm so sorry, Cameron."

I spun around, anger overcoming me. "What happened? Where's Camille?"

Sorrow shone in her eyes as she shook her head, unable to answer. It was frigid in the house. I stormed from room to room: every single door and window in the place was destroyed and the furnace was running full blast trying to heat the outside. I reached over to the kitchen sink to check the water – nothing. A pipe had to have frozen and burst somewhere. It looked worse than a crack house. Who would do this?

Grandma found me in my bedroom, staring at my most prized possession: a football trophy from my senior year when my team went to state and I was the MVP of the game. It lay broken to pieces at the foot of my bed. Her voice was soft, "I didn't want to tell you, but now I don't have a choice. Camille is unstable."

"Unstable!? You think!? She ripped my house apart! No way she could have done this on her own."

Grandma walked up to me. She was a little bit of a woman, at least a foot shorter than me and looked so fragile I was almost scared to touch her. I wanted to grab onto her, but I was afraid I'd break her. Her voice was gentle, "I'm so sorry. I'll pay to have everything put back. I'll have contractors here today to repair the house, and I can have restoration experts on a plane this afternoon. It'll be like it never happened, I promise."

"Don't bother. There's nothing left to restore. It's all destroyed. Everything, it's just gone."

Grandma took me in a hug, her warm embrace trying to soothe the anger just under my skin. "Everything can be repaired, Cameron. I'm so sorry I didn't warn you."

"How could you? I should have just been honest and told you she was staying here from the beginning."

"Don't be so hard on yourself. This whole life is new to you. There's no way you could have known who to trust. I, myself, have spent very little time with your sister. I brought her to my estate the same as I did you, but I could tell she was troubled from the start. I tried to get her counseling and even did my own 'tough love' campaign, but I wasn't strong enough. I failed her."

Grandma had a heart of gold. From the first minute I met her, she let me be who I was. She never forced any of this Centaur stuff on me. She said I could choose my life. I'd spent my first twenty-three years about a dollar away from poverty with a man who knew nothing about kids. Roger was nice enough: he made sure I always had enough to eat, he helped me with my homework, and he was kind – but he wasn't family. From the time I was old enough to understand, all he ever said was I should never look for my family – I needed to stay hidden. I wish I'd have had a lifetime with this lady instead of just the last couple weeks.

My eyes darted around the room. As I looked at the destruction, Roger's warnings to stay away from my family made sense. My twin sister must be schizophrenic to do this kind of damage. She seemed so normal on the phone. She warned me not to trust Grandma – that was a joke. Camille was the one I couldn't trust. She called me with an elaborate story that she and Drake needed a place to hide out. I couldn't tell her no – she was my sister.

I looked at the frail old woman standing just feet away from me. Grandma had had a tough life. Her husband of over fifty years was dead. She had two kids: one flew all over the world spending her money like the apocalypse was coming, and my mother ran away when she was a teenager after spreading lies about being abused. Grandma told me that Mom had slept with every man she could find. She ended up a single mother who could barely care for herself, let alone two children. That's why she'd given me away. Will seemed like a stand up guy – I couldn't understand why he didn't help her. Course, who knows, from what Grandma said about Mom, maybe he wasn't my father.

I wanted to feel sorry for Camille. I tried to tell myself it wasn't her fault. Mom made her this way. Maybe she didn't know the difference between right and wrong. Grandma cleared her throat and brought me back to reality, "I'm sure Camille didn't realize what she was doing. She might have thrown a party and maybe her guests got out of hand."

"Stop defending her, Grandma. If that's what happened, she could have picked up the phone and called me. No, this was on purpose. She wanted everything I owned destroyed. I just don't understand why."

Grandma sat on a frozen lump of furniture with stuffing ripped out of the cushions. From what was left of the material covering it, it had been my sofa, but there wasn't enough of it left for anyone other than me to recognize it. Grandma confessed, "That's probably my fault, too. Can we sit down? There's something I need to tell you."

I looked around my home. The whole place was in shambles, and it was just as cold inside as it was outside. I didn't want her to freeze to death. Despite the sun beaming outside, it was still ten below. I held out my hand to help her up, "C'mon, Grandma. Let's get back to the car. It's warmer there."

She took my hand and squeezed it, "Cameron, you are so thoughtful and kind. I'm not sure I deserve you."

How could anyone be mean to this lady? She had told me about my mom and Uncle Angelo. Both of them were jerks. And Cami, I couldn't believe she and I shared the same DNA. I led Grandma out through the living room, kitchen, front porch and back to the car. I held her door for her and helped her into the passenger seat before going around to my side. The engine turned over immediately as the welcomed heat blasted us.

I couldn't help but stare through the windshield at my shack of a house. I had had a small antiques store in an old building on the property,

Cameron's Collectables, it's door was hanging open, too. I took a couple deep breaths to keep from losing my temper all over again. How could Grandma possibly think any of this was her fault?

She held her hand up to the vent as relief filled her expression. "Better?" I asked.

Grandma reached over and took my hand again. I loved that about her. Roger had never been very affectionate, so I wasn't used to her motherly gestures. It hit me that this is how family treats one another. I'd seen it growing up when I went to my friends' houses, but I didn't realize how much I craved the comfort from another person until Grandma came into my life.

"Much better, thank you, Cameron. It's so thoughtful of you to worry about me, but I'm a lot tougher than I look."

Yeah, right. She was maybe ninety pounds soaking wet and barely five foot five. "I know Grandma. But no sense sitting in the cold when there's a perfectly good car whose windows haven't been smashed and with a heater that works."

"You're right."

"So, why do you think what happened at my house is your fault?"

She pursed her lips together and looked out the windshield. I could tell what she was about to tell me wasn't something she felt comfortable sharing. I gently prodded her, "It's okay, Grandma. I want to know."

She patted my hand but didn't take her eyes off the scene through the windshield. "You think I am old and fragile." She smiled, "I am much more fragile than I was twenty-five years ago, but I hold a prestigious position in our community."

That wasn't a surprise. She had her own plane, a huge secluded estate in Florida, and more men providing security than the president surrounded by the Secret Service.

"I was trying to establish a relationship with Camille. I inadvertently let slip that my position is passed to the heir of my choosing."

"I'm not following you, Grandma."

"Camille believes she will take my place leading the Centaur Council, by force if necessary. I had some reservations before, but after seeing what she did to your home, I'm certain – she is jealous of you and no doubt unstable. When I told her I believed she had a twin brother, she became angry – nearly to a rage."

My heart plummeted. "She didn't want a brother?"

Grandma squeezed my hand again but still didn't look at me. "Your half-brothers dote on her. Your father already has five sons, so he wasn't all that interested in finding you. You have to understand, Centaurides in our society can be traded for social status. Your father and his sons view Camille as their meal ticket. When she came to me, she had already been ruined by the Strayers."

My breath caught. "So what's all that have to do with me?"

"I choose who my position on the Centaur Council is passed to. I've known since Angela and Angelo were children that they were too reckless for such a position. I wish you could have understood my elation to find Angela had children."

Her gentleness warmed me, and I couldn't help but confess, "Probably the same thrill I had to find out I had a real family." When my words registered, she turned her gaze on me for the first time. I loved this lady. She was so selfless and kind, despite all the things she had been through.

"Camille believes she will take my place, by force if necessary, on the Centaur Council. I've called a special session to share with the Council my misgivings about Camille."

That was the second time she'd said Camille planned to take her position by force. My eyes were drawn to my home destroyed by the sister I didn't know. "Grandma, I'll support you in any way you need me."

"You're a good boy, Cameron: the son I'd always hoped for. If Camille forces my hand, I may have to step down."

I hated the idea of talking to Camille after what she'd done. All the memories I had were crushed, broken, and burned inside what was left of my home. Despite my desire to stay away from her until I'd cooled off, I couldn't let Grandma face her alone. "I could try talking to her if you want me to."

"That's so thoughtful of you. Judging from what she did to your house, I think she's past the point of a simple chat. No. Cameron, I want you to take my place."

"What? No. I can't."

"You can. I'm not going anywhere. I'll be with you every step of the way to guide you for as long as you want me to."

"I can talk to her and make her understand. You don't have to step down."

"It's time. I'm old. The Council needs new Chiron blood leading it. There is just one concern."

My mind was reeling. What did the Centaur Council do? Was it like being on a board of directors or something? I'd never been to college. I'd never been anywhere or seen anything. How could I lead a council of any kind?

As if she were reading my mind, she answered, "Don't doubt yourself, Cameron. You have what it takes. You are a natural leader and more fierce of a warrior than you know."

A warrior? The council went to war? With who, fairies? I shook my head, "There's too much I don't know."

"I'll be right beside you the whole time. The only problem we have is your father. He is of the Lost Herd, and you will need to renounce him if you are to take my place."

"Renounce him?" She said it like he was royalty or something. She'd explained the Lost Herd to me in Florida – at least a little bit. It was hard to believe the gods I'd learned about in grade school were real, even harder to learn one of my distant relatives had ticked Zeus off.

"There is much I haven't shared with you. I was pleased to have found you and did not wish for you to learn too much at once and fear for your safety. These last weeks I've watched you closely. You are strong enough for every truth I need to share."

While we sat in the overly warm car, she told me the history of my father's Tak bloodline, how we were banned from the pasture of Thessaly, how a death warrant was placed on our heads ever since then. She grabbed my arm, "Cameron, I can't lose you the way I've lost everyone else. Renounce your father's line, and I can protect you. You can take my place as Chairman of the Centaur Council."

I was shocked. Her story explained all the security at her estate. She didn't even know me but wanted to keep me safe. Grandma should have been more jaded after everything she had gone through – but she wasn't. What about Camille? She was in as much danger as I was.

Again, as if she had read my thoughts, her expression soured. "I offered your sister the same protection, and she disgraced me. She ran away telling lies to all who would listen of her mistreatment at my hands."

Bile rose up from my stomach. Grandma was right. It would just be she and I. We were all we had left. My father had phoned me and warned me to be careful of Grandma. Camille told me not to trust Dad or Grandma, but as I looked at what she'd done to my house – Camille was the one I couldn't trust. That loser Drake she was with stole my arrow right in front of me. Hatred bubbled up from within. I knew who I could trust, and she was the little old lady who had shown me nothing but kindness since I met her.

"I'll do whatever you need me to do, Grandma."

A smile spread wide on her face. "Good. I knew I could count on you. We need to find Camille."

Not what I had expected her to say. "What? After what she did? Why would we want to find her?"

"She is unstable. We need to get her help. Your mother made her this way. Maybe there is a chance we can get her some counseling. Will you help me find her?"

"I'll do anything you ask of me, but I don't want to see her." I was ashamed that I would be so attached to material things, but I needed to be honest. "She destroyed everything I had."

She patted my arm, and I could have sworn there was a twinkle in her eye. "Don't you worry about a thing. You won't have to talk to her. Just help me find her . . . , so I can make sure she is safe."

Grandma was a saint. After everything her kids and Camille had put her through, she still wanted to help them. My priorities changed in that moment. Roger had always told me to look out for number one. I could feel my heart grow as I would now be looking out for this sweet old lady, too.

"How do we find her? Credit card receipts?"

"You are her twin. You are Chiron twins. The two of you share a bond that allows you to find each other no matter where the other is. Open that connection and tell me where she is."

My eyes widened. Was she serious? Open what connection?

"Close your eyes." I did as I was told, but had no idea what she was talking about. "You've seen pictures of her. Can you visualize her face?"

I could. It was strikingly similar to my own. We shared the same brown eyes and brown hair. Grandma kept a picture of her in my room at the house. In the picture, her hair was over her shoulders, and she wore a white t-shirt with a stunning sapphire necklace. When I'd seen the picture, I remember thinking the combination was odd: the necklace looked like something to wear with an evening gown, not a simple white t-shirt. I thought back to the picture and could remember it with remarkable clarity.

"Good. You have her image, now, reach out with your mind. She is close. Where is she?"

She's close? She trashed my house but didn't skip town? Why would she stay?

"Do not waste your energy trying to find answers. Just tell me where she is."

My eyes snapped open. Had I said that out loud? Grandma was staring at me, and I didn't recognize her look. Tentatively, I answered, "I don't know how to find her."

"Yes, you do. I have a twin brother as well. Until we severed our connection, we could find each other anywhere in the world. You have the same connection. Use it. Help me . . . to help her."

There was a desperation in Grandma's voice. After everything Camille had put her through, it was hard to believe she still wanted to help her. "You have a twin? But you severed your connection with him?"

Grandma looked nervous. Maybe I'd struck a chord with her. She'd been so open with all my questions, but something told me severing her connection with her twin must have been painful.

Her body relaxed, "Zethus killed our parents. I could no longer stand the thought of any connection with him, so I terminated it."

I was wrong. Grandma had had more tragedy in her life than anyone I had ever met. Compared to a brother who murdered her parents, maybe Camille wasn't so bad in her eyes. Grandma said she held a prestigious position in the Centaur community. Maybe it was too much for those around her to handle. Maybe they had all cracked under the pressure. Her words "*I'm stronger than I appear*," resonated in my head. I would do anything she needed, for as long as she lived. Grandma had lived through too many betrayals.

I closed my eyes again, concentrating on Camille's picture from Grandma's house. I thought of the few times I'd talked to her on the phone and the way her voice sounded. I tried to make her words come back to me. I thought of the day Drake came to my house and showed me a picture of Camille on his phone. A homing beacon sparked to life in my mind. It was powerful enough that the spark made my heart skip a beat. She *was* close. Camille was still in the area.

Grandma's voice was shrill, "You've found her. Quickly, where is she?" The urgency of her voice took me off guard. How did Grandma know I'd found Camille? I hadn't said a word.

Grandma took a deep breath and relaxed her demeanor before speaking again. "Cameron, it's very important we find her. What did you see?"

"I'm not sure. She's close, but I don't have a specific location for her."

"As her twin, you should be able to find her anytime you try."

"Sorry. I can feel she's close, but I don't know where. At least I think I can feel her. I've never really met her."

"You shared Angela's womb with Camille. Your connection is stronger than any other. We need to find her." I understood what she was telling me in theory. I'd heard human twins shared the same kind of link, where one would get burned and the other would feel the pain. I'd never heard of being able to locate the other with nothing more than being a twin. Strangely enough, I had felt . . . something.

I'd grown up in this area my whole life. If all this supernatural stuff didn't work, we could just pop into a few of the businesses and ask if they'd seen her. That would be better than anything else. She would have had to have gone to a grocery store, a gas station or something. "Look, I don't know how this twin thing works, but I grew up here my whole life. I can ask around. Someone will have seen her."

She gently patted my hand, "However you think it is best to find her. But please keep trying."

"I will."

Grandma brought her hand to my face. "That's my boy." Almost absently, she added, "I can't understand why Angela chose Camille over you."

It felt like I'd just been sucker punched. I'd always had those thoughts, but had never said them out loud. What was wrong with me? Why wouldn't Mom have wanted me? I was a baby. I was only days old when she gave me away and never looked back. Roger told me he hardly knew Mom. Not only did she not want me, but she left me with a stranger.

I could hear the charity in Grandma's voice. "You are the last of the Chiron line. You will take my place as the Chairman of the Centaur Council. You will find your sister before she can take your legacy away from you."

I was confused, my feelings conflicted. "I thought you wanted to find her so we could protect her?"

ZANDRA

In the car, outside Cameron's house in South Dakota

"Protect her, and protect your future. You are my last hope, Cameron. Find her." My hand patted his arm. I couldn't believe he proved to be so easy to manipulate. I wish it were possible to tell Angela thank you. He had abandonment issues, and I was more than happy to use them to my advantage. The first few days were difficult; Cameron didn't trust me, and he questioned much of what I told him. Being cut off from all family and any bit of normalcy his entire life left him pliable: once I'd gained his trust, it was absolute. I needed only to tell him a few bits of information about how difficult life had been and we'd instantly bonded.

Camille was willful and headstrong. She questioned my motives and my authority at every turn. Cameron would do whatever I suggested and only wanted my approval in return. Passing my position onto him meant I could stay in power for the rest of my life. Cameron would deny me nothing. I merely had to keep the Strayers away from him a bit longer until the other herds would take care of them for me.

Frustration began to get the better of me. I couldn't understand why I couldn't find Camille myself. Cameron confirmed she was close. If she was within a hundred miles, I should be able to find her. How was she blocking me? It felt as though she were right under my nose. I was still baffled as to how she and Drake escaped from the assassination squad I had dispatched. I was told they were the best of the best, the most ruthless, and I was assured they would be successful.

When I learned of their failure, I was furious. I hadn't wanted to bring Cameron with me. I couldn't afford for the two to spend any time together, but I couldn't be sure of his safety unless he was with me. One of the guards on my estate learned he was from the Lost Herd and would have killed him if I hadn't intervened.

Now I was thrilled Cameron was with me. Seeing his home and his business first hand and believing Camille was responsible for the destruction of both worked better than anything I could have dreamed up on my own. He would never again trust her.

CHAPTER 12

Drake Nash – Katherine Newton's Home in South Dakota

All the others had gone to separate rooms. I stood in the doorway watching Cami. She was ten feet from me. It was just the two of us. We hadn't been like this, together, since Ireland. I savored the moment, anticipating her warmth and the feeling of her skin against mine. She was putting sheets on the air mattress we would share. I stood frozen, mesmerized by her graceful movements.

The muscles in my legs twitched, prodding me to go to her, to take her in my arms, to make her mine in every sense of the word. Her back remained to me. Details I had overlooked the last few weeks suddenly had my full attention. The gentle arch of her back, the way her hair fell at her shoulders, the way her body formed two perfect hearts from behind. Cami was beauty in its purest form.

She must have felt me watching her; without turning to catch my gaze, she asked, "You're just going to stand there all night?"

I looked around the room. It was crammed full of china on display, bookshelves overflowing, and a computer desk that was spewing papers in all directions. A large bay window looked out into the forest and was drafty enough it might as well have been open.

We were safe. For the first time since we were in Ireland, we were *truly safe*. I could let my guard down. I didn't need to be the Centaur Warrior tonight; I could simply be the man in love with the woman.

My feet moved of their own accord. The distance between us closed as my body pressed into her from behind. Cami didn't flinch or move to turn toward me. She stood with her face angled slightly, enough that if I were a weaker man, I could lose myself in her gaze. Her arms hung at her sides and made no move to touch me. I brought my lips to her ear, "You are beautiful."

My hands went to her wrists as my fingers caressed their way up her arms. Goosebumps danced on her skin where I touched. Her voice was soft, "I told you it was temporary."

Her love for me burned through her eyes, but the moment struck me funny, anyway. "I get it. Go ahead. Say the words."

"The words?"

"'I told you so.' Get it out of your system."

She turned fully into me. I waited for her to be a smart-aleck or to give me one of her smiles that could eclipse the sun. She wore a determined expression instead. Her fists went to either side of my t-shirt. The fabric was tight against me, but she was still able to pull it off as if it were no more attached than a towel.

Her lips pressed against my chest. Heat radiated off of me. Her fingers dug hard into my back as her lips made their way down to my abs. This wasn't happening. Not here. Not like this. Not in someone's dining room. Our first time together couldn't be on an air mattress on the floor of someone else's house.

I put my hands on either side of her face, my thumbs just under her chin, and brought her so I could look into those milk-chocolate eyes. My resolve began to crumble. I wanted her. . . all of her. My lips hung low and parted on hers. Her breath was as fresh as winter frost inviting me in.

Camille pressed her body against mine. The suppleness of her skin touching me set mine ablaze. My eyes shot open for fear that I had turned into a light storm again, fearing the transformation that accompanied the lights. I eyed my body: no pieces of light were there. It was the heat of my longing for her, as desire leaked from every pore on my body.

Camille's voice was breathless, "It's just the two of us. No one else but us."

I thought of her brother on the sofa and Daniel on the floor, just on the other side of the wall. There was no door for the dining room, no privacy whatsoever. I wanted Camille more than a seven-year-old wants Christmas morning – but not like this. Could I wait two more days for her? The vision I'd had of the two of us in the Caribbean, pictured us stretched out on the sand with no one around for miles. We would be there in a day, two tops.

I ached for her, and she opened up enough of her thoughts for me to know that she wanted the same. Could I deny myself the thing I wanted most in the world for some stupid fantasy? If I could, could I deny Cami? It was my fantasy, not hers. Our bodies needed each other. We were well past lustful thoughts and desires; it was a primal need that shot through both of us.

Was it just a fantasy? A couple hours ago I told her it was a promise. My words came out raspy, as if I couldn't find air, "Not here, Cami."

An exasperated sigh escaped her, "Yes, here, now."

I pulled her face up, making her look into my eyes. "Our first time together can't be like this. It can't be on the floor. You deserve so much better."

"I've waited. I've been patient. I would have waited for eternity if I had to. The place doesn't matter. Don't you feel it?"

I cradled Cami's face in my hands. My thumb caressed her lips. "You know I do."

"Show me." She slid up against me and my resolve disintegrated. Time and space lost all meaning. My need took over as I pressed myself to her. A low sigh escaped her and the room began to spin.

Cami lay down on the air mattress and stretched her arm up for me to join her. I didn't waste any time to lie on top of her. I was worried my weight would compress the air out of her lungs, but she wrapped her legs around me and crushed her lips to mine. The feeling was indescribable. Her heart raced underneath me. I leaned up on my elbow and placed my hand across her chest.

Eyes watched us. My lips let go as my head whipped around in all directions. She felt it, too. The eyes were watching from the doorway. I looked up to where I expected to see a person standing, but no one was there. A whine sounded at the doorway, and I located the eyes we'd felt, close to the floor, attached to one of the biggest Huskies I'd ever seen.

"Shooo, go away."

Instead the dog got down on the floor and began low-crawling toward us. I waved my hand and repeated, "Shooo, go on." The dog halted a few feet inside the dining room. I turned my attention back to Cami, but heard him moving closer again. "No, dog, stay." Every time I looked away from him, he inched closer to the air mattress.

Cami's hand gripped my face, forcing me to look into her eyes. "Ignore him. Pretend he's not here." She flexed her legs, and it was easy to forget about the dog. Cami's teeth grazed my ear, and a new wave of desire took me. I reached down to remove her t-shirt when a tongue licked my foot. I kicked at the dog, not hard, but enough to get him away from my feet. "Go on. Git."

The next thing I knew he was edging onto the air mattress. Cami laughed, not a giggle, but a full-blown roar when she felt the welcoming dog's tongue on her cheek. The sound was perfect. I hadn't heard Cami laugh like that since we were in Ireland. I forgot how much I had missed it. I swung her over to the side and put my back to the intruder who had invaded our air mattress.

"He licked my face!"

"I saw." His massive head leaned up over the top of my shoulder as more laughter erupted from Cami. I stood up thinking the dog would jump up and follow me out of the room. He didn't, he just took my place moving more solidly onto the air mattress. I tried to coax him out of the room, while he lay there with his tongue hanging out panting.

Cami, unable to stifle her smile, "Maybe this is where he sleeps?"

"Not tonight he doesn't. I found a leash by the door, fastened it around his collar and walked him out into the living room. Morning light was already shining in through a gap in the curtains. I leaned down at eye level with the dog and said, "Stay." I backed away from him, and he didn't move. Once I was in the doorway to the dining room, I turned my back and went back to Cami. The dog beat me to the air mattress.

Looking eye-to-eye with the dog who leaned over the mattress and into my face, I asked, "What are you? An escort?"

Cami reached up and patted his head. Still smiling, Cami said, "Okay, the Caribbean it is. But the dog's not coming with us."

I pulled Cami against me before the dog could wedge himself between us. Holding Cami on the air mattress of the drafty room felt incredible. My heart was full of love. All those times she'd told me my transformation was only temporary – I hadn't believed it. I wanted to, but somehow I got it stuck in my head that each person is only given a set amount of happiness in life. The week alone with Cami in Ireland had been more joy than I'd ever known. I'd exceeded my quota, never expecting to have this feeling again, this desire, this raw need.

She lay against my chest, my hands caressing her supple skin as I felt her drift off to sleep. I silently thanked Chiron for giving me the best gift I could have ever hoped for: the strength to defend her and the ability to make her happy – I would never take either gift for granted.

CHAPTER 13

Camille – Katherine Newton's Home in South Dakota

I awoke to Bianca standing beside the air mattress. "Hey, you two, everyone else is up. If you want to catch a shower, the hot water's almost gone."

Had it all been a dream? Drake's eyes peered down into mine. Under the floral blanket that covered us, my toes slid in his direction. I let them slide down his leg to his feet and under his toes. I reached over and flung the comforter off of us – it hadn't been a dream.

Drake looked amazing, better than I'd remembered. I didn't want a shower, or a day long car ride, or to see any of our friends. He brought his forehead to mine, "Ready to start the rest of our life, Love?"

His words elicited the tingles again from last night. I looked at the arch that separated the dining room from the living room; no doors had miraculously appeared for privacy. My hand found his shoulder and began sliding down his arm; as my fingers tried to explore further than his waist, Drake's fingers caught mine in his. "Soon."

Not soon enough. Maybe the garage was still empty – anywhere where I could be alone with Drake for ten minutes would be good. He chuckled at me after seeing my thoughts, "I thought you said you didn't care if I stayed a Centaur forever – seems you've changed your mind."

"I knew it was only temporary. You were the one who didn't believe me."

Drake gathered me in his arms. "I'll never doubt you again. You ready to get out of here and get to Cancun?"

"Yesssss."

"Gage and Bianca got married there. They thought we'd enjoy it."

"They're going with us, right?"

"Yes. We'll be there by tomorrow morning."

Drake let loose of me and stood up. He held out his hand to help me up off the floor. I could hear Daniel's voice through the open archway. "Vegas? Do you have a death wish? Lying low with three million people is about as smart as wearing your underwear over your skinny jeans."

"Watch your mouth, half-breed." The words didn't surprise me. I was used to everyone calling Daniel that by now. The surprise came from the voice who spoke the words – it was a female. Not Bianca. I listened harder to hear if it had been Katherine or Jessica.

"Sticks and stones. Name calling doesn't make your plan any less stupid. If you don't want your brother to find you, you may want to try somewhere a little more remote. How about Cabo?" Daniel was arguing with Jessica.

"Katherine will be there and I'll be fine."

"I hate to break it to you, but beauty and stubbornness don't make a good combination."

"Neither do conceit and arrogance."

"Actually, conceit and arrogance have served me well for twenty-three years. So have *sexy* and *charming*. Let me know which attribute revs your engine."

I shook my head, not believing my ears, "C'mon. We'd better get out there before Prince Charming gets a swift kick to the groin."

Drake tugged my hand back while I was in mid-stride. I turned to look at him, and he was all smiles, "Give her thirty more seconds – I'd hate for her to miss a golden opportunity on account of us."

I shook my head and pulled Drake's hand. He followed, still smiling. Brent was dressed and on the couch, sitting off in the corner of the dark room. All the activity was coming from the kitchen, and he didn't seem to be paying any attention to it. His eyes were focused on the other side of the room as if something were bothering him. I motioned for Drake to join everyone else in the kitchen while I took a seat next to Brent in the living room.

He looked at me as I sat next to him. Brent seemed so distant, as if he were worlds away. "Everything okay?"

He plastered a smile on his face. "Katherine let me use her phone. I got a hold of Cassie – my betrothed."

Judging from his far off gaze, I was sure of her answer, "She changed her mind?"

Brent shook his head. "No. She said she'd wait as long as it took."

"That's great! Brent, you've been chosen. She doesn't care about the Lost Herd. That's fantastic."

"Yeah." Brent's reaction didn't make any sense to me. He should have been over-the-moon excited. Why was he staring at the wood paneling on the other wall? Had she said something else? Did she give him news of our family? I tried to probe his thoughts, but all of them were locked up tight, hidden safely away.

"There's something you're not telling me."

Brent shook his head that there wasn't. "No, just need to decide where to go from here. I can't go back to South Carolina until after the Centaur Council convenes. Going back now would be suicide and would put Cassie in danger."

"You could go to Cancun with Bianca, Gage, Drake and me," I offered.

Brent shook his head. He reached over and took my hand, "No. You two deserve some time alone – just make it official first."

My cheeks blushed. My favorite cop from the morality police was back on the beat. "We will."

"What's wrong, Brent? I can't help if I don't know what's bothering you."

Brent put his arm behind my shoulder, "So much has happened. I was sure Cassie would have changed her mind. She had every right to, you know. I wouldn't have blamed her if she had."

I nodded. In fact, I, too, expected that was the news he had been trying to recover from. I'd never met his betrothed, but I decided I already liked her. It was a brave Centauride who would risk a death sentence of her own by keeping her betrothal to Brent intact. I wanted to ask him more about her, but whatever was bothering him – now wasn't the time.

Right on schedule, we were showered, dressed, fed and piling into Katherine's truck and Gage's rental truck at eleven o'clock on the dot. The dog that had so rudely interrupted Drake and me last night belonged to one of Katherine's neighbors. She'd come by to collect the dog this morning before we woke up. Bianca told me Katherine wouldn't accept her neighbor's money for taking care of the dog, but she had asked the neighbor to return Brent's rental car.

Gage, Bianca, Jessica and Daniel rode in Gage's truck. Katherine, Brent, Drake and I climbed into Katherine's truck. Everyone thought this was safest because if the vehicles became separated, Drake, Brent and I were the ones who needed Katherine to "cloak" us. No one would be looking for the other four yet.

I didn't ask Daniel where he'd been staying, but he didn't seem to mind that we weren't going to stop to pick up any of his things, either. Gage had given Drake clothes to wear, but his feet were too large for Gage or Brent to offer him a pair of shoes. Drake wore flops in the snow with his bright red toes looking nearly frozen. When we settled into the back seat of Katherine's truck, he told me, "Don't worry. There's bound to be a shoe store near the airport."

The first couple hours of the drive were quiet. I dozed off and on, each time waking up and looking at Drake's feet. I reminded myself that everything that had happened the last few weeks happened for a reason. Things were going to be okay – better than okay.

Brent sat in the front seat of the truck, remaining silent, his eyes fixed on the passenger side window. Drake and I spoke, but not out loud so the other two could hear us. We each pushed images to one another in anticipation of our impending alone time. Drake pulled me into his shoulder, and I loved the way we fit together.

Finally, it was Katherine's voice that broke the quiet while she searched for a new radio station. "So, tell me about her."

Brent peeled his eyes off of the window. "Who?"

"Yer betrothed. You called her this morning. What's she like?"

Brent's smile was warm. "She's great. Her family doesn't come from one of the affluent herds, so she works. She's a nurse."

"Nice. What kind?"

"In a doctor's office. The doctor is a Centaur, so I'd been to the office a couple times as a kid."

She gave up trying to tune in a radio station and shut off the radio in frustration. Katherine prodded gently. "Did ya meet her there?"

Brent looked over his shoulder at Drake and me as we pretended not to listen. Brent shrugged his shoulders and matter-of-factly answered, "I had an appointment with the dentist. The office where she works is in the same medical complex. As I left my dentist's office, it was late in the day, and she was changing her tire in the parking lot. She'd caught a nail on the way to work and hadn't noticed. I offered to help."

"Nice. Did that count as the third tenet?"

Brent chuckled, "Saving her life? Hardly. I didn't realize she was a Centauride until after I was tightening the lug nuts on her spare tire."

Katherine beamed, "If you think that doesn't count as saving her life, you've never been stranded with a flat tire before."

"Okay, if it had been up in this part of the country – maybe. Freezing to death is a real possibility. But, no, she just needed a hand, and I happened to be there."

"She chose ya because you helped her change a tire? You must have made a real impression on 'er."

Brent turned back toward the passenger side window, looking out over the snow-covered Badlands. "Yeah. I guess I did."

It got quiet again. The only sound was the rhythm of the road under the truck's wheels. A few minutes passed before Katherine asked, "So, did ya decide where yer going?"

Brent didn't turn away from the window. "Not yet."

"Vegas was my idea, but Daniel didn't think that was such a great plan."

Brent's eyes still remained locked on the window, but he answered, "Jessica will be safe as long as she's with you. You two should go somewhere fun. Vegas is as good a place as anywhere."

Katherine bit her lip as if she were arguing with herself, took a deep breath and offered, "If ya came with us, you could stay safe, too."

Brent finally turned his attention away from the window but said nothing. He was watching Katherine. I tried not to stare, but the energy between them was impossible to ignore. Was this why Brent looked so sullen earlier? Did he have feelings for Katherine that he needed to lock away because he had a Centauride waiting for him? His actions were starting to make sense to me. Drake nodded as if confirming my conclusion.

Katherine stammered, "I mean. . . if yer just waiting to go back ta yer life until after the Centaur Council meets, you could lie low with Jessica and me, if ya wanna."

Brent looked over his shoulder to see if Drake and I were listening. We were, but in that fraction of a second before he turned around, we both averted our eyes – pretending to be lost in each other. It wasn't much of a stretch.

Brent faced forward, looking out the front windshield, but didn't answer Katherine's offer. Katherine started fiddling with the radio again. Any station she had tuned in only stayed clear for about three songs, and now she didn't seem able to find even one. As she kept fiddling with the tuner, Brent's hand reached for hers. She looked at him as his hand coupled hers over the radio's dial. "I can't, Katherine."

Katherine sounded hurt, "Whatever. I just thought you were worried about being hunted."

"I am."

"Then why go off by yerself? I can protect ya. I can get ya home to yer Centauride."

Brent's reply was strained, "I'll be okay."

"Is it me? Ya don't want protection from a Lapith, is that it?"

Brent's voice was soft, almost vulnerable when he confessed, "It is you, and it has nothing to do with you being a Lapith."

The tension between them was thick enough to cut. Katherine drove for another thirty minutes then eased off the highway to a gas station. I looked behind us and saw Gage put on his turn signal as well. We pulled up to the front pump, and Brent got out to fill the tank. I zipped up my jacket to run inside to use the facilities. The four doors popped open behind us, and Daniel's voice, as always, was what I heard. "Hey, Brent, Jessica's made me a believer. We're going to Vegas, baby!"

Brent's eyebrows furrowed in response, but he said nothing, turning his attention back to the gas pump.

Everyone shushed Daniel, and he answered the glares with his typical smile. "Oh, right. The trees have ears."

Within ten minutes everyone's bladders were drained, the fuel tanks were full, and we had munchies for the road. Jessica stood with her back against their truck applying Chap Stick while Gage and Bianca made their way out of the gas station. Daniel walked up to Jessica, puckering his lips, "My lips are dry. Can I use that?"

Jessica capped it and tucked the little tube behind her back. "Gross. Go inside and get your own."

"Oh, come on. My lips are going to start bleeding."

Jessica didn't relent, "Go get your own."

"Fine." Daniel looked irritated as he walked back into the little convenience store. A few seconds later he walked back out and straight into Jessica. "They're out. I'll just use yours."

Jessica made a face and begrudgingly held out the little tube to Daniel. He shook his head at her, "No. That *would* be gross." Daniel put a hand on both sides of her face and pulled her lips to his. I didn't mean to watch, but I couldn't believe Daniel was kissing a Centauride. That broke every single rule I'd learned since I first learned about Centaurs.

I wasn't the only one staring as Gage, Bianca, Drake, Brent and Katherine stood in shock, mouths hanging open – no one flinched. After what felt like an eternity, Daniel let go of Jessica and smacked his lips, "Much better, thanks." He climbed in the back seat of the truck as if nothing had happened.

Gage and Bianca looked at each other over the roof of the car. Gage shrugged his shoulders and got in the driver's side. Bianca looked at me and smirked while she climbed into the front passenger side. Jessica stood leaning against the car – she was beyond stunned. Katherine stood by the driver's side door of her truck looking at her friend, trying to hide her smile with her fist.

I took my place in the backseat of the truck with Drake and asked Bianca, "*What was that?*"

"*I don't know, but it should make for an interesting ride to Omaha. I'll keep you posted.*"

CHAPTER 14

Jessica Baker – En route to Omaha, Nebraska

What a jerk. My body molded to the door. I didn't care how cold the window felt, I needed as much distance between Daniel and me as I could find. His thoughts were loud, nearly too loud to tune out – nearly.

Gage followed a decent distance behind Katherine's truck. Thank goodness I wasn't in her truck. If I were riding with Katherine, she'd be giving me a seriously hard time for what Daniel had just done. My eyes closed as the cool from the window helped diminish the burning in my cheeks. I used every bit of willpower I had to block all the errant thoughts flying inside the truck.

Daniel chatted with Gage like they were old pals. Who would have guessed that either of them knew anything about landscaping or that they could have talked about it for nearly an hour without a break. Better yet, who knew anyone could talk about landscaping that long? I didn't have my iPod. Strange to miss an inanimate object, but I had over a thousand songs on it, and I knew every one of them – every single word. It would be so much easier to tune the others out if I could pipe music directly to my brain.

"Shit." Gage's deep voice uttered to no one in particular.

Something about the sound of his voice made me open my eyes and face forward. It looked like a huge car accident in front of us. Police cars were stretched along the side of the road with their blue lights flashing. One, two, three . . . eleven, twelve. Twelve police cars?

There were two cars in between our truck and Katherine's truck. "Gage, you have to catch up to them."

"Relax, Jessica. If I speed up now, it'll look suspicious. I'm sure it's just a DUI checkpoint or something."

"Checkpoint? Not an accident?"

"Uh, no. The sign said mandatory state police safety inspection. This isn't normal then?"

OHMYGOD, OHMYGOD, OHMYGOD, we'resoscrewed, we'resoscrewed, we'resoscrewed. It couldn't be. There's no way Roscoe could have set up anything like this. Could he? He couldn't shut down an interstate to find me. He wasn't that powerful. That would take influence over humans, coordination, resources – no way could this be his doing. My heart was beating out of control. I took a deep breath, closed my eyes, and tried to relax my shoulders.

Daniel's hand slid onto my knee as his voice sounded concerned, "Hey, does this happen often?"

Why was he touching me? I stared at his hand, wordlessly letting him know he had crossed the line, again. "Oh, yeah, sure. We don't have enough criminals up this way so the cops shut down interstates all the time just for fun."

Katherine's truck rolled to a stop as a tall Centaur dressed as a highway patrolman leaned into her window. Katherine's truck stood seven feet, two inches, I knew because we'd tried to park it in a low parking garage in Rapid City that only had seven feet of clearance. The man leaning into her truck was tall, his hat cresting the top of the cab. He had to have been outside for quite a while because the exposed skin on his face and neck were bright red.

I reached out to see if any other Centaurs were near. One in a state patrol car on my right, another in a deputy sheriff's car in front, a couple humans, and another Centaur doing a vehicle inspection on a commercial bus that had been pulled to the side of the road. My attention went back to the very tall, beet-faced highway patrolman standing only inches from Katherine. Out of the corner of my eye, I saw a short, angry-looking sheriff and my heart skidded to a stop – it was Willie.

I ducked my head down; worried he'd see me watching him. Willie worked for my brother. He was a Council enforcer, and he had been along the night Roscoe and his boys went after Drake and Cami. He began walking toward the passenger side of Katherine's truck. It felt like it was happening in slow motion. I wanted to scream, to tell Gage to do a u-turn, to take a quick turn and make a break for it. Was it me, or the Lost Herd, they were after? Or both?

My words came out disconnected, absent the emotions sailing through me, "They're looking for us. See that short sheriff walking toward the passenger side of Katherine's truck? That's Willie. He's my brother Roscoe's second."

Gage and Daniel's face registered surprise. Bianca turned around; she must have realized at the same time. "It's okay. Katherine is with them, they won't know Cami or Brent are from the Lost Herd. If Katherine gets too far ahead of us to cloak you, here's our story: we'll tell them you and I were roommates in college and I popped in for a surprise visit. We're on our way to, to . . . where can we tell them we're going to that isn't Omaha?"

"Mitchell."

"Okay, we're going to Mitchell to. . . what can we do there?"

"See the Corn Palace."

"Seriously?"

"Yeah, it's a big deal. The whole thing is made out of corn."

Willie was motioning for Katherine to pull over to the side of the road. That's it. We're all done for. They'll take Cami, Drake and Brent away, and Katherine – they'll find out what she is. I started screaming thoughts towards Cami but she refused to answer. Why was she tuning me out? We had to make a run for it. If both trucks went in opposite directions – one of us might have a chance.

"*Cami! Cami!! Tell Katherine to get you all as far away as possible.*" No response. She was blocking me. "Bianca, tell Cami they need to make a run for it before Willie calls Roscoe or the other enforcers. Tell her!" We watched the tall Centaur who had been talking to Katherine shake his head at Willie. What was he saying? My mind was going fast, too fast to try to pry into the Centaur's thoughts. Willie shouted something at the tall Centaur while he gestured that he wanted Katherine's truck to move to the right lane for a more detailed vehicle inspection.

It was like watching a car accident. I could see what was about to happen, but I couldn't do anything to stop it. "*Don't pull over, don't pull over, don't pull over,*" my silent warning for Katherine kept replaying in my mind.

The tall Centaur shouted something over the top of Katherine's truck and waved her forward. Relief filled me. They were let through. Whoever the Centaur was in the State Police uniform had just overridden Willie. No doubt there'd be hell to pay for him later, but for right now, Katherine and the others were safe. Maybe it would be okay after all.

The two cars in between our truck and theirs both got routed to the right for a detailed vehicle inspection and it was our turn. I could barely see the taillights of Katherine's truck up ahead of us. I was sure she'd be waiting for us at the next exit.

The tall Centaur leaned in Gage's window. "License, registration, and proof of insurance, please."

Gage handed his license and rental car agreement through the window. The tall Centaur said, "South Carolina, eh? Whatcha doin up this way?"

"Honeymoon. My wife is up visiting her college roommate."

"Not the best time a year for a visit."

"We don't see snow that often."

"Yeah, you can take some of it back whicha."

Willie walked in front of the truck crossing to the driver's side where the tall Centaur stood. I tried to keep my eyes down, but I saw him through the windshield the same time he saw me. Willie shouted angrily, "Jessica!!" In an instant he was leaning in through Gage's window. "Are you okay? Roscoe's worried sick! You didn't come home last night."

I'd never been much of an actress, "Hi, Willie. Everything's fine. Bianca came up to see me for a few days. I told Roscoe I had a friend in town."

Willie looked at the other three in the truck. "No. He's got the boys on every interstate today – looking for you. Go on and step out of the truck; I'll take you home."

Bianca interrupted, "Oh, no. We flew all this way." She turned around in her seat, "I knew we shouldn't have stayed up all night playing cards!" She turned her attention back to Willie, "I am so sorry, sir. I was just so excited to see Jessica, and she told me there was a corn palace in Mitchell. Well, we don't have anything like that back home! Can you imagine? A whole palace made out of nothing but corn? I thought she was pulling my leg, but we looked it up on-line and I told her we had to go."

Willie looked at Bianca, "Sorry, miss. She's an unbetrothed Centauride. She knows better. If she wanted to go to Mitchell, her family would have arranged a proper escort." That was a slam on Daniel seated right next to me, and it was enough of one that he sat up straighter and scowled wordlessly at Willie.

The tall Centaur looked at the stream of cars behind us. He looked at Gage and said, "Mr. Richardson, go ahead and pull over to the right. They can work it out over there, we've got to get some of these cars through."

Bianca's voice sounded offended. "My husband and I are more than capable of providing escort. If I didn't know better, I would think you were insulting us. Now, if you want to follow us to Mitchell, you are more than welcome to come with us, but I've had about enough of all this. Gage, let's go." She sat back in her seat and faced forward as if her statement alone would make the car go forward.

Willie and the tall Centaur exchanged a look with each other. Centaurides were revered, and since neither had yet been chosen, they wouldn't want anyone to say they had been disrespectful to a Centauride. The tall Centaur looked at Willie and offered, "If you want me to go with them, Willie, I'll be happy to escort them."

Confusion was all over Willie's face. "Fine. Don't let them out of your sight. Call Roscoe and let him know we found her. I'll do a few more inspections then shut this down."

The tall Centaur who had been doing the inspections took a couple steps away from our truck, then turned back to Willie. "What about the others?"

"The Lost Herd isn't going to be on the interstate. They've been hiding for generations. You think any of them are dumb enough to drive through a checkpoint. Go on. I'll shut this down and send the boys home. You get your car and stay with Jessica."

I was paying attention to see if there was even a moment's hesitation. No one in the car smiled, giggled, sighed or even changed their breathing. The Centaur dressed as a state trooper turned toward Gage, "Go ahead, I'll get my squad and be right behind you."

Gage drove about fifty feet, then looked toward Bianca, "Where are they?"

"Two miles up on the right. They're waiting on the shoulder for us."

"One Centaur shouldn't be an issue. What'll we do with him?" Gage looked in his rearview. I didn't need to turn around and look; I knew he was behind us.

Bianca answered Gage, but directed her question to me. "I don't know. He's an enforcer, right?"

I knew most of the enforcers, at least the ones who worked for Roscoe. "I'm not sure. I don't know him. Most of the enforcers stop by my bar from time to time – I've never seen him before."

Bianca smiled, "Cami says Katherine's got an idea. Pass their truck and pull off on the next exit. Find a parking lot that's a little secluded if you can."

The minutes ticked away slowly. I didn't want anyone to put themselves in jeopardy over me. No doubt Willie had already talked to Roscoe. How had Roscoe set up checkpoints all over the place? I knew a few of his enforcers had jobs as small town cops, but there was no way they should have been able to block all the interstates. Maybe he could have pulled it off closer to home, but we were hours away. Maybe someone above Roscoe had ordered it, and Roscoe just had his men there looking for me, too.

Gage's foot eased off the accelerator as he steered the truck onto the exit. I wasn't familiar with this area of the state, so I was pleased to see a truck stop from the top of the exit with an enormous parking lot. Gage put his turn signal on and our "state" escort did as well. I glanced further back and saw Katherine's truck right behind him.

At the very back of the lot was a truck pulling a U-haul trailer. No other cars were in sight. Gage pulled into a parking spot, but left the truck running. The Centaur in the police car pulled up beside him, rolled his window down and asked, "Is there a problem?"

"No, no problem. We're just meeting a couple friends who wanted to see the corn palace as well." Alarm didn't register with the Centaur, he picked up his phone and seemed to be checking messages. Katherine's truck had parked on the other side of the police car. Cami, Drake and Brent stayed inside while Katherine leaped out of the truck and walked over in between Gage and the Centaur.

She wore her best smile, "Well, hi. You look familiar! Weren't you just at the vehicle inspection area?"

"Uh, yeah. New assignment. Do you need assistance, ma'am?"

"I'm a friend. My name's Katherine, what's yours?"

"Bill Blankenship."

Katherine squatted down, both her elbows rested on his open window. I could hear her perfectly through Gage's open window. "Well, it's nice to meet you, Bill. I'm sorry, but yer gonna be in big trouble."

"Big trouble, and why's that?"

"Because ya lost Jessica Baker. Roscoe Baker is gonna be furious with you. It's a good thing you work as a state trooper because you won't be an enforcer much longer."

"What are you talking about? She's right there." His finger pointed directly at me.

"That's not Jessica Baker. Jessica just hopped in one of the eighteen wheelers headed for Montana. Didn't cha see her? Were you too busy reading messages on your phone ta notice?"

"Look, Katherine, or whoever you are. Jessica is right there in the back of that truck. I'm not sure what you're trying to pull, but drop it or I'll have you hauled in for interfering with police business."

"Right. I thought Jessica had blonde hair? The woman in the back seat of this truck has jet-black hair."

Officer Bill's eyes stared at me through Gage's open window. He squinted several times as a look of panic started to show.

Katherine didn't let up. "Jessica Baker's only twenty-three, the woman in the back seat is at least forty."

Bill rubbed his eyes with both hands, then his head jerked toward the interstate, then back to Katherine. "Summabitch! Which truck?"

Katherine gave a relieved smiled, "I'm not sure – it had Montana tags and was really dirty." The Centaur flicked the switch for his lights and siren and roared out of the parking lot in the direction we had come from. As soon as his car was out of sight, Katherine collapsed against Gage's truck. Daniel jumped out of the back seat and caught her before she could hit the ground. I got out of my side and ran around to where Daniel was supporting Katherine.

"How did you do that?" Daniel asked.

"I can hide Centaurs, but I remembered my mom talking about how she was able to make Centaurs see things that weren't there. I'd never tried it before. It's a good thing he was a Centaur – that never would have worked on a human."

Drake, Brent and Cami had all gotten out of the truck just in time to hear Katherine's explanation. She turned toward them, "One of you is going to have to drive to Omaha. That wore me out. I need to recharge."

Smiles erupted in all directions. We needed to get out of here and quick. Katherine didn't know how long her "suggestion" would work, but she was confident he'd be able to remember where we'd pulled off, and since he had been following Gage's rental, the license plate would be on his dash camera. We hoped all the cops would be more interested in looking for a phantom semi with Montana tags instead of trying to piece together who I was with.

CHAPTER 15

Camille – Airport in Omaha, Nebraska

Drake parked Katherine's truck in long-term parking. Gage returned his rental. Drake and I found a shoe store where he bought something to cover his toes. We all met at a coffee shop inside the terminal.

Brent had intended to take off on his own, but after much prodding, Daniel convinced him to go to Las Vegas with the other three. I didn't know what to make of Brent. This morning he had seemed pleased that his Centauride hadn't changed her mind and his betrothal was intact.

Brent had feelings for Katherine, too – that was obvious from their interaction, or lack thereof, on the drive here. Maybe he was mad at himself for comforting a human, or Lapith, or whatever. He had always seemed to take the "no touching" policy to the extreme but had been openly affectionate with Katherine in the tunnel last night. Every time Daniel did anything remotely flirtatious with Jessica, Brent looked like he would explode. I wondered if Brent had a thing for all three women?

We had twenty minutes before our plane boarded. Now might be the last time I could talk to Daniel for a while. The last time we were in an airport together I'd pretty much accused him of doing something awful to Drake. In my defense, I had just flown in from Florida, and Daniel was being super secretive – but deep down I knew he'd never hurt me like that. As I stood up from the table, Drake stood up on reflex, but I motioned for him to sit back down and looked toward my best friend. "Daniel, can I talk to you for a minute?"

He glanced across the table at Drake then stood up. "Sure."

Drake looked like he was ready to protest, but this wasn't something that was up for discussion. It was my goodbye to Daniel; I needed to do it on my own. We started walking toward baggage claim, and I thought of all the times it had just been Daniel and I in the world. My friend, my cheering section, my rock – Daniel. Daniel was so much a part of me, could I tell him goodbye?

As we approached the escalator toward the first level of the airport, Daniel took my hand. It was warm and strong. I missed the comfortable friendship we'd shared for so many years. He squeezed my hand gently and asked, "You're sure about all this?"

"Am I sure about Drake?" He nodded and without hesitation I answered, "Yes." Words escaped me. There was so much I needed to say. I wanted him to know that no one would ever replace him. Every happy memory of my childhood was tied to him. The woman I'd grown into had a lot to do with our friendship. Nothing. I couldn't force any of the words out of my head.

"I still think he's a loser."

"I know you do. But could you try to be happy for me?"

It was colder downstairs as the frigid temperatures tried to force their way in from the outside. Daniel kept looking out the revolving doors. I could read his thoughts without even trying. He wanted more than anything for the two of us to go home, to hit a "reset" button and go back in time. I'd had the same wish many times in the recent months.

"I'll always be here for you, Cami."

Emotion threatened my eyes. "I'm counting on it."

Steel arms wound around me and crushed me into him, his voice leaking the pain he felt, "He loves you. Not as much as I do – but he loves you."

My body ached. It wanted the easy friendship we'd shared for so long – not professions of love or promises to stay in each other's lives. It wanted volleyball on the beach, snow skiing at Big Bear, surfing in Carlsbad, and movie premieres in Hollywood. All the time we shared, none of it was wasted. It was a part of me I'd carry with me every day for the rest of my life – but they were memories. Reality seeped in that Daniel, too, would soon be just the memory of a life that was never to be again.

I gripped him hard around the neck and buried my face into the crook of his neck. "I'll never forget you," were the only words I could choke out.

"Me either." He loosened his arms from around me and arched his back away from me, giving me one last long look at his face. "If you need me, just call. I don't care if it's twenty years from now. You call me."

I nodded as a tear rolled down my cheek. "Ditto."

Daniel released me completely from his embrace, looked at his watch and said, "You need to get back. Your plane boards soon." Daniel took my hand and led me back to the escalator. I couldn't see through the tears and stumbled onto the first step. His arm caught me, righted me, and a gentle hand wiped the tears off my cheek. "Stop it, or I swear I'll take you back to Cali right now."

My smile stretched wide against hot cheeks. "And face Pops after all this? No thanks. I'm staying as far away from your dad as I can."

Daniel laughed, hard and loud, "Yeah, good call. He hates you as much as he does me."

For the first time I understood why his father never wanted me in Daniel's life. All the times he found things for Daniel to do around the house so he couldn't meet me, or refused to let me talk to Daniel when I called the house – I got it. I finally knew why he wanted us apart. "He never hated you. He just didn't want you to get hurt."

When we emerged at the top of the escalator; I could see Drake watching us from the table where we'd left him. Daniel leaned down to my ear, his voice like gravel against it, "It was worth it. All of it. I love you, Cami." Daniel's lips brushed my cheek in a final wordless goodbye.

Drake was at the other end of the hallway, but through our betrothal connection, he shared my pain, the ache in my heart. Drake felt me coming apart at the seams, but made no move in my direction.

My words were hollow, I didn't believe them as they tumbled over my lips, "This isn't goodbye. We'll see each other again as soon as all this Lost Herd stuff is over. Drake and I'll find you."

Daniel led me by the hand back toward the others. I didn't mean to, but listened into his thoughts: he didn't believe me. He was sure we would never see each other again. I wanted to argue with him, stop him in his tracks and tell him this was just for a few weeks, but I couldn't. If we failed in convincing the Centaur Council – this might be the last time I'd ever see him.

As we approached, Drake stood up from the table and began walking to meet us halfway down the hallway. When Drake and Daniel stood eye to eye, it was Drake's voice that broke the awkward silence. "Thank you for everything. I promise you, I'll never let anyone hurt her."

Daniel let go of my hand. His hand cupped Drake's shoulder, "I know. Love her enough for both of us." His gaze fell on me, "Goodbye, Cami."

That was it. Daniel walked away and didn't give us a second look. I kept watching to see if he'd look over his shoulder – he didn't. I wanted to run back to him and tell him we'd be back, we were going to make it, everything would be over soon. I didn't. I watched him walk away. My feet wouldn't move no matter how hard my heart protested.

My childhood left with him. Images of bonfires on the beach, hot chocolate on the ski slopes, sharing a tube behind a ski boat with the wind blinding us – everything I loved about being young walked away. My lungs emptied as my voice screamed down the hallway, "Daniel!"

He stopped. Hundreds of sets of eyes looked at me, but he didn't turn back. He stood in the middle of the hallway as people dodging him headed to their gates. The statue of a man refused to look at me. He was letting me go – giving his blessing to go on without him. "*Turn around, Daniel. Please turn around,*" I begged him.

Seconds passed, my eyes fixed on his back. He straightened his shoulders and continued walking away. That was our final goodbye, and my body wanted to shut down. It was Drake's strong hands that kept me from collapsing as he pulled me into his chest. Drake let me implode in his arms – he didn't say a word.

We said our goodbyes to Brent, Jessica, and Katherine and promised each other we'd meet back at this same coffee shop in two weeks – *if* it was safe. Brent had seen my goodbye with Daniel. He swore he'd stay with Daniel until he heard from us. For anyone who didn't show up back here in two weeks, the others who did would work out a plan to help them. Something inside told me two weeks from now, no matter what happened in Africa, Daniel wouldn't be here. He'd go to Vegas with these three, but I wouldn't see him again.

We had all come together just over twenty-four hours ago. Finding Katherine and Jessica had been an amazing coincidence. If Drake hadn't have found Katherine's motel when he was on the run from Cameron's house, I hate to think what would have happened to us – to all of us. I was grateful to them and hated that we were parting ways, but Jessica didn't have her passport with her, and she wasn't too keen on leaving the United States.

Everyone believed the eight of us traveling together was too much of a red flag for any Centaur who saw us. I was ready to make the vision Drake had pushed to me last night a reality. It broke my heart to tell Daniel "good-bye," but it was time to start my life with Drake. Thoughts of sun and sand had consumed my thoughts throughout the drive.

The four of us went through security and walked up just as boarding began for our flight. Bianca and Gage sat two rows in front of us on the plane. Despite Gage's ribbing about the free upgrades, the tickets Drake purchased were all first class. It didn't take long to settle into our seats because Drake and I didn't even have a carry-on, just a magazine I'd picked up from the newsstand at the airport.

The stewardess asked if we wanted drinks while the remainder of the plane boarded. Without missing a beat, Drake ordered two mimosas. She handed us our champagne flutes. I'd never been much of a drinker, but Drake urged, "Relax, Cami. We're almost there. Short of the flight being hi-jacked, we'll be on the beach in time for breakfast tomorrow." He clinked his glass with mine as the image he'd given me last night played in my mind again.

I took a deep breath and enjoyed the champagne sweetened with orange juice. The stewardess took our flutes just before take-off, and the flight turned out to be uneventful. Drake pushed the armrest up that separated us; he held me the whole time, gently stroking my hair. The sensation was calming and lulled me into a restful sleep.

When we landed, it was early morning. Customs was a breeze. I'm not sure the agent even looked at my picture before stamping my passport. We waited by the luggage carousel for Bianca and Gage's bags to arrive.

Drake leaned up against the brick wall, and pulled my hand to his lips. "We've got five days before we leave for Centauride. You still up for a wedding on the beach?"

A smile erupted, "Just the four of us?"

"Well, and someone who can officiate."

My heart pounded loudly in my chest. This was it. Everything I'd wanted was finally going to be mine. "I'm in."

Drake's smile grew. "We're not going sky diving. I was expecting a little more of a heartfelt answer."

I stood on my tippy toes and whispered in his ear, "The wedding isn't the activity I've been dreaming about since I met you. It's just a means to an end." I leaned back from his ear to watch his reaction. "Better?"

His wide smile was gone. Drake's eyes smoldered and, instead of answering me out loud, it resonated in my head. "*You won't be disappointed – with any of the planned activities.*"

CHAPTER 16

Jessica Baker – Las Vegas, Nevada

None of us sat together on the flight, which was a relief. I worried I'd be bombarded by questions from Katherine about what had happened at the gas station with Daniel. She had regained her strength by the time we arrived in Omaha. Daniel's Chap Stick stunt had taken me off guard, so much so that I didn't react. . . I couldn't react. The remainder of the trip to Omaha, other than our brief detour with the state trooper, he chatted with Gage as if nothing had happened.

Centaurs didn't just kiss Centaurides. It wasn't done. Reality set in that no matter how charming Daniel was – he wasn't a Centaur. . . at least not one my family would entertain my choosing. Even if he were a pure-blood, I would never choose a mate that was so brazen, so shameless, so . . . Daniel.

I hadn't wanted to sit by Daniel on the plane, either. I didn't want to sit next to his cocky personality, or his flirtatious comments, or him. When we were waiting to board our plane in Omaha, something was bothering him – a lot. At first I thought it was me, that he was just deep enough to understand the turmoil he'd created in me. But Daniel grew up around humans and was oblivious as to how loudly his thoughts were broadcast. He wasn't at all remorseful for the embarrassment he'd caused me. The sadness in his eyes was only the first clue: it was the ache in his heart and his thoughts of losing Camille that clouded his disposition.

Why had he kissed me? Why had he done it in front of everyone? And why did he do it when I wasn't the one he wanted to kiss? The flight to Las Vegas had been a welcomed break. It was a chance to come to terms with what I had just done as well as the second guessing and obsessing about Daniel.

By now Roscoe would know I'd disappeared. My mother was no doubt already trying to locate me. Would she be able to follow us? She had always been able to find me, but I'd never purposely evaded her. I was never gone from her for too long. When I was with Katherine, I had always made it a point to call her so she knew where I was – so she never had a reason to ban me from spending time with her.

After Roscoe killed Gayle, it was hard to face Katherine. The three of us had been so close – three peas in a pod. Katherine understood Centaur justice at a theoretical level, but after losing Gayle, the implications of it were raw and painful. She was powerless. We were powerless. Mom provided no comfort to either of us, just the threat that she'd make me regret it if I ever got out of line the way Gayle had.

I knew several Centaurs in our community that were nearly aged out of eligibility. Up until now, it was just the threat that she could promise me to one of them that had kept me from disappearing. Now that I'd bolted, she'd surely have promised me to one of them. Goose bumps erupted on my skin at the thought. Ralph with his horrible hygiene, Jimmy with his disgusting thoughts broadcast for the world to see, or Spencer, the one who had anger issues – I could already be promised to any of the three right now as punishment for my abrupt departure.

The night Roscoe was brought home from his raid on the farmhouse was my first real ray of hope. Roscoe was the lead enforcer for our region – I couldn't understand what had happened to him. He was bruised, broken and bloody – ranting into the phone to whomever he reported to. Someone had gotten the better of him. Roscoe kept saying it was a Centaur Warrior; it wasn't until he'd shown Mom and me a hoof mark on his stomach that I understood what had happened.

I'd dug into his thoughts, something I rarely did for fear Mom would learn how powerful I had become, and saw the image of Drake in his mind. I couldn't be sure if it was true or something his mind "believed" it had seen, but for the first time, ever, Roscoe didn't have the upper hand on someone.

Last night when Camille wandered into my bar, I didn't know what to do – I wanted to try to dig through her thoughts to see if the image of Drake from Roscoe's memory was reality. I couldn't take the chance of asking her directly and having her head for the hills. When Roscoe showed up right before closing, I worried my one ray of hope was going to be extinguished before my very eyes. Thankfully, everyone else needed us as much as we needed them last night.

When we made our travel plans this morning, I wanted Katherine and me to stay with Camille and Drake – but it wouldn't have been possible to get my passport without going home to get it. I couldn't risk it, and we couldn't risk them staying in South Dakota any longer.

Katherine could keep me hidden, but Drake could keep us all safe. Seeing him in Katherine's entryway last night had left me speechless. Roscoe hadn't been wrong. Drake was enormous. Strength emanated from him.

"What'll it be? Gambling first? Maybe a show?" Daniel's voice brought me back to reality. I'd been standing by the baggage carousel lost in my own thoughts. I didn't realize the other three were waiting on me.

Katherine answered, "Let's find a place to stay first. Something mid-scale: not Motel 6 and nothing ostentatious where other Centaurs may be staying – think: blending in."

Daniel turned on his heel and headed for the door, "I know the perfect place."

That was just like him. Taking charge, no discussion, no consideration for anyone else – it infuriated me. He might as well have been a pure-blooded Centaur. I looked at Katherine to see if she would call him back; instead she reached for the handle of her suitcase, shrugged her shoulders, and followed him out into the sunlight.

We emerged from the airport and shed our winter coats. The sun shone brightly off the awaiting taxi cabs' windshields. Fumbling in my purse, I dug deep to find my sunglasses. It had been a quick direct flight from Omaha, and I knew the weather would be a welcomed change, but the bright late-day sun was a surprise.

He had already flagged down a hotel shuttle and was hefting our bags into the luggage rack. The MGM? Did he not listen to a word Katherine said? One day. That was it, one day and Katherine and I would be on our way somewhere else. Daniel was putting us all at risk, and this seemed to be one big joke to him.

As we piled into the shuttle, I tried to hold onto my frustration toward Daniel and his ill-thought through plan. As we drove, the excitement of the city got the better of me. Las Vegas was just as over-the-top as I'd expected. Palm trees seemed to flank every hotel, people were crammed on every street corner, and the roads were choked by more limousines than I'd seen in my whole life.

The shuttle deposited us at the curb outside the hotel. The photographs I'd seen of it didn't do it justice. It was enormous, with bright lights framing its outline just coming on as the sun began to set. A brilliant marquee advertised shows, restaurant specials, and welcomed a wedding party.

Before we'd moved off the sidewalk, Katherine's frustration spilled out of her, "Not what we were looking for, Daniel."

He smirked, "Don't worry. I've got this covered; I've been here tons of times. We'll blend in no problem."

We had all taken as much cash out of our bank accounts as the ATM would allow at the airport in Nebraska. No one seemed too worried about being traced to Omaha since we didn't stay there, but we needed to be cash only while we were here.

Daniel walked straight up to the registration desk while the three of us stayed back a few feet desperately trying not to make eye contact with anyone. In a friendly tone the clerk said, "Hello, I'm Bryan. Do you have a reservation with us?"

Daniel answered in a loud whisper, "Keep your voice down. I'm here with Jessica Baker's party – we're in one of your Sky Lofts."

I froze. He'd just used my real name. Was he an idiot? We didn't have a reservation, and what the hell was a Sky Loft?

The clerk started tapping keys on the keyboard then looked up in an apologetic way, "I'm sorry, sir, I'm not showing a reservation for a Jessica Baker."

"You're new, aren't you? Check under Mickey Mouse."

The clerk's fingers whizzed over his keyboard, "I'm sorry, sir. I'm not finding a reservation under either name, and all our Sky Lofts are booked."

Daniel's voice sounded angry, "Dammit, Katherine!" He turned back toward us, "Jessica, I'm sorry. This is the third time. I want her fired." He pointed an accusing finger at Katherine, "How do you intend to deal with the Paparazzi? She has a release in two weeks. This was to be her break before her media frenzy, and you've screwed it up again. If they don't have our room ready, how much do you want to bet they don't have the security detail, either?"

Katherine's eyes were the size of quarters. She was stunned speechless. I couldn't understand what he was up to, and Brent stood just a few feet away with the same dumbfounded look.

Turning back toward the desk clerk, Daniel's tone changed, "My apologies, Bryan. The mix-up was with our publicist's inability to coordinate the simplest request. I'm afraid I'm going to have to ask you to move some people around. We require a Sky Loft for the next week and a four person security detail."

The desk clerk's eyes grew to the size of Katherine's although he somehow maintained his ability to speak. "Um, I just check people in. We don't have any Sky Lofts available, but we have some very nice adjoining suites." The enormous smile he plastered on his face did nothing to hide the clerk's nervousness.

In a seriously condescending voice, Daniel answered, "I'm sorry. This is not your fault. Could you have the hotel manager come help us?"

My heart stopped. We were probably on a surveillance feed right now. Our pictures would be broadcast on the evening news when we were taken away in handcuffs. How long would it take for enforcers to collect us? An hour, maybe two? I stepped forward and took Daniel's arm, "It's fine. Let's just go."

He turned toward me in a flourish, "Ms. Baker, I can't have you walking the streets. What would the studio say? You get mobbed two weeks before their premiere and who would be held accountable? Me – that's who. No. I'm certain the hotel manager will be able to fix this in a jiffy." He patted my hand that was still cinched tight on his arm in a dismissive way and turned back toward the counter.

As if on cue, a nicely dressed man with an expensive suit and impeccably manicured nails eased his way up next to the desk clerk. I was right, there was surely a panic button behind the desk, and it would be a matter of minutes before the police arrived. I was mortified. How were we going to get out of this one? I looked at Katherine and Brent: both wore the same "deer in the headlights" look.

Daniel leaned in across the marble counter and whispered quietly to the man I had to assume was the hotel manager. He wore no name tag but glanced in my direction several times while Daniel continued with some enormous lie about me being a Hollywood movie star. I couldn't hear everything said because Daniel was speaking so quietly. I tried to concentrate on the conversation, giving up my attempt to hear their words and focusing on the hotel manager's thoughts.

Adrenaline pumped freely through my body: anger at Daniel for pulling such a stupid stunt, fear that in a matter of hours I'd be back in South Dakota. If that happened, I'd be lucky to just be under lock and key. The anger and fear gave way to rage that he could be so obtuse about the whole situation. The adrenaline interfered with my concentration, and it was a full minute before I could calm down enough to get a clear read on the hotel manager's thoughts.

My anger, fear and rage melted into astonishment in that second. He believed Daniel. How could it be? I wasn't a movie star. I was a big fat nobody. I continued watching the hotel manager, waiting for him to realize this was just a horrific prank – he didn't.

Instead he motioned for the desk clerk to move to the side and took charge of the reservation computer. I heard his fingers type hard on the keys and then answered, "Miss Baker, ah, I've found your reservation. We're so pleased to have you staying with us this week. My name is Malcolm, and if there is anything I can do to make your stay more comfortable, please let me know."

I had to speak. I had to say something. Words eluded me. He hadn't called the police. We weren't being shown to the curb. How did Daniel pull that off? "Uh, thank you. . . Malcolm. I will."

"Very good, Miss Baker." Malcolm whispered conspiratorially, "We understand your need for discretion. We would love to see you take advantage of our amenities. Could I schedule you for a complimentary spa treatment?"

Daniel jumped in before I could answer, "You don't mean in the spa with your other guests?"

"Oh, of course not, sir! If Ms. Baker would like to choose a time, we'll have our staff come to her room."

Daniel nodded, "Excellent. Yes, if you could have your staff stop by tomorrow, say about 11 a.m.? And we'll need security posted outside our door."

"Already taken care of, sir. They have orders to escort Ms. Baker throughout the premises." He nodded to two men standing behind us wearing dress shirts, dress slacks and sports coats. "Now, I'll show you to your suite and make sure everything is to your liking."

The ride up the elevator was excruciating. I kept expecting him to change his mind and security detail to handcuff us or something. When we exited the elevator, Malcolm was quick to open the door to our suite, then handed me the card key. He stood just inside the door. I had no idea what I expected, but two walls lined with windows overlooking the Las Vegas strip was not it.

I saw Brent opening his wallet for a tip when Malcolm waved it away. "No, sir. You are our guests this week. We're thrilled you chose our hotel." Almost sheepishly, Malcolm looked toward me while he fished in his pocket, "If it wouldn't be too much of an inconvenience, I'd love to have my picture with Ms. Baker."

I should have been more in character with more of a Hollywood air, but I wasn't an actress, or a movie star. I nodded and moved closer to him and forced a smile onto my face. He handed his phone to Daniel who took our picture and handed it back.

When the door closed, everyone was still speechless. Thoughts began picking up speed as I tried to slow them down enough to say anything. What would happen when he found out I wasn't someone important?

He had my name: what if he called the police? If the police found out, would my picture be on the news? How much did a room like this cost, and how were we going to pay for it?

Daniel was the only one who was able to talk. "Not bad, huh?"

Brent spat out, "Are you insane? Now everyone in the hotel knows we're in this room. How is that blending in?"

"Relax. Celebrities get special treatment. No one is going to get past the two armed men standing outside the door. We got the best view in the city and don't forget – there's a casino right downstairs for entertainment. We couldn't be safer."

The shock of what he'd just done began to wear off when I accused, "You used my real name."

Daniel rolled his eyes, "Of course, I used your real name. The trick to pulling off an exceptional lie is to have as much truth as you can get away with mixed in."

"So anyone looking for me just has to look at the hotel registry."

Daniel shook his head and pulled out the registration slip and handed it to me. The "guest name" was Mickey Mouse. Still angry, "So how do you think we're going to pay for this?"

His finger slid along the paper and tapped the area that showed the nightly rate column: it was $0. I couldn't believe it. "They comped the suite?! Are you kidding me?"

Daniel's only answer was a cheesy grin. I didn't know how to respond. I should be angry; he had put us all in a lot of danger. In five minute's time he could have had us in jail, our picture out on the wire, a beacon for everyone looking for us. But he didn't.

Daniel took my hand in his then looked toward Katherine and Brent, "Excuse us for just a minute."

My hand felt stiff and cold in his warm hand. He tugged me toward the staircase and led me up the steps to the suite's second floor. I had noticed the view when we first walked in but hadn't paid attention to the furnishings. It looked like they came straight out of a home design magazine. Everything was perfectly coordinated, the pile of the carpet was thick and lush, and I was sure no matter where we stood, the view would be breathtaking.

When we were upstairs and out of earshot from Katherine and Brent, Daniel continued holding my hand as his blue eyes stared into mine. "I know you're still mad about the kiss."

My eyes slid to the carpet on impulse. Was I still mad? Embarrassed, yes. Irritated, no doubt. But, mad? "Look, you're a lot of fun, but. . ."

Daniel cut me off, "Stop. Once you say the word 'but,' it negates everything you said before it. I'm not asking for anything from you. I don't have any expectations beyond wanting you to have fun. Is that so bad?"

Wanting me to have fun? Was he serious? What kind of game was he playing? I knew how he felt about Camille. I didn't have to be able to read his thoughts: it had been written all over his face before we left. Who was this guy in front of me now?

When I didn't respond he said, "Live a little. You've been muzzled your whole life. We've got a few days before you and Katherine figure out what you're doing next. While you're here, we have fun. No strings. No expectations. Okay?"

"What are you?"

"Just call me the Morale Fairy."

Somehow teaming the image of Daniel with any kind of title including the word "fairy" seemed absurd, but if he was trying to make me laugh, it worked. He was tall, with light brown hair, blue eyes, wide chest, and a perfect smile – definitely not a fairy. I stood motionless, realizing that he still held my hand in his. "No strings?"

"No strings. Maybe a thank-you would be nice."

I shook my head at him in disbelief. As much as I hated how he went about it, we were in an amazing room that couldn't be traced to us. We had armed security provided by the hotel to make sure no one sneaked up on us. We were being treated like royalty, and we were in the city whose motto was: *What happens in Vegas, stays in Vegas.* He had exceeded my wildest expectations, and we'd only been here for less than an hour. "Thank you."

"I was thinking of more of a personal thanks." Daniel eased toward me. We stood only inches apart. He let go of me and shoved both his hands in his back pockets. He leaned closer, enough that I felt the heat off of his skin. Every fiber of my being told me to back up – I didn't. Alarm bells sounded in my head warning me to move away – I stood motionless, mesmerized by the blue of his eyes. I watched his eyelids close slowly as his lips descended to mine.

The softness of his lips flush against mine created a fluttering in my chest. Instead of the shock of our first kiss in the bitter cold and in front of everyone, this one was slow, gentle, inviting. I forced my mind to quiet, allowing my senses to focus on his lips and how they felt against mine. Too soon, he eased his lips away, but rested his cheek against mine. In a breathless voice, he murmured, "You're welcome."

Daniel leaned over the banister looking down onto the living room below. "You two up for the Casino?"

Katherine answered, "You three go ahead. I'm just gonna order room service and park it in front of the TV."

Brent's voice still sounded frustrated, the way it had when we arrived, "No. I'm going to stop by the business office. Mom set up a Facebook page where I can check on my family. I want to see if anyone's left messages."

Daniel grabbed both my hands, his voice sultry, "Looks like it's just the two of us."

I wasn't sure if it was his devilish smile, his fiery touch, or his smooth voice, but heat spread through me. I tried to remind myself Daniel was dangerous. No strings. He was good for some laughs, and laughter was exactly what I needed right now.

"We should quit while we're ahead." I recognized the look in Daniel's eyes. It was the same one Katherine had when I helped her win the motel in Deadwood. Being able to see what cards were going to be dealt made winning too easy. We had plenty of winnings already, so there was no good reason to keep playing. If anything we'd attract attention that we didn't need if we continued.

"One more hand. I've never had this good of a night before." Daniel's excitement would be short-lived if I told him I was helping him. Of course, what little I knew about him – maybe not. We were already up several thousand dollars. If by some chance the hotel manager figured out we weren't who we said we were, at least we had money to settle the bill.

"I'm beat. Come with me." I tugged his arm in a playful way.

He made eyes at the dealer as if I were asking him to sacrifice his first born son. "If you're beat, why would I want to come with you? You'll just be snoring."

My hand let go of his arm and slapped him harder than I probably should have, but the dealer thought it was hysterical. She'd noticed our security entourage, but didn't ask any questions.

I pushed all of my chips toward Daniel. As far as we knew, no one was looking for him. He looked at the enormous pile and asked, "You sure?"

"What, you're going to skip out on me after the lights go out tonight?"

Daniel quickly scooped up both our stacks of chips and poured them in a plastic bucket. I didn't wait for him so he had to sprint the few strides to catch up to me. Slyly his hand went to my waist with a gentle pinch, "Unless you can think of a way to keep me occupied, you'll never know what I've got up my sleeve."

"Says the human to the psychic Centauride."

"Psychic?"

His surprise caught me off guard. Didn't he know? He had to know. Cami was his best friend: she would have told him. Well, maybe not. Not all Centaurides had the same powers. If he didn't know, was there was a reason Cami had kept it from him?

CHAPTER 17

Jessica Baker – Casino in Las Vegas, Nevada

Daniel looked at me like I'd lost my mind. "What do you mean psychic?"

We were walking toward the cash office. The two security guards assigned to us were a few steps behind, so they wouldn't overhear us, but I felt weird talking to him out in the open. "Cash out first. I'll tell you when we get upstairs."

Within minutes, Daniel's wallet was full of cash. One of the security guys yawned, and I looked at my watch. It was already after 2 a.m. I was so used to closing my bar that my body rarely wanted to find sleep until after 4 a.m. I didn't feel like going up to the room right away, but the constant chiming of the slot machines was grating on me. I remembered seeing an atrium near the registration desk and led Daniel toward it.

A few benches set in the middle. Although the casino never closed, no one else was here, and we wouldn't have to share this part of the hotel with anyone else. As we walked on the path toward one of the benches,

I turned back toward our security detail, "Would you boys give us a couple minutes?"

They both nodded and posted themselves on opposite sides of the atrium.

Daniel looked almost giddy, "You're psychic? For real?"

"No, I'm a fake psychic." I shouldn't have made fun of him, but the answer was folded up neatly in his wallet. "Where do you think all the chips came from? Your lucky day?"

"Maybe. Prove it."

"It's not that big of a deal. All Centaurides have powers."

"So, you can't prove it?"

Frustrated at his disbelief, "I didn't say that."

"Quick, how many quarters are in my pocket?"

"This is silly. Can't you just believe me?"

"I knew it. You aren't psychic. It's okay, babe, a smokin' body and a sense of humor are fine – you don't have to have cool powers, too."

Was he serious? I was rationalizing with a juvenile. "I'm not going to do parlor tricks for your entertainment."

"What would you rather do to entertain me?" He wagged his eyebrows like an eighth grader.

Did he really think he was funny or did he act this way just to annoy me? "Grow up."

"Just tell me you can't do it."

"I said I'm not going to, I didn't say I couldn't."

He reached his hands into his pockets and jingled the change together. "C'mon, take a guess then."

"You want to know how many quarters are in your pocket?" I couldn't believe I was going to stoop to the equivalent of a magician at a 5-year-old's birthday.

"Yeah."

"If I tell you, will you drop it?"

"Of course."

"Fine. Five."

Daniel reached into his jeans and pulled out a handful of change. "Oh, so close. Sorry, babe. Four."

"Check your other pocket."

He pulled a lonely quarter out of the other pocket, and the smug look on his face was gone. His cockiness ebbed a little, "Lucky guess."

"Sure. It's your story. Tell it any way you want."

"Oh yeah?" Still not believing me, he asked, "What's my dad's phone number?"

"716-4210."

This was more fun than I'd expected. Daniel was seriously clueless about Centauride powers. He was sure I'd made it up. There were rules about revealing our powers to humans, but he was more Centaur than human – none of this should have been a surprise to him. If his mom were a half-blood and his father a pure-blood, maybe there was no one who would have told him. I guess it made sense that he might not know.

"Is Cami psychic, too?"

Of course. Everything always went back to Cami. I shrugged my shoulders. "She's a Chiron."

"So, she's psychic, too?"

"You should ask her."

"Yeah, that's not going to happen. She left, remember?"

"It's not like you won't see her again."

His shoulders slumped and he looked away from me. The glee disappeared from his voice. "She told me goodbye, Jess."

"Weren't you listening? We're all meeting in Omaha in a couple weeks. Ask her whatever you want then." He didn't say anything. I was so used to him talking a mile-a-minute, it was odd for him to remain quiet. Didn't he plan to go back to Omaha with the rest of us?

He stared at the floor. If I didn't know better, I'd swear he was memorizing the geometric patterns on the tile. His words were distant, "You ready to go up to the room, or what?"

What wasn't he telling me? I began searching his thoughts, but they were strange, different from before – detached. He said he didn't like the cold – maybe he was swearing off Nebraska because of the temperatures. Maybe he was homesick and wanted to go back to his family. "Do you miss home?"

He looked at me as if I'd grown a third eye. "Why would you ask that?"

"I don't know. Just wondering."

"No. Not much anyway."

"So why aren't you going back with us to meet the others in Omaha? Is it the cold? Winter doesn't last forever, ya know."

Daniel shook his head. "She told me goodbye."

"Cami? She told all of us goodbye."

"You wouldn't understand."

"I bet I understand more than you know."

"Really?"

"You have a crush on her and she's with Drake now. You're jealous. Get over it." Wow, that felt good to say out loud.

Daniel shook his head, "Not even close. You don't know what you're talking about. Drop it."

"Yeah, right."

"Okay, fine, I'm jealous. There. I said it. Let's go upstairs." He stood up and started walking toward the elevators. Something wasn't right. I was really confused: he was lying to me – I could feel it. He wasn't jealous of Drake, or if he was, it wasn't jealous the way I'd believed.

"Wait. Daniel. Stop. I don't get you. Are you angry with her or something?"

"Let it go. I'm fine. It's been a long day."

I couldn't miss the defeat in his voice if I'd tried. I tapped him on the temple with my index finger, "Tell me what's going on inside that thick skull of yours."

"I can't, Jess." Only two people had ever called me Jess – Katherine and Gayle. It shouldn't have mattered, lots of Jessicas shortened their names to Jess – but not me. I wanted to tell him it wasn't okay, that "Jess" was reserved for people I couldn't live without. Reality hit me – I had found a way to live without Gayle.

Since Katherine and I ran away – thoughts of Gayle seemed to consume me. If she were here, she'd tell me to go for it with Daniel. She'd still be laughing about how he checked us into the hotel. I missed her. I wanted to know why he was being so evasive. I tried a different approach: lowering my voice, I looked up into his eyes, "Just try. Please. I want to know."

"Fine." He sighed. "When she told me goodbye, it was like a piece of me walked away – a big piece. I've known everything about her – her whole life. I know why she won't wear red shoes. I know why she's scared of pigs. I know why she hates roses. I know everything about her past, but there's no place for me in her future. I'm glad she's got Drake. If I can't be around, at least someone's looking out for her."

"She won't wear red shoes? Pumps or flats?"

"What?" He shook his head as if "idiot" were printed on my forehead. "It doesn't matter – she doesn't wear any red shoes, ever. Why she won't isn't important. The fact that I know that and I've known it since eighth grade is what matters. How is Drake going to know that? What if he buys her a pair?"

"You're not making sense. So she tells him she doesn't like them. Are you sure you're not upset that they're together?"

Daniel shook his head. "I'm not human and I'm not a Centaur. I don't fit anywhere. So, no, I'm not going to be *that* guy, the one everyone keeps around because they're too kind to tell him to leave. I get that no one wants me around, and don't worry, when you're done with me – no hard feelings."

Daniel held out his hand to walk me back to the room. I was speechless. No one wanted him? I was at the airport when Camille screamed his name and he refused to turn around. I was at my bar when she first saw him and she lit up like a Christmas tree. I was in Katherine's entryway when he risked his life to give her the man she wanted – even though Drake's fury could have been a death sentence. Was he blind, deaf and dumb?

"What makes you think I'm anything like Cami?" The words were out before I could take them back. I couldn't lead him on. He wasn't a Centaur – not really. A radical thought occurred to me. If I never went home, who would tell me I had to choose a pure-blooded Centaur? Who would tell me I had to choose anyone?

We were kids when Gayle announced she was going on a date with a human. I thought she was kidding at first, but when I realized she was serious, I remember being so envious – jealous even. If my family couldn't find me, I could be with whomever I wanted.

"Duh, you're both Centaurides. So you have the same powers and everything, right?"

I covered my mouth to try to muffle the laugh. "Are you serious? Uh, no. I can't do a tenth of what Cami can do."

Daniel turned his head as if he didn't believe me. "Why not?"

"Centaurides usually have two *skills.* They come from the two dominate blood lines in them. Most can read minds, a lot of us can see hidden objects, some can communicate telepathically, some can move objects with their minds, some can see the future, and a few can communicate with spirits – only a Chiron has all the abilities."

"Wait, how do you know?"

"Everyone knows. It's always been that way. I've never been telepathic, but when Cami wants to talk to me that way, I can hear her and she can hear me. When you two came to my bar she started talking to me telepathically – it was amazing. I had heard about telepathic connections, every Centauride shares one with her betrothed, but I'd never experienced one before."

"Seriously? Why didn't she tell me she could do all that stuff?"

Because you're not a Centaur. That's what nearly slipped out. I shrugged my shoulders, "It's not something easily worked into a conversation."

"Yeah, I guess not. But you're really psychic?"

"I can see objects, like cards. I can hear thoughts, and with some people I can dig through their minds to find thoughts."

Daniel blushed. Not a rosy pink, but a bright red embarrassed blush. "You know what I'm thinking?" An image of the two of us in a passionate embrace danced across his thoughts.

My eyes went to the escort standing half way across the atrium. I lied. "Only if I try. I'm used to blocking everybody out. It gets a little overwhelming to hear thoughts in a crowded place like this."

Daniel looked relieved. "You ready to go upstairs? Ten bucks says Brent's wrapped up in a snowmobile suit hiding in a closet, so he doesn't inadvertently come in contact with Katherine." Daniel's hand rested on the small of my back as he led me toward the elevator. He didn't mean anything by it. I'm sure it was a harmless gesture – something gentlemen do. His touch gave me a strange sensation – his hand didn't bother me; the fact that I didn't want him to move it scared the crap out of me.

CHAPTER 18

Camille – Cancún, Mexico

Was it possible to melt, either from the burning sun or the heat Drake generated next to me? My stomach knotted into a tight ball, and my palms began sweating. This was no longer insane flirting. In a few short hours Drake would be mine in every way possible. I leaned into his chest and shared a few choice thoughts in return.

Gage and Bianca towed their luggage over to where we stood. Bianca looked us up and down and shook her head. We had nothing but the clothes on our backs and our identification. They had been in the area just weeks before, so Bianca took charge, "Gage and I will take care of the rooms; you two, go get some clothes. Meet us on the waterfront pier in two hours. We'll take a ferry from there."

"A ferry?" I looked at all the high rise hotels surrounding us; any one of them would have been perfect.

Bianca smiled, "A ferry, a bus, and then a cab. We've got the perfect place for you two for some privacy. We need to get it set up here because we didn't want to make the calls from the states."

Drake and I did as we were told.

Inside the city, stores were stacked on top of each other with owners standing on the street trying to usher us into their stores. The streets were clean, the weather was warm, and almost everyone spoke English. Two hours later we each had enough clothes for a week. We even invested in a suitcase so we could blend in with the wintering tourists.

The beauty of the area didn't escape either of us. We waited on a bench by the pier as Bianca had instructed. The water looked just like the image Drake had pushed to me at Katherine's house. We sat in front of the tranquil ocean, Drake's arm draped over my shoulder and my head nestled into the crook of his neck.

He was quiet and kept his thoughts to himself. This was our wedding day. I couldn't help feeling that I should be nervous – I wasn't. I pictured us standing in the surf exchanging vows. "For better or worse" had an especially sharp meaning. We'd had the "worse" a hundred times over. I was ready for some "better" for a while – even if it was just for a few days.

Drake's voice startled me when he broke the silence, "We could stay here, you know."

"And not catch the ferry, bus and taxi? What fun would that be?" I eyed the beautiful hotels. Each had breathtaking views of the ocean as I silently wished Drake would lead me to one of the lobbies.

Drake squeezed my hand gently, "No. I mean we could *stay* here. Not go to Africa." I lifted my head off his shoulder and looked at him. His eyes remained focused on the surf.

"We have to go. If we don't, it's a death sentence for my family."

His voice was steady but low, "I can't protect you like this – I'm human. I can't lose you."

"I'm right here."

Drake didn't tear his eyes away from the surf, but his hand began caressing my arm. "When we talked about going before – it felt like we didn't have anything to lose. My transformation had sealed the deal. Going up against the Council with you, fighting for the Lost Herd – it felt right."

I didn't understand what Drake was getting at, "Nothing's changed."

Drake slowly shook his head, "Everything has changed. We've got a real future now. We could hide here, make a life for ourselves: buy an estate and lock ourselves inside and never see another Centaur."

I didn't even want to consider it, because it sounded too enticing. "No. That's not who we are. Like it or not, I'm the last Chiron Centauride. You are more of a Centaur warrior than the world has known in thousands of years. There are thousands, maybe tens of thousands, of Centaurs from the Lost Herd who are counting on us."

A single tear slid down Drake's cheek, and he made no move to wipe it away. The words slid out of him quietly, "I don't know how to change back."

When he'd been transformed, he thought of himself as a different species – I never felt that way. I knew it was only temporary. I was sure eventually he'd be human again, so our circumstances never impacted what I believed we needed to do. "If we fail, we fail together – you already promised me eternity in the pasture. If we succeed, we can live wherever you want, except South Dakota!"

Gage and Bianca found us sitting on the bench. They were all smiles. We spent the first forty-five minutes on a ferry; it let us off on a pier where a bus was waiting for us. We rode the bus over nicely paved traffic congested roads for the first thirty minutes and then another thirty minutes on rougher country roads. When the bus let us off in a smaller city, a line of taxi-cabs was waiting for passengers on the street.

The four of us squeezed into the back of a mini-van and rode for another thirty minutes. I was beginning to wonder if we would end up in South America! The large canopy of trees hung over the poorly-maintained roads until the cab pulled up in front of a large gate. Bianca got out of the cab and pressed a security code into an awaiting keypad. Large iron gates swung open – inviting us into its private paradise.

The cab driver set our suitcases on the curb, collected his fare, and was out the gate headed back to the city. I looked around at the sprawling estate in front of us. The sound of the surf was close, and little bits of turquoise ocean peeked through the trees.

Bianca grabbed hold of her suitcase handle and said, "Follow me." She didn't walk toward the steps of the main house. Instead she walked on a path toward the ocean, her bag's wheels struggling against the loose sand. As we walked along the path, the view of the ocean was gorgeous. The water was so clear, even from twenty yards away we could see fish swimming in the shallows. The sound of the waves rolling onto the sand was a gentle reminder that we were thousands of miles away from the Centaurs who hunted us.

At the end of the path stood two small cottages, both nestled directly in front of the ocean.

"Ta daaaaa," she announced with a flourish.

I didn't know what to say. She handed us a key and pointed to the one closest to us. A man in a pressed white shirt and white pants stood in front of the cottage. I looked at Drake, not sure what to make of it. It was already ninety degrees, and the poor man must have been sweltering. When we were only a few feet away, he spoke, "Welcome. Lunch is ready."

Lunch was ready? I was hungry, but I would have preferred to starve and get some alone time with Drake first. Perched behind the back of the cottages was another man sitting by himself in the shade. Well, not by himself – a large iguana sunned a few feet away on a rock sticking out of the ground. An inviting glass of water set in front of him while an automatic weapon lay across his lap. I froze. Drake noticed him the same time I did and eased his body in front of mine.

Bianca looked in the same direction and shook her head. "Would you two relax? He's part of the security detail we arranged."

I was surprised at this little amenity, "Security detail?"

"Uh, yeah. You think it took me two hours to rent beach front bungalows?"

"What all did you arrange?"

"Let's see, the cooking and cleaning staff, security, a priest who will bring a marriage license with him, a couple disposable cells, a boat in case you want to go exploring, and all of the transportation here."

I could hardly believe my ears. "A priest who brings a marriage license with him?" It should have occurred to me that there were more details required than simply standing together and saying, "I do."

She gave me a smug look. "Luckily we had just gone through the process a few weeks ago, so we filed for your license when we got here. He's picking it up on the way."

I took Bianca in a tight hug. I wanted to tell her that she was the best wedding planner ever . . . or that I'd never be out of her debt . . . or that she was the sister I'd always wanted, but the only words that came out were, "Thank you."

She squeezed me back, "None of this would be possible if it weren't for you. I just want you to be as happy as I am."

She flashed a memory to me of me prying bars off the window of Zandra's guest house, where she and Drake had been held captive. Zandra had told Gage and me that Bianca and Drake were both dead. It was her twisted way of getting Gage and me to go through with an arranged marriage to each other. It almost worked, too. In the end we all escaped that day. Gage and Bianca didn't waste any time saying their "I do's." Now it was our turn.

After lunch Drake and I explored the little cottage. It wasn't lavish by any stretch of the imagination. The floors in each room were stone tiles. Huge windows opened to catch the ocean breezes, and each room had a ceiling fan. There was a small kitchen with an efficiency stove and single sink. The countertops were Formica and the furniture well worn. Despite its humble appearance – the cottage was perfect. I looked around for a thermostat when Drake shook his head. "Your first time to this part of Mexico?"

I nodded. Drake smiled, "We aren't in the states, and modern conveniences aren't common here. If you're cold – close the windows, if you're hot – open them. If you're really hot, cool off in the ocean."

"Really?" The temperatures were well into the nineties, and I couldn't imagine living here without air conditioning. Maybe it felt so hot because we'd just left the winter of South Dakota.

"There are lots of homes here without electricity. We're lucky to have ceiling fans."

No electricity? I'd grown up poor by US standards, but every place we'd ever lived had electricity, heat in the winter, and air conditioning in the summer. Will had set up a pretty hefty account for Drake and me in the Caymans, so money wasn't an issue for us. We could afford to stay anywhere in the world – I liked that Drake was quick to point out we were lucky to have electricity and ceiling fans. The cottage was charming, and enjoying it with Drake was truly a gift.

We changed into our swimming suits and grabbed beach towels from the linen closet. After the temperatures in South Dakota for the last few weeks, and before that the cold wet temperatures in Ireland, it felt incredible to lie in the sunshine. We soaked in the sun's rays as the heat penetrated all the way to my bones. Just when I thought my core temperature was ready to spontaneously combust, the man in the nicely pressed white shirt appeared with two cold bottles of water.

I drank mine down greedily before I realized Drake was watching me. He hadn't said much, and I figured we were both enjoying the bliss of the day. When his expression didn't change, I wondered where his thoughts were. Our telepathic connection only worked when we purposely shared our thoughts with the other, and he'd kept his hidden from me since the airport. It didn't bother me to have the silence. It was a nice break, but I was curious, "What're you thinking?"

He turned away from me and looked out into the turquoise ocean before us. "Nothing that I need to share right now."

"Keeping secrets already? We haven't even made it official yet."

I got a grin out of him. He shook his head, "I'm content."

"That's what you're thinking? Not trying to be high maintenance or anything, but *content* wasn't a word I was hoping to hear you describe us with for at least another twenty years."

Drake scooped me up against his chest as we both looked out into the ocean. "*Content* means different things to different people."

"So you're generally happy with how things have turned out?"

Drake's fingers lightly caressed my arms as he kissed my neck. "I'm not happy that we've had to go through so much to get here, but if this were our last day together on earth, I'd go without any regrets."

That was a strange thing to say. Did Drake know something he wasn't telling me? I tore my eyes away from the incoming waves and craned my neck around to look at him, "No regrets?"

His grin widened to a smile. "Assuming Bianca's plans go off without a hitch and I get some much needed privacy with you after – no, no regrets."

My face warmed as my blush grew, "So why do you look so sad?"

Drake didn't answer right away. Instead his hand caressed my bare skin from my shoulder to my wrist and back – sending tingles all the way to my toes. His eyes stayed fixed on the surf. "Our days may be numbered."

I understood. He'd said as much when we were waiting for Bianca and Gage on the bench in the city. He didn't think we would make it out of the Centaur Council alive. I knew better – we needed to go. We could change things. I didn't need to see our future to know the Centaur

Council wasn't something we could avoid. If we didn't take the fight to it, it would only be a matter of time before they found us.

Drake's voice remained quiet, but it was absent the emotions that were coursing through him. "If things don't go well in Centauride next week, I'll regret that I wasn't able to convince you to stay in paradise with me. That's what I'll regret."

Nothing I could say would change the way he felt. Zandra only needed to be within a hundred miles of us for her to find me. Even if I agreed to go into hiding, eventually she'd stumble across us, and we would be in an even worse spot. On some level I agreed with him, but there had to be a reason so much had happened to us. Even if the worst possible scenario happened – it wouldn't be in vain. I stood up and tugged Drake to his feet. "Enough of watching the waves. Come swim with me."

CHAPTER 19

Camille – Bungalow Outside of Cancún, Mexico

I stood in the bedroom staring at my reflection in the mirror. My hair was down, loose just over my shoulders. I wore a white bikini top and a sheer white wrap at my waist that hung to just above my ankles. Not exactly the wedding dress my mom may have wanted me in, but I couldn't imagine a more romantic setting or a more appropriate outfit. I looked out the window into the surf. It was late afternoon, and the breeze off the ocean was cool.

A soft tap sounded at the bedroom door, Bianca on the other side, "Can I come in?"

"Yeah, are we all set?"

"The priest just arrived." Bianca looked at me and smiled. "Hmmm, something's missing."

I laughed, "Yeah, a real dress, a veil and shoes, but I don't think Drake will mind, and I don't have to worry about wrinkles in this."

"No. If anything, we are about traditions. Something old:" Bianca held out her hand, in which a pair of diamond earrings sparkled, "these were Gage's great-grandmother's. He wants you to have them, so you always carry a little of Aphrodite's magic with you. Something new: I think your swimsuit is new, right?"

It was. I bought it as soon as we had gotten off the airplane this morning. "Definitely new."

"Something borrowed and something blue:" Bianca reached into her purse and pulled out a handmade necklace of beautiful turquoise and blue stones strung between seashells. "Gage gave me this on our wedding day – so I want it back. You're covered for borrowed and blue. Here, let me try one more thing."

Bianca turned me away from the mirror and started braiding my hair. It only took her a few minutes. When she was done, she turned me around, and I could hardly believe my eyes. It looked like a style a goddess might wear. A thick braid wove around my head with a few loose strands of hair hanging down framing my face.

"What do you think?" I was speechless. My inability to answer put Bianca in panic mode, "If you don't like it, I can take it out. I didn't spray it or anything." She reached for the pins she'd put in to hold it in place, but I grabbed her hands before she could let it loose.

"No. It's perfect. Everything's perfect."

Bianca checked her watch. "We've got some time to kill. What do you want to do?"

Time to kill? If the priest was already here, what were we waiting for? I decided it didn't matter. I wasn't nervous, and spending a few minutes with Bianca was a treat. We'd spent almost no time together, just the two of us, and I doubted I'd be able to rip myself away from Drake any time soon.

I shrugged my shoulders. It seemed silly to stay in here. It was bad luck for the groom to see the bride before the wedding, but we'd already had more than our fair share of foul luck. Standing in the surf, waiting to say “I do” to Drake seemed like a better idea than standing around here at the bungalow. “Let’s go wait on the beach.”

Sharply, Bianca answered, “No!” Surprise at her reaction must have colored my face. Did she have a momentary meltdown? She cleared her throat, “I mean, no, seeing Drake before the ceremony is bad luck.”

I shook my head at her. “If the priest is already here, what are we waiting for?”

“Gage went to get the rings.”

The rings. A pang of disappointment shot through me. Why hadn’t Drake and I thought of that? It shouldn’t matter, but it felt wrong using rings Gage had picked out. I wanted the ring I’d wear for the rest of my life, regardless of how short or long that time might be, to be one Drake had selected. I didn’t want Bianca to feel my disappointment, so I asked, “Why are we doing this so late in the day?”

She bit her lip. If I didn’t know better, I’d think she was hiding something from me. “The priest’s schedule didn’t allow for an earlier time.”

“Oh, that makes sense. Is he the same priest who married you and Gage?”

She smiled, “Yes. We wandered into his chapel down by the ocean right after we arrived from the airport. You’ll like him.”

“What names are on the marriage license, anyway?” Drake and I had flown in with the fake passports Will had gotten for us before we left for Ireland.

“Your real names.”

Just to clarify, “Benning and Nash, right?”

Bianca nodded, “Yes. Why didn’t you ever change your name to Strayer or Chiron?”

I smiled, “Yeah, with all the abundance of free time I’ve had lately, standing in line at a court house to file legal documents should have been higher on my priority list.”

“I’m sure your father could have had his lawyer do it for you.”

I didn't like the way I'd left things with Will the last time we spoke. So much had happened in South Dakota that I couldn't be sure if Will and Zandra were in cahoots with each other or not. Since I found Drake, I'd only talked to Will on the phone long enough to let him know we were safe. From what Brent told me, he and Gretchen went into hiding just days after we spoke on the phone.

I shook my head, "It doesn't matter. I'll be Mrs. Nash in an hour."

"Um, if you do, you'll be the only Chiron Centauride in history to take on her husband's name."

"Call me a trend-setter. My mom was Angela Benning my whole life. That was one she picked out of thin air, so taking Drake's name shouldn't be a big deal."

Bianca's eyes went to the floor. Now I *knew* she was hiding something from me. "What? What aren't you telling me?"

"Normally I wouldn't say anything, but I think Gage is ready for you to switch last names. At least not to be a Benning anymore."

"What are you talking about? I've always been Camille Benning. That's the name on my birth certificate."

"You know Gage's Dad, Kyle, hid your mom, right?"

"Yes, but that's not a big secret anymore. Everyone knows that."

"Gage's dad was in the Army for a while. Did you know?" I shook my head that I didn't. "He was stationed at Fort Benning in Georgia. He bought Angela a small house on the outskirts of the base. After she disappeared," Bianca did air quotation marks, "he went to see her there a few times – but they decided it was too dangerous for both of them. She left for California, and that's when she changed her last name to Benning. She told him it was so she'd never forget the few weeks of happiness he'd given her after he helped her escape."

I couldn't believe that Bianca would know this about Mom and I wouldn't. There was more I didn't know about her than what I did, or the parts I thought I knew turned out to be lies.

Another tap on the door: this time it was Gage. He let himself in and closed the door behind him. "Okay, we're just about ready for you. Any last minute jitters I need to calm down?"

That was just like him. Gage and I had nearly been married; in fact, Bianca, Drake and I escaped the day before Gage and I were to walk down the aisle together. If we had been human, a friendship between the two couples after everything that had happened would be no more likely than hitting the lottery.

"No jitters. I'm ready." I wondered why Mom and Kyle's relationship bothered Gage? It happened way before either one of us was born. As long as we had some time to kill, it wouldn't hurt to find out a little more about my mom. "Gage, Bianca told me your dad and my mom hid in Georgia for a while. What else don't I know about her?"

Gage gave Bianca a confused look. "I'm not sure what all Bianca told you." Gage shrugged his shoulders, "I heard stories about Angela most of my life. She was more than a crush to my father. Truth be told, I'm glad things worked out the way they did with the four of us. You look so much like her that I don't think his sanity would have survived having you as a daughter-in-law." Gage smirked, then added, "Mom heard all the same stories I did about Angela, and she would not have been the best possible mother-in-law for you, either."

I didn't want to pry, but so many questions had bothered me since Zandra's. Gage might be the only one with real answers. "If he loved her so much, why didn't he just marry her and keep her away from Zandra?"

"I asked Dad the same question lots of times. She needed to escape more than just Zandra's home. She didn't want anything to do with being the Chiron Centauride. She didn't want to oversee the Centaur Council. She didn't want every decision she made scrutinized. She didn't want people to pretend to like her because of her lineage. The one thing she wanted more than anything else was freedom from Zandra. Dad couldn't deny her after everything she'd gone through. He gave her the freedom she wanted and, in the process, tucked his love for her away."

There was something else in this whole "hiding scenario" that bothered me, "So, if Mom did all this with your dad's help, why was there a Blood Debt? How come he was going to make me marry you?"

"Only Angela and Dad knew it. I heard stories about Angela growing up, but he didn't tell me about hiding her until after Zandra took you. When he found out you were there, he sat me down and told me everything."

"All those years, he wrote her off. He never tried to rekindle anything with her."

"That's the part of the story you're missing." Gage looked at Bianca as if arguing about whether or not to let me in on his father's secret. "Dad pledged your mom."

Now I was really confused. Drake told me the betrothal pledge was sacred. A centaur could only give it once, and if the Centauride changed her mind and broke the betrothal, the Centaur was still bound to her for eternity. Gage must not have known that I understood what it meant because he explained, "It doesn't matter that he married my mom and had a family. When he reaches the pasture, Angela will be waiting."

"Wait, so they could communicate telepathically? The same way I do with Drake?"

"Yes and no. When they were relatively close, he in South Carolina and she in Georgia, they probably could. But after she moved to the west coast, no. That was too far away."

"How far can two be away from each other and still communicate?"

Gage wound his fingers around Bianca's, "We've been more than 50 miles apart and still been able to talk, but we haven't been further apart than that."

"Further after you were married?"

"Uh, no, it doesn't work like that. The betrothal pledge is what ties the souls together. Being married doesn't act like an amplifier for the pledge if that's what you're asking."

It still didn't make sense to me. Mom and Kyle loved each other. He'd tied his soul to hers by giving her his betrothal pledge. Why would she go into hiding, and, more than that, why would he help her stay hidden? "I still don't understand why he let her go."

"All I know is I'm glad you're marrying Drake so Mom doesn't have to be reminded of Angela every time she sees me for the rest of her life. She already knows she'll spend eternity alone." I'd never met Gage's mom, but I could only imagine her pain. Drake had told me most Centaurs were in loveless marriages; it sounds like the Richardsons were no exception.

Gage watched me as my confusion refused to subside. He leaned over and gave my arm a gentle squeeze. "I wish I had all the answers for you. If it's important to you, maybe you can talk to Dad about it one day. But right now you have a couple people waiting for you on the beach. One Centaur in particular is getting pretty antsy. You ready?"

I was. I pushed all the thoughts of Kyle and Mom out of my mind. Whatever stupid decisions they'd made when they were young had no bearing on me today.

Gage held out his elbow to escort me down to the beach. He leaned down and whispered, "By the way, you look beautiful. I'm glad history didn't repeat, and we both got our happily-ever-after."

I squeezed his arm, "Me, too."

Bianca trailed us out of the cottage. She had heard us and added telepathically, "*Me three.*"

In the same place Drake and I had sunbathed earlier, Drake stood next to the priest waiting for me. Drake looked amazing. He stood in a loose fitting white button-down shirt and baggy cargo shorts, barefooted with his toes buried in the sand. Drake's blue eyes were fixed on mine as Gage led me to the beach.

This was it. I never imagined myself married at twenty-three, but I wasn't nervous. I didn't question my decision or worry that I'd regret it later. The certainty that washed over me was surreal. I carefully stepped across the hot sand, on the way to my awaiting destiny – Drake.

I didn't notice anything but Drake standing in front of me, waiting patiently with an enormous smile. His eyes looked brighter in the sun, his skin a dark contrast to the sand beneath him. Someone cleared his throat behind me, but I didn't break eye contact with Drake to see who it was. A hand stretched out from behind a tall palm tree, stopping Gage and me. I looked to see who it was attached to, and my heart nearly stopped. "Gage, thanks for standing in for me. If it's all right with Camille, I'd like to be the one to give her away."

CHAPTER 20

Camille – Outside of Cancún, Mexico

I couldn't believe my eyes – Will was here. I looked to a small group sitting in white plastic chairs set up under a clump of trees, hidden from view of the cottage by shrubs. Beau and Lacey, Bruce and Hannah, Bart, Ben and Gretchen were all sitting in the shade. Drake's mom, Hallenjah Nash, sat in between Gretchen and a Centaur who looked like an older version of Drake. Bianca walked up and stood next to Gage, her smile beaming, "Surprise."

I was stunned. "How did you. . . ?"

Will's arms gathered me in a tight hug. "Bianca always has a few tricks up her sleeve." He was smiling so hard that his eyes wrinkled. I let go of Will and leaped the few steps to Lacey and Beau, who both stood up and hugged me hard.

I hadn't seen them since they left South Dakota and went into hiding. She leaned down close to my ear, "I told you it would work out." Lacey was the seer. Before she and Beau left South Dakota, she told me not to worry, things were going to work out. The realization hit me: it was *her* voice that I had heard in my head. All those times I tried to convince Drake his transformation was only temporary – it was because Lacey had seen it. She told me before she left.

Bruce and Hannah hugged me next. Drake and I first met at their wedding, and I couldn't believe they'd risk exposing themselves to come to ours. Bart and Ben were all smiles, too. Both gave me a quick hug and a kiss on the cheek.

Gretchen stood on the other side of Ben, and when she hugged me, it wasn't a quick embrace. She held me so tightly it nearly crushed my lungs. I couldn't believe my eyes; everyone was supposed to be in hiding. Why would they risk coming here?

Gretchen heard my thoughts and answered aloud, "We couldn't let you get married without your family." She motioned to Drake's parents, "Your whole family."

Drake stepped up to hug his parents then wound his arms around my waist as his lips went to my ear, "Sorry. Gage and Bianca made me promise not to tell. They wanted to surprise you. We should get started before we lose the priest in the surf. Don't worry – everyone is staying for the party afterwards."

"Party?"

"Let this be a lesson to us both. If Bianca tells us she needs two hours to make room reservations, she is probably doing more than making a couple phone calls."

Hallenjah held out her hand and I took it. She looked almost regal. I had only met her once, briefly, when she told me Drake was still alive, and she took the dreadful shock collar off of me so we could escape Zandra's house. Her voice was warm, "You look radiant, Camille. Welcome to our family." Her words nearly brought tears to my eyes. She knew I was from the Lost Herd, yet she willingly accepted me.

Drake's father was a different story. He took my hand awkwardly, and his palm felt stiff around mine. "Mr. Nash, it's great to finally meet you."

Drake's Dad looked from me to Bianca and back to me. His eyes held nothing but loathing – it was obvious he didn't want to be here. I remembered Drake telling me his father had wanted him to collect a Blood Debt when Bianca had run off with Gage. Drake had stood up to his father and told him it was his idea to call things off with Bianca.

The smile I'd plastered on my face began to falter. I looked to my right, where Drake had appeared beside me. "We're both glad you're here, Dad."

His father huffed, "Didn't have much of a choice, did I? Couldn't let your mother come here by herself."

Hallenjah's voice was irritated, "Don't you start, Nathan. When your only son gets married, you drop what you're doing to be a part of it."

In an unfriendly tone and wearing an angry look, Nathan said, "You are lovely." I didn't know why he bothered to say something nice if he didn't mean it and he didn't want to be here.

Drake and I had been through so much: two kidnappings, the belief that he'd died, his transformation into a Centaur Warrior, running for our lives – too much for anyone to get to spoil today. I didn't listen in, but I believed Hallenjah was silently scolding him. Drake's words were soft and sweet in my head, "*He doesn't do well with surprises. Don't pay any attention to him.*"

I nodded my answer to Drake, but turned my eyes on his father. "Mr. Nash, could I have a word with you?"

Hallenjah and Drake froze. My tone was sharp and anyone within ten feet knew it wasn't a request. "Do I have a choice?" He raised his eyebrows.

"No." As I started walking back toward the bungalow, Drake and Hallenjah took a step in our direction. I turned around and shook my head, "No, we'll just be a minute."

We were back on the porch of the bungalow before either of us said a word to the other. He stared at me with angry eyes. Maybe he was mad that I'd pulled him away from Hallenjah. Maybe he was embarrassed I'd been so forceful in front of everyone. Maybe he was just a jerk. "Can I call you Nathan?"

He nodded. With more confidence than I was feeling, "Okay, out with it. This is the 'speak now' part – before you have to 'forever hold your peace'."

Nathan's words were sharp, "I've got nothing to say to you."

"Really? Maybe I can get things going for you. How about: you're not good enough for my son. Let's start there."

"I didn't say that."

"Don't let me put words in your mouth. Whatever problem you have with Drake and me getting married, I want to know what it is now."

"You want to know what my problem is?"

"Duh" was sooooo the wrong answer, and in spite of myself I almost let it slip out. Instead I just looked at him, waiting for a response. I didn't want a shouting match, and I wasn't sure that I'd be able to fix whatever his issue was, but he was Drake's dad, so I was going to listen.

"Fine. You're from the Lost Herd. He marries you, his future's over."

"That's not a secret. Drake loves me, and he doesn't care who my parents are."

"Of course, he doesn't. It's his life. His choice. It doesn't matter what I think, so I'm not sure why we're wasting time. You want to get married so bad, go do it."

"You know we wouldn't be here right now if it weren't for Hallenjah, right?"

His words were slow and hateful, "Don't remind me."

Anger began mauling my insides. I leaned up against the beam of the bungalow, steadying my legs. If he felt this strongly – should I go through with it? Did he already blame Hallenjah? "So, you wanted Drake and Bianca to marry."

"That's not a secret, either. She was perfect for him."

I couldn't keep the frustration and anger from my voice, "She was in love with Gage. Drake wouldn't have been happy. They both would have been miserable."

His words rushed out, "They would have had a future. He could have had children with her. He could have taken over my business and had an honorable life. Instead, he'll be looking over his shoulder for what's left of his life. You've effectively destroyed our blood line by choosing him. Now you want me to be happy about it? Fine, I couldn't be happier that you're getting ready to exchange vows with my son. You're signing his death warrant. For the love of Zeus, don't have any children – the loss of Drake and grandchildren would kill Hallenjah."

Nathan looked out into the surf. I felt like he'd given me a swift kick in the stomach. The anger was gone, so was my rage that had steadily built up toward him. This didn't have anything to do with him being angry about me being from the Lost Herd – at least not the way I was picturing it. All those times Drake said his father didn't care for him or didn't approve of him, nothing could have been further from the truth. My answer was calm, "I can't promise you any set number of days you'll have left with Drake. I don't know if we've just got today, or ten days, or ten years, or a lifetime. The only promise I can give you is every day he has left will be spent with a Centauride who can't live without him."

He blinked but didn't turn away from the ocean. "I know you don't approve of me. If I were in your shoes, I'd probably feel the same. But you know as well as I do, Drake isn't like other Centaurs. Drake would do more than sacrifice his life for me, he'd sacrifice who he is, and do it without regrets. I'll never forget who he is. He's your son and he learned how to be who he is from you."

Nathan continued looking off into the distance. Drake said the two had never been close, but after this conversation, I knew it wasn't because Nathan didn't care about him.

I eased over toward him, understanding him better than maybe his own son did. "Drake told me that you wanted a big family. He remembers Hallenjah trying to convince you to try again, to have more children. Drake said he remembers her screaming at you about it, but you wouldn't."

There was something different in his voice when he spoke. A tenderness that hadn't been there before. "You don't know what you're talking about."

"Hallenjah had complications giving birth to him. You wouldn't try to have any more kids because you couldn't bear the thought of losing her." Nathan's eyes wouldn't meet mine, and his silence told me I was right. "That's how much I love your son. No matter how impossible the odds, we're going to succeed, because I can't stand the thought of a day without him."

He turned toward me and looked into my eyes. Nathan shared the same color eyes as Drake – the same piercing ice blue. "I don't know if we'll be successful. I can't guarantee that we won't be hunted like dogs. But if you ask him, he'd tell you he'd take a few days of bliss with me over a lifetime without me. That's how I feel about him, too." I waited for him to argue with me, but no words came. "Deep down, you know I'm right, because that's how you feel about Hallenjah."

His gaze refused to drop mine as he pursed his lips together hard and nodded. We stood there in silence. The only sound was the surf gently lapping against the beach. I waited for him to say something epic, or maybe just kind, or anything. Nathan pushed himself off the wall of the bungalow and held his hand out to me, "I see now why Drake was so taken with you. Not only are you lovely, you are compelling." That didn't sound like much of a compliment, but he gave me the same smile Drake had with the dimples that made me want to melt. "C'mon, the others are waiting."

"Slow your roll, Speedracer." That was one of Daniel's phrases, and I'd always wanted to say it. In twenty-three years, this was my first opportunity. "You're okay with the wedding?"

He nodded, "I'm more than okay with it. I forgot what it felt like to be young and in love. Thank you for reminding me."

When we got back to the beach, Drake and Hallenjah looked nervous. I'd purposely blocked Drake from the conversation so he couldn't listen in. I didn't know if Nathan had done the same, but from her questioning look, I'd bet that he had, as well.

Drake took my hand in his and led me to the awaiting priest.

The ceremony was perfect. I barely heard the priest's words, and even if I had, his accent was so thick that they sounded like he was speaking in Spanish. It was Drake's ice blue eyes that held me captive on the sand throughout the short ceremony. His fingers caressed mine as he held my hands and a warmth baked from inside me.

Drake gently slipped the ring on my finger, "*Mom brought these with her. They belonged to my grandparents. When my grandfather passed in a car accident, my grandmother left for the pasture a week later. She couldn't stand the loneliness of losing her Centaur, and her body refused to live without him. Mom told me she saw the same love in your eyes that she always saw in her mother's and wanted us to have them.*"

Goosebumps erupted on my arms. The priest announced, "I no' pronuse yo man e wife."

Drake and I turned around while a photographer was snapping pictures rapidly. Bianca really had thought of everything. Ben and Bart walked straight up to us and said, "Welcome to the family," then proceeded to tackle Drake into the ocean.

Laughter erupted from all sides. Drake stood up and was soaked from head to toe. He walked out of the water, all smiles, shaking the salty water from his face. He wrapped his arms around me and bellowed, "I don't know what you're laughing at." Within seconds he had brought me down into the ocean with him.

The priest excused himself and the party commenced. Tables full of food were carried down to the beach by more men wearing nicely pressed white shirts. Caribbean music echoed out on the beach, and a full-blown party ensued well into the night.

Drake's parents were not at all what I had expected. Both could dance, like dancing I'd only seen on music videos. His father threw Hallenjah in the surf before the night was over, too. As Hallenjah's laugh echoed along the beach, Drake watched his parents play in the water. I stood next to him, intertwining my fingers with his, "Your dad isn't what I expected."

Drake let go of my hand and wrapped his arms around me, still staring at his parents goofing around in the ocean. "I've never seen him so happy." He stopped watching his parents and looked down into my eyes. "You have that effect on people."

"Sure, his son marries into the Lost Herd and he's thrilled."

Drake shook his head, "I haven't seen him like this since I was a little kid. What'd you say to him before the wedding?"

"Nothing really. Only that if he tried to stop us from getting married I intended to take him for a swim with a brick hooked to his ankles."

Drake's eyes flexed and I couldn't help but laugh at his reaction. "Just kidding. We just spent a couple minutes getting to know each other, that's all."

Drake swung me around so I was facing him. We began swaying to the music together as he rested his chin on my head. Our bodies moved together slowly, and even if I had tried, I couldn't drown out the love that poured out of my heart for him. For a long time everyone disappeared, and it was just Drake and I molded together in the moonlight.

Will cleared his throat. I opened my eyes and saw him patiently standing off to the side. "May I have a turn?" Drake kissed my cheek and let me loose, handing me over to Will. The music was slow, a soft ballad playing as he danced with me on the beach. Will's voice was quiet but strong, "Congratulations, Camille. I couldn't have chosen a Centaur better than Drake for you."

His words were meant as a compliment to Drake, so I didn't allow myself to make a snide comment about arranged marriages. It wasn't anything he had dreamed up; it was just a part of the Centaur culture I didn't like and would thankfully never endure. Will looked at me with heavy eyes, "Drake told me you two intend to address the Centaur Council next week."

"We do. Gage and Bianca are going with us."

Worry spread across his face. I could feel his discouraging words coming before he spoke them. "It's not their fight."

I leaned back so he could see my resolve. "It's everybody's fight, Will."

He pursed his lips together. I had struck a nerve. We'd spent remarkably little time together for a father and daughter, but he knew me well enough to know not to give me any type of ultimatum. Mom always told me I was strong-willed. He must have already come to the same conclusion. Will collected his thoughts before he asked, "What do you intend to say?"

"I don't know. I think pretty good on my feet."

"I know you don't think of me as your father." His words hung heavy in the air. I did think of him as my father – but I wasn't sure if I could trust him. How do you put that into words in a nice way? It was several minutes before he offered, "If you could spare the room, I'd like to go with you."

"Why?"

"It wasn't your sin against the gods that brought you and Cameron into this world. It was mine. If the Council feels they must exact revenge against the Lost Herd – it should be me who pays the price."

I leaned away from him, unable to process what he was saying. Was he offering himself up as a sacrificial lamb to the Centaur Council? "No. Whatever creed, or warrant, or whatever it was that Zeus handed down was wrong. Centaurs exterminating a herd for the actions of one Centauride thousands of years ago is insane. We aren't sheep. We don't blindly follow. We were born from adversity and no one, god or otherwise, controls our destiny."

I waited for him to argue, to tell me I was wrong, or to try to convince me to go into hiding. He didn't. William took both my hands in his, gripping them as if his life depended on them, "You *are* Chiron's daughter."

"I am Chiron's daughter *and* daughter to the Lost Herd of Centaurs. Chiron protects me. The Council will see reason or they will be dissolved. It is their place to preserve and protect, and they have lost their way under Zandra."

The music played on, but neither Will nor I still swayed to the beat. He stood still, looking at me, searching for one morsel of doubt in my features. He didn't find it because no doubt existed.

Will wore an astonished look, saying the words out loud as if he didn't believe them. "You do not fear her."

It wasn't a question, but I answered him anyway. "No."

"She is the most powerful Centauride in history."

"Power is just power. True strength is in the wisdom of our actions."

Will still held both my hands as he went down on one knee, bowed his head, and said, "Guardian of the Lost Herd, hear me now. Camille needs the protection you have afforded my family for generations. Keep her safe. Shield her from harm. Allow her to lead us out of the Dark Ages."

I didn't know what to say. Guardian of the Lost Herd? Brent had told me one of the gods had to be secretly helping the Lost Herd. Who was it? Did Will know which god was helping us? Will stood up, hugged me to him and said, "I've never been more proud of another in my life. Our legions stand at your disposal. You need only say the word."

"Legions? What the heck are you talking about?"

"Camille, the Lost Herd has been in fear of their lives, fear for our children's lives for longer than anyone can remember. We've been waiting for the right time, the right place in history, the right leader to set us free." His eyes were glossy as he looked down into my eyes, "That leader is you."

Drake had been a few yards away. I didn't notice him until he took a step toward me; it was obvious he'd been listening. Pride shone through his eyes. I didn't believe he would ask me to hide from the Centaur Council or any of their Centaur enforcers again. Drake understood what was to take place when he said, "I'll be at your side."

Drake eased over to me while Will stood up and walked over to where Gretchen was waiting. Drake took me into his arms. His voice was low, his desire clear, "Have we spent enough time with everyone else?"

His words sent shivers up my spine. Today had been magic, more than I'd hoped for. I tugged his shirt toward the cottage, not even bothering to tell everyone goodnight. They would all still be here tomorrow. Drake didn't hesitate in following me, his hands on my hips, guiding me in the moonlight. Just as we reached the threshold of the little cottage, Drake hoisted me up in his arms, his lips softly brushing mine. "I've loved you since the first moment I carried you in my arms. If this has been a dream, I hope I die in my sleep so I never awake from it."

I reached for the door handle so Drake could carry me over the threshold. A high pitched cry followed by a bloodcurdling scream echoed up to the cottage. It was Lacey. Drake set me on my feet in front of the doorway. He turned and sprinted toward the beach without a word. I stood frozen, "*Lacey, what happened?*"

"They're here, Cami. Run. Run now!!"

CHAPTER 21

Camille – Outside of Cancún, Mexico

Despite my fear, I asked Lacey, *"Who's here?"*

"The Council's enforcers. Save yourselves."

A bright flash of light shown through the trees, so bright I raised my hand to cover my eyes. The white light was as brilliant as the sunrise magnified by the reflection of the ocean, but it was hours too early for that. I closed my eyes and shouted through my thoughts, "*Drake, where are you?*"

"*Hide. Hide in the jungle until I come for you. Now. I can't fight them off if I think you're in danger.*"

I wanted to go to him – to help him. More screams echoed off the water – was that Gretchen? What was happening to my family? I took a step toward the ocean. If I lost Drake now, my life would be over. I'd die the same death his grandmother had – death from a broken heart.

Drake's voice was loud in my head, "*Cami, hide. I promise I'll come for you.*"

I have no clue how he did it, but he let me see what he was looking at through his eyes. In that moment I knew where the bright light had come from. It wasn't an explosion. It wasn't muzzle fire from a weapon, and it wasn't the sun rising. Drake had transformed back into my Centaur Warrior and was attacking the Council's enforcers on the beach.

He didn't need my help. I hated the idea of hiding, but I mentally reached out to the beach where all the commotion was going on – there were fewer Centaur enforcers here than had ambushed us in South Dakota.

I begrudgingly did as I was told. I stayed within the confines of the estate, but away from any paths, and stayed well camouflaged by the vegetation and darkness. I needed to keep my mind from running through all of the worst possible scenarios. I connected with Drake's mind, to see what he was seeing. The images through Drake's eyes were fierce. The enforcers seemed to be concentrating on just him, ignoring the others and assaulting him.

Ben, Bart and Beau were lobbing rocks at one. The three took turns charging the enforcer, trying to keep him off guard. He was bobbing and weaving better than any welter-weight fighter I'd ever seen, but they were getting the better of him with their assaults. A second enforcer got in the mix, but, he, too, couldn't stave off their assault.

Four enforcers were attacking Drake. One enforcer wielded a sword so quickly it was nothing but a blur in his hands. I saw everything through Drake's eyes and couldn't help but cringe as the Centaur attempted to sink his sword into Drake's flesh. Drake was too fast, so each time the blade came down, he was a fraction of an inch to the side. The three other enforcers circled him, carrying daggers; each attempted several rushes but couldn't catch Drake with his guard down.

I didn't see Hallenjah, Lacey or Gretchen and was too enthralled with the assaults to try to locate them. I looked for Will and Drake's father, but they, too, weren't in the fight. Bianca stood on the beach by herself, easily fifty yards from the action. I could see an enforcer stalking her in the shadows. Couldn't she see him? He was right there! "*Bianca! Behind you!*"

Before her response sounded in my head, I watched an enormous palm tree fly through the air and crush the enforcer to the ground. "*Whoops, can't imagine how that could have happened.*"

I wanted to laugh, and, if I hadn't have been so freaked out a second ago, I would have. "*Did you just set a trap?*"

"*Of course not. We're not the warriors, right? We're just defenseless Centaurides.*" Gage jumped down from a neighboring tree and tied the enforcer's hands. It seemed like overkill, no way was he going anywhere unless Bianca moved that tree trunk. Man, I loved Bianca. I'd forgotten she could move objects like that.

I crumpled down to the ground, watching the battle unfold, unable to do anything from this distance. I counted seven enforcers total. The four were still attacking Drake, and although he hadn't yet been touched, it was only a matter of time before they wore him down. I stood up. He couldn't do this without me. I took several big strides when his voice warned in my head, "*Don't do it, Cami! I can handle them, but I need to know you're safe. Stay put.*"

I paused, arguing with myself. What if I could distract one of them? Wouldn't that be some help? I could climb a tree and manipulate objects, something. I concentrated on the four Centaurs circling Drake. I'd never tried to manipulate objects from a distance, so I focused on one with long dark hair that looked to be the largest of the four. He crouched down readying to pounce on Drake, when he did I made sand fly in his eyes. He took two steps back as his hands flew to his eyes to brush the sand away – Drake landed a hoof to the Centaur's chest.

When we were attacked at Cameron's house, he'd taken on thirty Centaurs without so much as a scratch to show for it afterwards. He'd be fine. He had to be fine. I cleared my mind and started counting, slowly down from twenty to calm myself. I was at seventeen when I made my decision, I couldn't stay here hiding. It wasn't in my nature. It wasn't what Chiron would want me to do.

If Drake put his life on the line, I would stand beside him. Either we'd win or we'd lose, but we wouldn't be apart. I took three large strides, watching the ground beneath my feet. I ran directly into the awaiting arms of an enforcer. I'd caught him off-guard and pushed him with every ounce of strength I had. It was enough to knock him off his feet, but his hand reached up and caught my ankle, bringing me to the ground, too.

I didn't have a weapon of my own. Somehow he had tracked me here. I refused for him to see me try to crawl away. We were both on our feet at the same time. I stood tall, extending to the full measure of my height, my hatred for what he stood for glaring through my eyes.

The enforcer froze. He stood just feet away from me, trying to anticipate in which direction I would flee. I tried to read his thoughts, but they were blocked. His expression was a stone, giving nothing away of his intentions. I glared at him – daring him to try to strike me down. He reached for me so quickly and grabbed my throat with such speed that I was in his choke hold, my feet dangling inches above the ground, before I realized he had even flinched.

Not like this. This was not how I would die. I willed the muscles in my throat to go rigid under his touch, to refuse to yield to the pressure put on them. I closed my eyes and concentrated on a tall tree that was just on the other side of the path. The lack of oxygen started to give me tunnel vision, but I concentrated on the tree.

I couldn't identify the type of tree, but it had large thick vines hanging from it. When I opened my eyes, one of the vines was suspended in mid-air as if it were a snake, ready for me to tell it to strike. I envisioned the vine wrapped securely around the Centaur's throat, squeezing his larynx, denying him the air that his hands held hostage from me.

In an instant, the vine coiled around the Centaur's throat and yanked him hard away from me. The Centaur's eyes flew open, as his hands clawed at the vine – desperately trying to remove it from his neck. I fell to the ground, sucking in as much air as my lungs could take.

The Centaur coughed and gasped as the vine squeezed the fight out of him. When his body went limp, I willed the vine to release his throat and wrap around his body. I leaned down to the Centaur's limp body on the ground: he had a pulse. I didn't want him dead – I didn't want any Centaur dead. I just wanted my family to be safe.

Drake's voice called to me. "*It's over. Where are you?*"

Relief spilled over me, "*Here. I'm near the main house.*"

His voice was heavy, "*I'm sorry, Cami.*"

"*Sorry?*" Had he not gotten there quickly enough? Was it Beau? Or Bart? Had Will been hurt? Before I frantically asked the question of who hadn't made it, Drake's face appeared through the trees, along with the rest of him. All nine-hundred pounds of him stood before me in the moonlight – he towered above me, my Centaur Warrior.

I threw myself at him, grateful that he was okay, then I steadied my voice, "Is everyone okay?"

Drake exaggeratedly looked at his body, but nodded. "There were only eight. They must have been sent to do reconnaissance and couldn't pass up the opportunity to try to take out a few from the Lost Herd whose guard was down." Drake saw the unconscious Centaur who lay at my feet, "My mistake, nine." He took both my arms and held them out away from my sides, looking up and down my body, searching for any sign that I'd been hurt.

I wasn't sure if my neck was bruised, and if it was, it might not be visible in the moonlight. Any injury inflicted would heal quickly, Drake might not even see it. "I'm fine. Where are the others? And why did you say you were sorry?"

"Gage's standing guard over the enforcers. Everyone is fine, not even a scratch. We're going to have to get out of here. We don't know how long until the others arrive."

I shook my head. No matter where we went, the Council's enforcers would find us . . . unless. Another idea occurred to me. "Can we get a hold of Katherine? See if we can get her down here."

As if the thought had never occurred to him he asked, "Why?"

The answer seemed obvious. "She's the only Lapith I've ever met. If she were with us, no one would be able to find us – none of us. Our families are here. She could keep everyone safe."

"Lapiths are the sworn enemy of the Centaur. No matter how persuasive you are, she won't put herself at risk to come here and protect us."

"You heard her in the car yesterday. She cares for Brent. If she knew Brent's family was in danger, I bet she'd be on the next plane."

Drake leaned down and extended his hand to me, "If anyone could track her down, I'd put my money on Bianca. Let's go get her."

Images of my family started flashing in my mind. I'd been so preoccupied with the Centaur who'd come for me that I hadn't tried to find out what happened. Deep down I knew they were okay, but I asked Drake for confirmation anyway, "You're sure everyone's okay?"

"Yes. Everyone's fine. Well . . . Dad's a little shaken up, but he'll be fine in a minute. He didn't know that I had the ability to . . . trot." Drake gave me a lopsided grin, and I put my fist over my mouth to hide the giggle.

Drake had transformed so quickly, I wondered how he'd done it. "But how did you. . . ?"

He smiled sheepishly as his thumb caressed my hand. "It wasn't anything I consciously did. As soon as I saw the enforcers on the beach, my body took control and transformed on its own."

Bianca's voice called to us from the beach. "Drake? Cami? Where are you two?"

When the two of us stepped out onto the sand, faces full of fear, exhilaration, and shock at what had just happened looked back at us. Will was the first to recover. He took a step toward Drake, held out his hand and said, "You are the only Centaur worthy of my daughter. Thank you for protecting my family."

Drake shook his head. "There will be more. We may not be able to stay here."

I squeezed Drake's hand. He nodded toward Bianca, "Unless our party planner can get four more guests to join us."

She didn't hesitate as she read my thoughts and her smile grew. "I think I can convince them." She turned toward Will, "We're going to need to charter a plane, and we're going to need a couple passports."

William looked confused while Gretchen's smile stretched from ear to ear. She saw what Bianca and I were thinking, then relief filled her, "You know how to contact Brent?"

Bianca nodded vigorously, "We'll have to pull him away from the roulette wheel, but it shouldn't be too hard to convince them."

Gretchen looked at me and silently asked, "Brent came to see you?"

I nodded, "Yeah, we all got out of South Dakota yesterday. He went to Las Vegas with the others."

"Will told all the boys to go into hiding. We left right after Beau. We can message him through a Facebook account we sent up, but we didn't know where he'd gone."

Drake stood off in the distance – away from the others. He had been right beside me when we walked up, but all the stares must have bothered him. As I moved toward him, he was forcing a smile on his face. Did he not want Katherine here? Did he want to go on the run instead?

"Why are you off by yourself?"

Drake's voice was hollow, "I just pictured tonight a lot differently."

"The night's not over yet."

"I haven't exactly mastered this body yet, Cami. I don't know how to change back."

"Do it the same way you did at Katherine's house."

"You were there. The only reason it worked was Daniel was goading me on. It's not a light switch I can flip at will." His hoof stomped in frustration.

I looked around for something to stand on. He was too tall for me to look directly into his eyes. I spied a fallen tree trunk a few yards away and motioned for Drake to come over to it. I stood on the decomposing trunk and held my hands out to help me balance. Once I was steady, I put my hands on either side of his face. My thumbs caressed the tender skin just below his eyes.

I let my mind's wall crumble. All my thoughts lay open for him to see. Flashes of memories of the two of us faded in and out of my conscious thought: the moment he caught me in mid-air the first time I met him, just after I had stumbled off of Will's stairs. . . the overwhelming desire I had for him the first time we kissed. . . the relief I felt when he sneaked into my room at Zandra's house and told me everything was going to be okay. All these emotions and images were rolled together for Drake to see and experience through my eyes.

Flashes of light began peppering his back, just as they had in Katherine's entryway when Daniel sent him into a jealous rage. I pushed images of the two of us harder: the memory from two nights before in Katherine's garage immediately after Drake had transformed . . . the raw desire we had shared. The more images I pushed, the brighter the lights became, until there was an enormous explosion of light, and before me stood Drake, the man.

The transformation to his human form brought him back to his normal size. I hopped down off the log and buried my face in his chest. Drake was acutely aware of the attention his transformation had brought from the wedding guests and the heavily guarded enforcers. Bart, Beau,

Ben, Bruce, and Gage surrounded them. Each enforcer's hands had been bound, and from all the cuts and bruises, it looked like each had been in a title fight and lost.

A bright red blush appeared in front of me before Drake reached for some nearby plant's enormous leaves to cover himself.

All smiles, I asked, "Now, tell me again how you pictured tonight?"

Drake balanced the two leaves covering himself, holding each firmly in place on his front and back. "Come with me and I'll show you."

CHAPTER 22

Camille – Bungalow Outside of Cancún, Mexico

We made it as far as the entryway inside the bungalow. I'd wanted Drake since he knelt in front of me giving me his betrothal pledge on the way to Ireland. Want wasn't a strong enough word – craved. He stood in front of me, my back to the door as his hands let the two large plant leaves covering him drop to the floor. It was the first time I'd seen him naked; my breath hitched and my heart felt like it would beat out of my chest. Drake looked like a sculpture, a true work of art.

My hands went to his chest, tracing the broad lines defining his muscles. When I saw him waiting for me on the beach with the priest, I didn't think it was possible for him to look more handsome – I was wrong. A body like his should never be covered up with clothes.

It was here, finally, the day he would be mine in every sense of the word. Drake's strong hands reached up and untied my bikini top. It fell to the floor with the leaves. The sheer wrap around my waist and my bikini bottoms joined them. Drake's eyes took me in as his hands glided all over my exposed flesh, creating goose bumps in their wake. He brought his mouth to mine, hard – his tongue greedily penetrating. Drake stepped into me, his erection hard as his gentle glides across my skin morphed into harrowed kneading. A husky moan escaped him as tingles ripped through my body.

I didn't want to take things slowly; the pent-up desire wanted free, and I had no strength nor ability to try to cage it. The ache that had been with me screamed to the surface. I put my arms over his shoulders as I wrapped my legs around his waist. There would be no more enforcers, or transformations, or dogs to interrupt us.

He held me in place and walked into the bedroom. His teeth grazed my earlobe as his voice whispered, "I love you."

"I love you, too."

Drake eased me onto the bed. I lay on my back as Drake's lips kissed, caressed and tasted every inch of my body. When I was sure I couldn't take one more second without him inside me, I grabbed the back of his head and demanded, "Now."

I awoke to bliss. Bright sun rays fought their way in through the gaps in the window's shutters. The sound of the surf had been our background music all night. In the light of day, the crashing waves sounded angry against the backdrop of the chirping birds.

Drake's naked body lay against mine. I'd never known a truer friend, a fiercer protector, or a deeper love than the man I could now call my husband. If Drake were right, and more enforcers were on the way, this is how I wanted to spend my last few days on earth: not running . . . not hiding . . . not working on a strategy to bring down Zandra. I wanted only to lie in his arms, to feel his breath against my neck, and to watch the images of us that play in his mind while he dreams.

His hand brushed a stray strand of hair behind my ear as his lips drifted to my neck. His voice was gravelly next to my ear, "Good morning, wife."

I jerked slightly, unaware that he, too, was awake. My hunger for his touch was acute, and his word spoken against my ear – "wife" sent tingles to my toes. My body was exhausted in a delightful way. Our families waited for us at the main house, but I only wanted to stay where we were: tune out all the chaos that our lives had become and simply stay wrapped up together as one.

"I know what you're thinking." Drake's voice was smoother than it had been moments ago.

"Really? And what's that?"

"That the enforcers should storm through the door now and kill us where we lie."

My body went rigid as I spat, "What?! No. Why would I be thinking that?"

In a hushed tone, "For as long as we live, we'll never have a better day than the last twenty-four hours. If I died now, I'd die a happy man." He was close to right, but I didn't want either of us to have a death wish.

I wrenched myself free and turned over to face him. "Yesterday was just the first of many years of the same. Get used to it."

Drake's eyes bore into mine as his smile warmed me from the inside out. "I don't know. I've had some pretty vivid fantasies these last couple months, but none prepared me for last night."

I buried my face in his chest, drinking in his scent and memorizing this moment. He was right in a small way; if anything did happen to us, I could retire to the pasture without regrets. I forced myself to believe that in spite of any struggles we had ahead of us, there would be days just as perfect in our future. "Road blocks are no more than stepping stones as long as you're with me."

His soft lips gently kissed mine, then he pulled back with a smile, "I believe you." Drake slid out of the bed and offered his hand to me, "C'mon, I'm sure Gage and Bianca have had to put up a security detail to keep our families away. Let's go get some breakfast," he winked with a mischievous grin, "you'll need your strength for later."

When we entered the main house, everyone else sat around a large table, happily chatting away. Bart stood up from his chair and motioned for me to take his seat. Everyone was still talking about Drake's transformation, the wedding, and the enforcers who were locked up in the basement.

Silver trays were warming on a buffet table along the far wall. We filled our plates and joined in the chatter.

A panel of television screens covered a wall in the same room, a stark contrast to the buffet holding the food on the opposite wall. The entire estate was being monitored: the beach where Drake and I had exchanged our vows, the bungalows, the pool, hallways in the main house, the main gate, and areas of the property that I couldn't identify.

I thought of the events last night and wondered how much it had cost Bianca to keep the footage of Drake transforming into a Centaur from being posted on You-Tube. The man monitoring the televisions kept stealing glances at Drake, and I was sure he had to have seen the whole thing. It occurred to me that I hadn't seen any of the security detail last night when all the action was going on and made a mental note to ask Bianca where her thugs with guns had been.

I watched the screens as a taxi-cab pulled up to the main gate. After zooming the camera in on the passengers and speaking in Spanish to the driver, the man monitoring the security system buzzed it through the large metal gate into the estate.

The four passengers piled out of the taxi in front of the estate's main house: Brent, Daniel, Jessica, and Katherine. Bianca must have noticed my surprise at seeing them, because her voice resonated in my head, "*They called ahead after they landed, so we were expecting them.*"

Gage was absent from the room; Bianca must have noticed I was looking for him. Her voice resonated in my head, "*He volunteered to keep a watch on the Council's enforcers locked up in the basement.*"

Something bothered me. I turned to Bianca and asked, "Hey, any idea why the enforcers were only carrying swords and daggers instead of Uzis and sniper rifles?"

"We don't know and they're not talking. We're not counting on being as lucky the next time. Your brothers went on a late-night weapons run. All the humans on the security detail are using armor piercing rounds now, too. If more come, we'll be ready."

I didn't like the idea of taking anyone's life, but I refused to be unprepared. I nodded a silent thank you and went outside to meet Daniel, Brent, Jessica and Katherine.

My goodbye to Daniel in Omaha had been awful. At the time I wasn't sure if I'd ever see him again, and I couldn't have guessed I'd see him just two short days later. Before I could grab hold of him and crush him in the too-warm air, Daniel positioned himself in front of Will, held out his hand and beamed, "It's nice to see you again, Mr. Strayer."

Will's lips were pursed together firmly. I'd always heard that absence makes the heart grow fonder. Will remembered exactly who Daniel was, and he hadn't miraculously grown a soft spot for him.

Daniel had nothing but contempt for Will, and although his words had been kind, his tone made no effort to hide his disdain. Daniel took it upon himself to introduce everybody. "Obviously, you know our favorite America's Most Wanted: Brent." Will took Brent into a hug as Brent welcomed our father's embrace.

Daniel stretched his arm around Jessica and pulled her to him. Jessica's body went rigid and her face blushed in response to his touch. "This is Jessica

Baker, fabulous bartender, blackjack master, and Centauride extraordinaire." Will and Gretchen smiled a warm greeting as Jessica nodded her, "hello."

Daniel held his arm out with a flourish and announced, "This is her human friend, Train Wreck."

Brent shouted a few steps away from Will, "Stop calling her that!" Brent re-introduced Katherine to his parents, "Mom, Dad, this is Katherine Newton. She helped us get out of South Dakota."

Gretchen's gaze was fixed on her son. She turned her head as if contemplating something she saw, but said nothing.

Daniel interrupted Brent's introduction with a smirk, "Tomato, tomato," Daniel said the first tomato with a long a sound and the second tomato with a short a sound.

"Enough, Daniel." Brent grimaced.

Daniel was definitely getting under Brent's skin. He called to Jessica and Katherine, "C'mon, I bet the water's great." Daniel saw Beau emerge from the house, and it looked like I'd been replaced. His face lit up like a toddler with his first sucker. "Beau!! Crap, they didn't say you were here!"

Beau walked straight over to Daniel and hugged him. "I thought I was going to be the only one in the surf today." It shouldn't have bothered me, but Daniel didn't even seem to notice I was standing there.

Lacey peeked out from behind Beau, "Beau, there'll be time for that later. I think your family wanted to catch up first."

"Right. Daniel, we'll be down in a few." Beau hugged him a second time, "I'm glad you're here, man."

"You, too, Bra."

Instead of Daniel, Katherine, and Jessica heading down to the surf right away, we all walked over to an outdoor patio set and told the four what had happened the previous night.

Brent's reaction surprised me. He didn't seem the least bit worried that we'd been found by enforcers. He looked hurt when he searched our family's eyes and muttered, "You were all here for Cami's wedding and no one invited me?"

Daniel leaned in and whispered, "Yeah. Nice ring. I better see some pictures later."

Guilt washed over me. I had been elated that Will, Gretchen, Bruce, Hannah, Beau, Lacey, Ben and Bart surprised us; it never occurred to me that Brent would feel left out. Gretchen reached out and took Brent's hand, "We didn't know where you were when Bianca called us."

"You all took off. I didn't know where any of you were." Brent had been left out. My feet walked toward him, but I couldn't bring my eyes to meet his. I recognized the loneliness in his expression – he believed he had lost his entire family before he came looking for me in South Dakota.

His voice was strained, "When I couldn't find any of you, I went looking for Cami."

I felt horrible. He knew Drake and I were getting married but didn't want to be a fifth wheel. By not coming along, he'd nearly missed seeing our family – maybe for the last time. In a strange way I was silently thankful the enforcers had shown up, so we had a reason to bring him here.

No one said anything right away. The realization of our thoughtlessness weighed heavily on me. As I looked around at the others, I could only guess that they felt the same.

Jessica and Katherine said very little, Brent looked solemn – as if he would rather have been walking on hot coals than sitting on the little patio. I couldn't help but notice – it looked like the four were hiding something. None would make eye contact with me, and all seemed to be in their own little worlds. What happened in Las Vegas?

Daniel put his arm around Jessica and motioned to Katherine, "Let's go change. I bet you two have never caught waves like these." He looked between Beau and Brent, "See you two soon." The three of them disappeared into the house.

Gretchen was pleased to have her family surrounding her; she didn't need to say it: the joy emanated from her. It was surreal for all of us to be together when just days ago I had worried I might never see any of them again. Brent remained quiet. He'd watched the three walk up the steps, but made no move to go with them.

Will and Gretchen shared a wicker love seat, his arm lovingly draped around her shoulder. Bruce sat with Hannah on an overstuffed chaise lounge. Lacey sat in a chair as Beau sat on the ground with his back propped up against her legs. I sat on Drake's lap in the matching chair next to Beau and Lacey. Bart and Ben completed the circle on two rusty metal chairs they had dragged over from the back of the house. Brent looked awkward, as if uncomfortable in his own skin, as he took a seat in the sand.

It was a great afternoon catching up with everyone. Lacey and Beau had spent the last few weeks at her father's cabin at Lake Tahoe. Will and Gretchen had stayed at a friend's chateau in France. Bruce and Hannah never left Charleston but had rented a house on the Isle of Palms where all the tourists flocked to in the summertime. Ben and Bart had been skiing in Colorado. Brent had been left to fend for himself.

After we were all caught up, I excused myself to go see if more food had appeared in the dining room. Breakfast had been cut short when the others arrived, and I was starving. Brent followed me inside while Drake stayed to talk to Beau.

Daniel's was the first voice I heard as we got inside, "Hey, Train Wreck, you want a soda?"

Brent shouted from behind me, "I told you, stop calling her that!"

Whatever the inside joke was between Daniel and Brent – Brent did *not* think it was funny. It almost seemed like Daniel was purposely calling Katherine "Train Wreck" just to get under Brent's skin.

I tried never to probe anyone's thoughts who might want them to remain private, but my curiosity started to get the better of me. Daniel hadn't grown up around Centaurides, so he wasn't used to nor did he try to hide his thoughts from anyone. After sifting through a few x-rated thoughts he openly had for Jessica, I abandoned my search and decided to satisfy my curiosity the old-fashioned way.

I asked, "Okay, what gives?"

Daniel pretended to be surprised with my question, "Huh?"

"Why do you keep calling Katherine 'Train Wreck'?"

Daniel's lips set in a sly grin as his eyes darted to Brent. Brent glared at Daniel, silently warning him to keep his explanation to himself. Instead of answering my question, Daniel went in a different direction, "You know, I've spent a lot of time with Beau and Brent. Those are two Centaurs who couldn't be more different. Did you ever notice?"

I had noticed. Beau was thoughtful and kind; he'd go out of his way to do anything for anyone. I'd seen his thoughts lots of times; Beau rarely tried to hide his. I wasn't surprised because he never had anything to be ashamed of if others saw what he was thinking.

Brent was very different from Beau; he seemed more like a card player – keeping his hand close. Brent was kind and accepting of a sister who had essentially dropped out of the sky, but he rarely let his guard down. Brent was opinionated and very *in favor of* Centaur traditions. If I had to guess, I'd say it was that he liked the security it gave him, all the rules made sense to him, and anyone who didn't follow the rules was wrong. He looked at all situations as if they were black and white. Brent had suspected we were part of the Lost Herd, but when the truth came out in the open, Brent had a tough time dealing with it.

It felt odd talking about Brent with Daniel while Brent was in the same room. "They look a lot alike."

"Yeah, and I look like an Olympic swimmer, but it doesn't mean I can hold my breath for two minutes."

"What?"

"I'm not asking you if they look like they share the same genetic make-up, I asked if you noticed how different their personalities are."

Before I could answer, Brent warned, "Leave it alone, Daniel."

Daniel put on his best innocent face, "Leave what alone? I'm just making an observation."

As Brent continued glaring, and Daniel feigned innocence, I decided a more direct approach was better. "What does Beau have to do with you calling Katherine 'Train Wreck'?"

Brent blew out a large breath he'd been holding and answered me before Daniel could. "He's trying to be funny." Anger welled up in him, "And he sucks at it."

Daniel held his palms up to Brent, looking as if he were being robbed. "Whoa. I suck at it? If you weren't wound so tight, you'd think I was hysterical."

"I'm only wound tight because I've been subjected to you and all your commentary for three full days. Just drop it."

Katherine had been standing at the door watching the ribbing that Daniel had been dishing out. She looked sad. Next to her sat an enormous suitcase. When she turned to go up the entryway, Brent bolted toward her from where he'd been standing within arm's reach of Daniel. "Can I get that for you?"

She shook her head but no words came out. As she turned to walk out of the room, Brent reached over and put a hand on her shoulder. "Let me help you." He looked nervous but didn't remove his hand. He added, "If Mom sees you carrying a big suitcase up three flights of stairs while I'm hanging out with these two, I'll never hear the end of it."

Katherine looked at his hand on her shoulder, but she didn't tell him to let go. When her eyes met his, the tension between them was thick in the air. Her voice was monotone – absent any emotion, "I've got it."

Katherine was two strides away from Brent when he swooped up behind her, took the suitcase out of her hand and went up the stairs in a blur. She stood at the bottom of the stairs, put her hand on the banister for support, took a deep breath, and stealthily wiped her eye. Something was wrong, but asking Brent or Daniel wasn't the right way to go about it.

"Hey, Katherine. You're already in shorts, any chance you'd go for a walk on the beach with me?"

Relief spilled over her features as a half-smile emerged. "Now?"

I nodded and she eagerly opened the front door. I wouldn't press her, but something had happened in Las Vegas. I tried not to jump to conclusions, but whatever it was, if she needed to get it off her chest – I'd listen. She looked like she was ready to implode.

CHAPTER 23

Camille – Outside of Cancún, Mexico

The sand was soft and wet between our toes. Every few feet I'd see a crab or water bugs feverishly trying to get back into the ocean after the surf marooned them on the shore. Katherine was deep in thought. Trying to see into her thoughts was like looking at an empty whiteboard – blank. I wasn't surprised. If just being near her were enough that other Centaurs couldn't see us, I shouldn't have expected her thoughts to miraculously broadcast to everyone.

Katherine's red hair blew in the breeze, obscuring most of her face. I kept expecting her to smooth it away or to hold it to the side, but she didn't. She walked with one foot in front of the other, unable or unwilling to talk. We passed a massive pile of driftwood stuck on some concrete blocks. Maybe someone had piled the blocks there for a dock that was never built. The trees swayed as the wind picked up; the monkeys and noisy birds who were screeching quieted as we passed them. It felt like a storm was almost on us, but there wasn't a cloud in the sky.

The pile of concrete blocks was so far behind us we couldn't see the defined pile anymore when I asked, "Mind if we sit?"

Her voice carried over the gusts of wind without her having to shout. "I thought you'd never ask."

The wind had steadily picked up, so I suggested, "Can we get off the beach so we won't be pelted with the sand?"

Katherine shrugged her shoulders but walked to the shelter of some trees just behind the beach. I was struggling for a way to kick start my interrogation. "You know I never got a chance to say thank you."

Katherine looked at me, still absent any real emotion and said, "Ya just did."

She'd shut me down quickly as I heard my own voice trail off, "I guess I did." She looked like she was a million miles away, and I wished I could see what was on her mind. "Are you worried about your family?"

She shook her head, but the far off gaze she had fixed on the ocean remained there. I didn't want to pull what was bothering her out forcibly: I couldn't risk offending her. We needed Katherine. Instead I prodded softly, "I don't know how to help you if I don't know what's wrong."

Her words were gentle, almost lost to me in a gust of wind that blew hard through the trees. "Ya can't help me. No one can."

"I'd like to try. Sometimes just talking about a problem helps you solve it."

"Not this time." Her lips crushed together in a forced smile. The turmoil was just under the surface, but I was clueless how to help.

"Is it Daniel? I know he can be difficult. If he's bothering you, I can get him to back off."

Her forced smile morphed into a genuine one at the mention of Daniel. "Naw, I like him. He's one of the lucky ones, ya know?"

She liked Daniel? That was a surprise. Most people just tolerated him. "Lucky? How do you mean?"

"Humans get ta breeze through life. They're the only species who truly have free will." The only species? What else was out there? Before I could ask her, she continued, "Centaurs live within the confines of some very rigid rules. In addition to the rules, you pretend ta be human and pretend you're making your own choices."

"We make our own choices. Some of them just . . . conform better than others," I countered defensively.

Her smile grew as if she didn't believe me. Going with the flow must be a typical Centaur trait. She confessed, "Lapiths look like humans and think like humans, but we have our own issues to deal with. Humans have the world in the palm of their hand and no idea what ta do with it."

"Maybe in some respects, but they don't get to do all the cool stuff that we do."

Katherine chuckled to herself, "That's the thing: Daniel would trade anything to be a pure-blooded Centaur right now, but if he got his wish, he'd be stifled by all the rules he'd have ta follow."

"So Daniel *is* what's bothering you?"

"No. He's the one who's made the road trip bearable. Do ya know, when we got to Las Vegas, he went to the MGM and got our room compted?"

"Compted? Like from gambling?"

"Uh, no. That wouldn't be all that remarkable. He went into the lobby of the hotel and started spouting off this outrageous lie." Katherine proceeded to tell me about how they got checked in, and by the end of the story, my stomach hurt from the laughter.

I could see Daniel pulling that kind of stunt. It was just like him. "Yeah, that's Daniel. I'm surprised Brent didn't try to reel him in."

"None of us could believe it. The three of us didn't say a word. The next thing we know we're in a Penthouse suite and the manager wants his picture with Jessica. Only a human would pull something like that."

"Oh no, that's more of a Daniel thing. An idea like that wouldn't even occur to most humans. They'd just have laid a credit card on the desk and hit the casino after they dropped off their bags."

That was one of the reasons I'd always been drawn to Daniel. He could make even the mundane a true adventure. I still didn't have the answer as to why she looked so unhappy. "So, if it's not Daniel, what is bothering you? Did Brent say something rude?"

"It's not what he said or anything he did."

My curiosity hadn't diminished. "Why does Daniel keep calling you Train Wreck?"

Her gaze fell to a small patch of grass on the ground, but she nodded. "So, Daniel and Jessica are really into each other. Ya noticed, eh?"

Not sure where her question was going, I decided just to follow her lead. "Yeah, it would be hard not to."

"Jessica likes him, a lot, but she's not ready to write off her family completely until all this stuff plays out. He's like a Snickers bar for her. She can't get enough of him. The two of them decided they were going to the casino for some middle-of-the-night black jack. Brent and I were in the hotel room watching a movie, one thing led to another, and when they came back. . . ."

I waited for her to finish, but she just let it hang in the air. I couldn't have imagined how one thing had led to another knowing Brent's personality. When after too long of a pause she didn't finish, I asked, "What led to what?"

"Daniel and Jessica walked in on Brent and me kissing. He completely melted down. One second he was apologizin', the next he was shouting about betraying his Centauride, then he started mumblin' about embarrassing his family."

"So the nickname?"

"Once Brent started to calm down, Daniel started ribbing Brent about his perfectly laid out life. How he came from money, he had all these great brothers and led a charmed life. Daniel told him he should have stayed down in the mine shaft in South Dakota because his life has officially been derailed."

"Train Wreck, I get it. But that's just Daniel. He wouldn't keep saying it if it wasn't ticking Brent off." Katherine reached down and picked up a twig, poking a little patch of grass. I was worried she might go back into silent mode, so I asked, "So, do you like Brent?"

"No. I don't' know. Maybe. Do you know what my family would do to me if I brought home a Centaur? I'd be disowned."

"Really?" The thought hadn't occurred to me before. All I'd heard since I learned about Centaurs was how the Centaur was viewed by "settling" for a human. Without any real knowledge of Lapiths, I hadn't considered a Centaur would be undesirable.

"Uh, yeah. I only invited Jessica and Gayle over ta our house once. I swore I'd never do that again."

I picked up a stick, and we both started poking at the ground. "So, if you don't like him, how did one thing lead to another in the hotel?"

Katherine looked at me shyly, her hair still blowing in the breeze, but she made an effort to keep it out of her face. "Well, he's not hard on the eyes. When we were walkin' in the mine shaft, he took me by surprise. . . a little."

"Yeah, I was there." I didn't want to tell her that I'd been just as surprised as she was by his kindness. Brent wasn't a jerk. If anything, he was the brother who had gone out of his way to make me feel like part of the family when I first arrived in South Carolina. But it wasn't long before he was the first to openly disapprove of how Mom had raised me.

The stick she'd been poking the ground with had uncovered an interesting piece of wood. We both kept poking at it, but only partially paid attention to the object in the sand, "I was raised ta hate Centaurs. Gayle and Jessica were the only two I ever had time for. Both of them had brothers around when we were growin' up. If they knew what I was, and I was lying on the side of the road bleeding ta death, none of them would so much as hold a towel against an open wound to save me."

I didn't want to try to guess what had come over Brent in the tunnel. I remembered he had been furious when he found out Katherine was a Lapith. The two of them had shouted at each other, and I was worried we might never get out of that tunnel. "I think your story about Gayle really touched him."

"Yeah, what he doesn't understand is that he never should have touched me – not like he did."

Puzzled, I didn't understand what she was trying to tell me. She must have seen my confusion, "Okay, so Lapiths are all supposed to be long gone, right?"

"That's what you guys told me; I learn more every day. Up until a few months ago, I didn't know Centaurs were anything more than bedtime stories and one of the constellations."

"Did you know that one of the rules Centaurs have about no touching came from a Lapith?"

My eye muscles flexed, "How do you mean?"

She bit her lip. She wanted to answer my question, but she hesitated, no doubt struggling with how much she could share. Her voice shook but her gaze was steady, "Okay, so a male Centaur won't physically touch a Centauride once he's betrothed, eh?"

I nearly laughed, "Yeah, that's the custom as I know it." My mind immediately returned to the day Drake and I met at Bruce and Hannah's wedding. He'd caught me in mid-air and kept me from doing a face-plant on the driveway. Afterwards, I'd held out my hand as a thank-you, but he refused to touch me.

"That tradition didn't start because a Centauride got offended that her betrothed made contact with another Centauride. It wasn't a jealousy thing at all."

"Well, what was it?"

"You've heard of Rupert, eh?"

"The father of the Lost Herd."

"He was supposed to be some wild Centaur who was kicked out of the pasture of Thessaly, right?" I'd heard that from Brent, Will, and Drake and had no reason to doubt what they'd told me.

"Right. He had a bunch of wives. Back then, I think they all did. Shortly after he was banished from the pasture, he met Lila, a Lapith. He was hurt or something, I don't remember that part of the story, but Rupert embraced her as a thank-you for something she'd done."

"So, what happened to Lila?"

"He became obsessed with her. He ignored all of his Centauride wives and refused ta stay away from the pasture where Lila lived."

"But, he'd been banished. Weren't Centaurs hunting him by then?"

"Lila was able to hide him because she was a Lapith, the same way I'm able to hide you and your family now. It was unheard of back then, Centaurs and Lapiths never got along, so no Centaurs ever looked for him on her property."

Now I was really confused. "Did he have children with her?"

"Not right away. Centaurs all still had hooves back then, so the two just lived a quiet existence together. But Lila wanted children, and after a few years of Zeus screaming for their deaths, Rupert knew his children had been slaughtered. She prayed to Athena for protection."

"Athena? Zeus's daughter?"

"Yes."

"Did she help them?"

Katherine nodded her head. "By the time Athena offered ta help, Zeus had already changed the other seven herds ta look human. It was easy for the herds to hunt down Rupert's descendants – they were the only ones with hooves. Rupert was the last true surviving Centaur from his own blood line."

No wonder everyone was convinced the Lost Herd had been completely extinct. Katherine continued, “Athena took pity on Rupert and Lila – she vowed to protect ‘em both.”

“His whole family had been killed? That’s why everyone believed the Lost Herd was extinct.”

It wasn’t a question, but she nodded anyway.

“So the Lost Herd is descended from Rupert and Lila? They were able to go undetected for centuries because of her Lapith blood?”

Katherine nodded again.

“So, how are the enforcers finding us now?”

“I’m not sure, but I think the Lapith blood has become diluted over the generations. Some families from the Lost Herd mated with only other Lost Herd families. Those probably still have a good bit of Lapith blood in them. Most of Rupert’s descendants all blended in with the other Centaurs, following the rules set down by Zeus.”

“How do you know?”

“Your father is Will. He’s of the Lost Herd, I can sense it. His wife, Gretchen, she’s not.”

“But how can you tell who’s from the Lost Herd?”

“I’m descended from Lily and Rupert. I can just tell.”

“But you’re not a Centaur?”

“No. Any Centaur blood in my family tree has been gone for generations.”

“Does anyone else know this?”

She shook her head, “I couldn’t say. My great-grandmother told the story when I was very young. But now that I’ve met ya, all the pieces make more sense.”

“Does Athena still protect Rupert’s descendants?”

She shrugged her shoulders. “I don’t know. Until all the action with Roscoe last week, I thought the Lost Herd was something my great-grandmother had made up. She told me their blood would call ta me, but I never felt it ‘til I met you and Brent.”

It had never made sense to me why everyone was shocked that the Lost Herd was still around until now. All but Rupert had been hunted down and killed. Athena was a protector. I remember learning about her from Zandra. Athena was Zeus's first child, born without a mother – she sprang from Zeus's head. I spoke more to myself than to Katherine. "Lila couldn't have chosen a better protector."

It hit me that my initial questions had gone by the wayside when Katherine told me of my bloodline. "But, what does all this have to do with you and Brent?"

"Don't ya see? Brent isn't attracted to me. When he tried ta comfort me in the tunnel – his concern for me sparked the connection: the same connection that happened between Lila and Rupert. I've screwed everything up for him. He was already chosen – he has a Centauride he cares about who's willing to wait for him ta return."

"So, he's having second thoughts. Did you ever think he's having those thoughts because he likes you?"

"He likes me 'cause of the spark between us in the tunnel – nothing more."

"I don't know, Katherine. Have you told him any of this?"

"No. You saw his reaction when he found out I was a Lapith. What do ya expect he'll think when he finds out the only reason he's feelin' what he is toward me is because he was kind enough ta comfort me."

"But, you do like him."

"It's not a question of liking or not liking him. It's the turmoil I see in his eyes every time he looks at me. It's the way he pulls away from me just as he gets within inches of me. I don't want to be the woman he chooses 'cause he's obsessed."

"You have to come clean. You have to tell him."

"I wish there were a way to have Cassie here. If she were here everything would be fine. He'd forget about me and could ignore what happened in the tunnel."

"What if she were here and nothing changed?"

She ignored my question. "When he called her, she said she still chose him. If she were here, none of this would be happening. Daniel's right, Brent has the future he's always wanted within his grasp. I can't take it much longer. If he keeps this up, I'm gonna give in, and his future – the future he wants – is over.

"And if he still wants you?"

Heartache shown on her face: she'd already thought through the possibilities. "Brent's a Centaur. He wants a Centauride. He felt sorry for me when I told him about Gayle. If he'd never touched me, none of this would be happening right now. Can you convince Bianca to get Cassie here? Like she did us?"

My mind went back to the enforcers who stormed the beach last night. How safe would it be to have Cassie here, too? Would Brent want us to put her in danger? I wanted Brent to be happy, but no matter what Katherine said, the feelings weren't one-sided. It wasn't all Brent, and there was more there than some simple spark ignited in the tunnel.

I started racing through the possible scenarios. What would happen to Katherine if Cassie were here and Brent chose Cassie? Or to Cassie if Brent still wanted Katherine? Or worse, what if she were here and he couldn't choose?

Katherine stared at me woefully. I sighed, "Bianca's pretty amazing. I'll ask her." Katherine's expression turned grateful. I'd been right, even if Bianca couldn't get Cassie to join us, telling me what had been bothering her had reduced the burden she was carrying.

I still had trouble wrapping my mind around everything she'd told me, but one question burned inside me. "So, am I a Lapith?"

She smiled genuinely, "No more than a drop."

"A drop?"

"My great-grandmother told me that Rupert and Lila had ten children. Five considered themselves Centaurs and five Lapiths. The children who thought themselves Centaurs were able to disguise their Lapith blood. As they mated with Zeus's Centaurs, they were able to stay hidden for centuries until their blood once again ran pure. The same happened with the five who considered themselves Lapiths, the blood never crossed."

"So, I am a pure-blooded Centauride?"

"Cami, this was centuries ago, at least thirty generations back. I'm sure whatever Lapith blood your ancestors may have had is long since gone."

"That's too bad. I figured that was why you were so willing to help me."

Her eyes darted to the ground. There was more to the story than she told me. I couldn't see what it was, but I could feel her trying to hide something.

"Not just you, Cami. All of the Lost Herd."

"You protect the Lost Herd?"

"Lila promised Athena. She vowed she would defend their children. It carried on with her descendants. My great-grandmother told me the stories so I knew it was my duty to Athena to protect the Lost Herd. I thought she was crazy at the time. There are Lapiths around who aren't descended from Lila and Rupert – they are enemies to all Centaurs."

My mind sped up, the possibilities threatening to envelop me. "So, how do I know who I can trust?"

"There aren't many Lapith families left. If you ever run across a human who hates you for no reason, and you can't read their thoughts – that's a Lapith. If I weren't bound to protect ya, I'd be the same way."

Embarrassed by her answer, my first inclination was to lash out. What drove their hatred of Centaurs? "You don't like Centaurs very much."

"I loathe Centaurs. The stupid rules they follow blindly. The Blood Debts they inflict on one another. They pretend ta be humans, yet think they're superior to 'em."

I reached out and squeezed her hand, "Not all of them." I wanted to tell her how welcoming my family had been when I had no other family in the world. I wanted to tell her how Gage risked his own life pretending to want to be betrothed to me just to make sure I was okay. No matter how much I wanted to tell her she was wrong – I couldn't bring myself to do it. She was right. When I thought Drake and Bianca were dead, I was prepared to marry Gage to get away from Zandra. The idea of her friend Gayle losing her life over something as simple as a high school crush was barbaric. No, there would be no argument from me.

Instead of arguing with her, I fished for more information. Of everyone I had met in the last several months, Katherine was the least likely to sugar coat or withhold information from me. "So, how are you able to protect us? How does it work?"

"Think of me as Kryptonite. Or a black hole, heck, maybe even a magnet."

"I'm still lost."

"Centaurides can't use their powers against me. It's a proximity thing because they can't use them on other Centaurs or Centaurides that I am physically close to. Kind of like a black hole."

I didn't want to burst her bubble, but I could still read other Centaur and Centauride thoughts who were close to her, but I wanted to hear what she had to say, so I didn't interrupt. "That night the Centaurs and Zandra were looking for you in the woods in South Dakota, she could probably tell you were in the area, but she couldn't pinpoint where you were. We were directly under Gage and Bianca, and Bianca is convinced Zandra didn't even see her."

That much I already knew. "But a magnet? I don't understand your meaning."

"Brent touched me. When he hugged me in the tunnel, I felt the change in him myself. The longer he denies his feelings for me, the more obsessed he's going to become."

"The same thing would have happened if any Centaur touched you?"

She shook her head, "It was the way he touched me. Casual contact, no. But when he tried to comfort me after telling you all about Gayle, his heart opened up to me – the same as Rupert's did with Lila. I don't know how ta break the connection he established with me. It's part of the reason that Lapiths walled ourselves off from Centaurs. It's how that crazy rule of no touching came ta be."

Gently I asked, "Do you want it broken?"

She answered a little too quickly, "Of course, I wanna break it." She continued digging at the piece of wood she had unearthed, speaking almost to herself, "Why would I wan' a Centaur?"

"When we were driving to Omaha, you just seemed, I don't know. . . interested."

Blush spread bright on her cheeks, "He was nice ta me, okay? Is it a crime to wanna be around someone who's nice to you?"

"No. Not a crime. It's completely understandable, unless you're denying your feelings."

Katherine stood up – our conversation was over. "Let's get back ta the others."

I was grateful for all I had learned. There never seemed to be a shortage of questions on my part, no matter who I was talking to, but the idea that she was a Lapith descendant of Rupert had been completely unexpected. Would other Lapiths in her family come to the aid of the Lost Herd?

CHAPTER 24

Camille – Beach Outside of Cancún, Mexico

The few days we spent together were amazing. I had quiet time with Drake; since we were newlyweds and remained in the little sea-side cottage, no one bothered us during our alone time. My whole family was treating it like a vacation. Mornings were spent playing volleyball on the beach and goofing around in the surf. The food was amazing. Each of my brothers took turns guarding the Council's enforcers in the basement. Having Katherine around worked out perfectly: everyone was able to let their guard down. Although the captured enforcers refused to talk to us and were extremely proficient at blocking their thoughts, no more came looking for them.

It was Wednesday morning before we knew it. Gage, Bianca, Drake and I made preparations to leave for the airport Thursday morning. We'd planned to use a chartered plane that Will had arranged.

I was doing a quick clean up of all the rooms in the little cottage when Will knocked on the front door and let himself in. Drake assumed Will wanted privacy, so he chose that minute to go check on the prisoners.

Will took a seat on the tattered couch and motioned for me to take a seat in the chair adjacent to it. "We haven't talked about your trip since your wedding."

"The less you know, the better, for right now."

"I'd like to go with you."

"You're not going to offer yourself up as some sort of sacrifice."

"It's more than just me who wants to accompany you."

"No. You guys lay low. If I need your help, I'll call."

"Do you remember what I told you when you said Gage and Bianca were going with you?"

I didn't like his argument then, and I wasn't ready to entertain it now. "They don't have any ties to the Lost Herd. They haven't broken any tenets. They are the safest companions to take along. No matter what happens to Drake and me, they'll know the truth, and we're guaranteed that they'll be free to go about their lives."

"Don't be naive, Camille. If they stand with you, they stand against Zeus."

"They aren't going to be doing any of the fighting."

"You know both of them better than that. Neither will stand by if anything happens to you or Drake. What about Cameron?"

"What about him?"

"You know he's going to be there."

"No! Why would he be there?"

"He's been living with Zandra. She's spent time with both of you now. Everyone expects her to name one of you as the next Chairman. No one is expecting you to be there. So, who do you think will take her position?"

"But I thought it was always the Centauride?"

"Traditionally it is the Centauride, but the Chairman picks the successor."

Maybe I was naive. There was so much I didn't understand and no time left to learn it. "How do you see this playing out?"

"From what I've seen, Cameron isn't as strong-willed as you are. I haven't been allowed to spend much time with him. I can only think the worst because Cameron has been cooped up with Zandra and Angelo since he left South Dakota."

"They wouldn't let you see him?"

"It was different with Cameron. When you were at Zandra's estate, she forbade me from seeing you. With Cameron, she allowed me as much access as I wanted, but *he* didn't want to see or to talk to me."

"But Chiron protected me. Doesn't that mean the Council will see me as the rightful successor?"

"The Centaur Council is made up of the head of each of the original lines from the pasture. The Tak line has not been represented since the Council was formed. Phineas is the head of our family. If you intend to put an end to the extermination of our family, he should be there with you, taking his place with the others."

I couldn't believe what I was hearing. "Phineas kidnapped me. He plotted to kill you. He had his daughter try to insert memories in my head, and, eeeww – he wanted me to marry his son. He's wrong on so many levels I don't even want to get into it. I don't trust him. He has no place on the Centaur Council."

"Phineas is my half-brother. He was desperate, and he made an incredible error in judgment. You don't know what it's been like living this way."

"You're right, he did make an error in judgment, and there is no excuse for him. He will not accompany me, and if he shows up, I guarantee he won't like what I have to say."

Storming out of the bungalow, I didn't know which direction to go. Anger coursed through my veins. Phineas really was my uncle? How could he have kidnapped me and tried to marry me off to his son? I felt violated.

It was bad enough thinking he had betrayed me when he was my protector at Zandra's, but he was more than that. He was my own blood.

Who was I kidding? Zandra had tried to marry me off, too – at least Gage wasn't any relation. My mind started to wander. When I first found out who my father was, Will insisted I come to his house right away. If I would have refused, would he, too, have taken me against my will? How much did I really know about my family?

I had started on the path toward the main house, but veered off toward the beach. Drake and Beau were sitting together on beach chairs staring out in the ocean. I wanted to join them, to put my conversation with Will out of my mind. I heard Drake ask, "But her brother wasn't pledged?"

I held my ground just inside a decent distance that I could hear them but not close enough that they would notice I was eavesdropping. Beau answered, "No, he was of age, but hadn't been chosen."

"Maybe the two of them will be hanging out and not bother you."

"You know the rules, the first pledge has claim. Losing her now would kill me, because there's a real chance that there could be nothing after."

Their conversation made little sense. First pledge? A betrothal pledge? That was the only kind of pledge I'd ever heard of. What was Beau talking about that a first pledge had claim? I eased closer, as if proximity could somehow bring clarity to their words.

"She loves you. You've gone past betrothal; you two are married."

"Yeah, but she married into the Lost Herd. You think her brother or betrothed would look the other way if she shows up in the pasture and it's my fault she's there?"

"She chose you, Beau. She did it knowing the truth. You're worrying about nothing, anyway. Cami and I are going to make the Centaur Council listen. We're all going to have a long life. Stop worrying."

My heart swelled. There was no doubt in Drake's voice. I'd finally understood their words. Lacey was betrothed to a Centaur before Beau.

Her fiancé and her brother were both killed in a car accident, the same car Beau had pulled her out of before it caught on fire.

When Centaurs became betrothed, the Centaur had a choice. If he really cared about the Centauride, he could give her a betrothal pledge that tied their souls together and guaranteed they'd be together for eternity. Beau was worried because the Centaur she was betrothed to before him had given her his betrothal pledge.

Drake told me, generations ago, during herd quarrels it wasn't uncommon for one Centauride to be given up to twenty betrothal pledges. In life, if pledged, the Centauride and Centaur established a telepathic connection so the betrothal pledge to multiple Centaurs allowed her to have an army of protection. If a Centauride had several Centaurs pledged to her, she could communicate with all of them. It was an added safety measure for the Centauride.

I'd asked how that worked if the souls were tied because a Centaur could only ever pledge once. He told me in the pasture the only pledge that counted was the first one. Beau was right to be worried. I'd embraced that part of being with Drake; if something happened in this life, at least we'd be together after death. Beau didn't have that assurance.

We had to make the Centaur Council see that exterminating the Lost Herd was wrong. We had to do it for a lot of reasons, but feeling Beau's pain – we had to do it for him. His only time with Lacey could be this life; eternity in the pasture would belong to the Centaur who died in the car crash.

The waves and seagulls beckoning me, I turned away from Beau and Drake, not wanting to intrude. I walked down the beach and lost myself in my own thoughts, jumbled around my family and what we were really up against. It wasn't until the surf was at my ankles that a peace washed over me. Motionless, I allowed the waves and the serenity of the turquoise water to calm me.

"I thought you'd be spending your last day with Daniel."

Wheeling around to the voice who had invaded my privacy, auburn hair flowed back from her face as Jessica sat ten feet away on a towel. Had she been there before? What happened to her platinum blonde color I'd seen just yesterday? As I continued to take her in, she was an absolute beauty. The colored hair and dark make-up had hidden the real Jessica.

"I was headed toward the house; I just took a detour. What are you doing here?"

"Same thing you are. Hiding from the chaos." She patted the towel she sat on as an invitation.

I didn't want to talk. I didn't want company. Where could I go to be by myself that would be far enough away?

"What's the deal with you and Daniel?"

Here we go again. My whole life everyone had assumed Daniel and I were more than friends. I thought I'd put all that to rest. I was married to Drake. If that didn't send a strong enough signal, nothing would.

"He's my best friend."

"You've got a funny way of showing it."

"Daniel knows how I feel about him."

"Does he?"

"Look, I'm leaving soon. If you've got something to say, say it."

"Just an observation."

"What?"

"So you take off to find your family and you stop calling him. He goes looking for you and you've vanished. You keep reemerging, and each time you don't have any time for him. You run off and get married without so much as an invitation, and then your new BFF calls and says you need us all to come running. When he does, you're so wrapped up in your own drama, you hardly even notice he's here."

"That's not true. Besides, he's been so occupied with you he hasn't missed me a bit."

Jessica shook her head. "Go on and keep thinking that."

Begrudgingly, I took a seat next to her on the towel. "What, so he's mad at me now?"

"Not mad. He feels left out. He misses you."

"I'll talk to him before I go."

"Yeah, you do that." Jessica buried her toes in the sand, wrapped her arms around her knees, and stared out into the water.

I didn't want to be rude to her. On some level she was right. Daniel had been so much a part of my life for so long that not having him with me through everything left a big gaping hole. Drake and I had had one thing after another thrown at us. These few days when I could finally catch up with him, my thoughts had been all consumed by the Centaur Council and what it would mean for my family.

"You're right. I've been a crappy friend. I didn't want to intrude on his time with you."

"What's that supposed to mean?"

Surprise rocked me. Weren't they a couple? The two of them were everywhere together. On the beach they had been the pair who beat everyone else at volleyball. Daniel had this great idea to sneak into town before anyone woke up a few days ago and showed up at lunch time on a wave rider, towing three more behind him. It was only a few hours later when the two of them were airborne together in the surf. Every meal we'd eaten with the others, the two had been sitting together. Could I have jumped to the wrong conclusion? Even Katherine thought the two had a thing going on.

Her stare told me I needed to answer, "I mean, you two seem to be good for each other."

She answered dismissively, "Daniel's a great diversion."

The hair on the back of my neck stood up, "A diversion?"

"Well, yeah. Don't get me wrong, we've had fun together, but there'll never be anything serious between us."

"Why not?"

She rolled her eyes at me as if I were the densest person on the planet.

CHAPTER 25

Daniel – Beach Outside of Cancún, Mexico

A diversion? Screw her.

Looking at the pail of ice in my hands, I silently placed it on the ground and walked back through the trees. I'd seen my two favorite ladies sitting on the beach and had been ready to give them both a surprise, but the surprise was on me.

Dad was right all along. He told me not to get mixed up with Cami – she'd just break my heart. One time wasn't enough, either. I'd let her break it over and over and kept coming back for more. When I saw her in the bar in South Dakota without Drake, I thought maybe, just maybe things would finally be put right. I'd finally get the girl.

I'm such a chump. A few hours later and sure enough, there was Drake, and he'd proven her love for her again. No way for me to compete with a frickin' horse. I'd kind of resolved at that point that it was really over. The way she looked at him – she'd never leave. Something about seeing them together at Katherine's house finally did it for me. Cami could be happy. She'd finally get what she deserved. I swore I'd be happy for her no matter what happened. In Omaha, I thought I'd said my last goodbye to her, that I would finally move on with my life.

But, Jessica? She was into me. I felt it. Why was I suddenly only a diversion? Ben made some stupid comment about her hair yesterday, and the next thing I knew she went into town to get hair color, and now she's a brunette. I thought she'd done it so she wouldn't stick out around all the others, but maybe she had a thing for Ben. Centaurs were jerks. Centaurides were even worse.

The jungle stretched out for miles. I wanted as far away from the ocean, the house, and all these jerks as I could get. Behind the main house was a stump with a machete waiting for whatever animal would be butchered for the next meal. I stalked straight past a few people on the porch of the main house. I couldn't say who it was because no way was I going to make eye contact with anyone. I was done with the whole lot of them.

A diversion? That's as bad as being a television show – something to keep her attention until someone better came along.

My hand wrapped itself around the worn leather handle of the machete. Bracing my foot against the stump, I pulled hard and the knife broke free. The jungle lay directly in front of me. Sweat already formed on my chest and ran down my hairline. My bare feet felt the first pangs of pain as I stepped onto some plant that sliced it with papercut-like precision. The main house was still in sight, but I refused to go in for shoes.

The machete slashed through the plants hanging in front of me, and they fell to the ground at my side. My arm slashed again and more fell. I kept walking. My heart pumped so loud in my chest, I could hear the sound in my ears. Birds laughed at me overhead.

A diversion? A toddler's toy – shiny and fun in the beginning only to be tossed aside when a new toy presents itself.

Pressing on into the shadow of the jungle, the machete continued ripping through the plants that tried to block my way. Pops' warning echoed in my head, "Stay away from my world." Hatred began seeping through my blood stream. I stepped on another plant with razors for leaves. Blocking out the pain, I refused to stop, refused to turn around, refused to be a diversion.

I don't know how long I continued slashing. When I finally stopped, my arms were stiff and shaking. I allowed the machete to drop to the ground, just missing my big toe. My body was soaked in a combination of sweat and humidity. Blood flowed freely from my feet and showed no signs of stopping. My body crumpled to the ground as I allowed my mind to wander.

There was nothing but jungle in all directions. The path I'd made was barely big enough for me to fit through. My feet throbbed, my arms ached, and my mind was numb. A diversion. Something for entertainment purposes – that was me.

The day I first met Cami came back in living color. I'd been a little scrawny when I first met her in the third grade. There was this boy who had repeated third grade, like twice, so he looked like a fifth grader. He was on the playground and took my kickball. I pretended like I didn't care, but Cami saw what he'd done, walked straight up to him, doubled up her fist, and punched him in the nose. The kid grabbed his nose and let the kickball fall to the ground. Cami picked it up, walked over to me, and asked if I wanted to play.

That's what life was always like with Cami. For years, at least until I was twelve, I always got a new red kickball for my birthday from her. She didn't take crap off of anyone, and she was always sticking up for others – even a scrawny kid she didn't know. I should have kept her from ever going to South Carolina.

Tears threatened to release as I squinted my eyes closed to hold them in place. No way was I going to let either of them get to me like this. No stinkin' way.

My mind wandered to Jessica. The first kiss I stole under the premise of needing Chap Stick. She was out of my league. What was I thinking? I let myself be deluded enough to believe she'd fallen for me, a half-breed.

There was nothing comfortable about the ground or comforting about the sounds screeching from all directions. My energy was gone. My drive was gone. My desire to see another human, Centauride, Centaur or even Lapith was gone. I allowed my eyes to close, hoping when I opened them again, everyone would be gone. The world would spin on without me, and everyone would think I'd blended back into the world, and I wouldn't have to hear another good-bye.

SEVERAL HOURS LATER

Throbbing in my feet awoke me. The heat had diminished, but it was still hot enough to roast a turkey. I leaned up against a tree, with dusk just setting in. The jungle I'd thought was alive before was now something more – awake and alive. Leaves rustled above me from the scurrying of little feet. The howl of creatures in the distance and the sound of insects calling to the predators around me ushered in my first pangs of fear. My mind went to the *Anaconda* movies I had laughed at. Cami and I had watched them all – those nights together in California seemed a lifetime ago.

I pushed away the movie memories with Cami only to be replaced by YouTube videos of men being eaten alive by snakes and unsuspecting adventurers slashed to pieces by wild cats.

My pulse began picking up even as I willed it to slow. The more blood pumping through my heart, the more my feet ached. I awkwardly pulled my foot up to my groin for a closer look. What had I done? Gashes slashed across the surface. I pulled off my shirt and ripped it in two pieces then bound up both feet in the material. I took a deep breath while I tried to carry my weight – the pain was too much, and I collapsed back to the jungle floor.

My throat was dry. When was the last time I'd drunk water? Breakfast? No, last night before bed. The sky told me it had been nearly twenty-four hours. I hated the idea, but I couldn't get back on my own and needed help, "Hello?! Can anybody hear me?"

More rustling in the trees above. "Hello?! Anybody. Help!"

I couldn't walk, but I could see the general direction I had barreled through. Careful where I put my hands and knees, I began crawling back toward the house.

CHAPTER 26

Brent – Jungle Outside of Cancún, Mexico

Mom, Jessica, Cami, Hallenjah, Hannah and Lacey had all tried to find Daniel remotely. None had ever purposely tracked a human or a Centaur before. Collectively they believed he was in the jungle, but none could pinpoint his location. Jessica started freaking out because she said his thoughts were usually so loud that he must be unconscious for them to be so silent. They had tried for almost an hour before we broke ourselves into two person search parties.

This was it. I couldn't put it off any longer. My heart swelled when Katherine partnered up with me to look for Daniel. Security cameras showed him going into the jungle hours ago in late morning. No one knew why, but I had a suspicion he couldn't bear the thought of telling Cami goodbye.

Jessica started freaking out around noon and took Cami into the trees to start looking for him. When they came back two hours later with nothing, everyone partnered up to go look for him.

Katherine's hair was pulled up on top of her head. She walked behind me through the dense trees, and I found myself turning around to make sure I hadn't lost her. Her steps were so light, I couldn't even hear her most of the time. Each time my eyes locked on hers, she gave me a half grin. What would I give for a full smile? Almost anything. That was something I noticed more than anything – Katherine almost never smiled. It was as if she had this armor shell around her, and she wouldn't let anyone in.

The story she had told me about her friend Gayle had rocked me to my core. I'd never lost anyone close to me in a Blood Debt, but seeing one paid when I was young soured me on the process. The day I'd seen the Blood Debt paid, I couldn't look at the fallen Centauride, bleeding on the ground. My eyes were fixed on her friend. Her friend was a girl of the same age who wailed beside her.

Katherine had that same look that night in the tunnel. The helplessness, the hurt, the anger – she was distraught at reliving what had happened. All the emotions of losing her friend were rolled into eyes brimming with tears. I had no choice but to comfort her, to hold her and to promise to help her with anything she needed. I'd been too small to help the grieving Centauride as a child. I could offer no comfort at the time, and could only look on, soaking in the girl's pain through my eyes.

I knew better than to touch a woman when I was betrothed, but I couldn't help it. There was something about Katherine that moved me. It wasn't her sweet demeanor; in truth, she'd been abrasive to us from the first moment we met her. Maybe it was her vulnerability in the tunnel. I couldn't say.

Her voice nearly startled me. "I'm sorry Bianca couldn't persuade Cassie ta come down."

Was she serious? I didn't even want Bianca to make the call. I shrugged my shoulders, "Probably for the best."

She paused before answering, as if she were trying to find the right words. "I'm glad she hasn't changed her mind." Her green eyes were sincere. She couldn't feel that way, could she? The kiss in the hotel, didn't she remember? All those times our hands had brushed each other, the pull I felt to her, didn't she feel it, too?

"Yeah."

Katherine stammered, "She told. . . she said. . . she was worried she might draw more attention to you and yer family if she came here."

"Cassie's smart. She's probably right." Turning, I couldn't keep up the facade. I couldn't talk about Cassie that way. She was a great Centauride. She'd chosen me. Me. But I didn't want her, not anymore – maybe not ever. Since I met Katherine, my world had been upside down, my priorities renumbered, but did she feel the same?

Drake was the only Centaur I'd ever known to back out of a betrothal – my circumstances were nothing like his. What would my family think? Dad told us from the time we were children we had to carry on the blood line: it was our responsibility. Would he ever forgive me if I backed out? What would my brothers think if I traded my family's future for my own desires? Maybe they'd treat Katherine like she was a human and shun us. Worse yet, would Katherine think I only wanted her so she could protect my family?

Lost in thought, I realized I couldn't hear Katherine. Turning around, she was still two steps behind me, head down, watching the ground below her. When I turned back toward the front, my head slammed into a low hanging branch. Stumbling backwards from the jolt, I crashed into Katherine, sprawling us both on the ground.

I scrambled off of her as my vision blurred. Her eyes were wide. I wiped sweat from my forehead; the pain was sharp as sweat continued to pour into my hand. The sweat streamed into my eyes, blinding me, as Katherine's voice spoke softly, "Ease back, Brent. I've gotcha." Her hand laced behind my head as she pressed a cloth onto my forehead.

Her cloth wiped my face, and once she got the thick sweat off of me, my vision came back into focus. As she held the cloth away, the crimson surprised me. It wasn't sweat; the cloth was full of blood. Her voice echoed through the jungle, "Hey, we need some help over here! Brent's hurt!" Blood from the wound on my head poured down my face, scarcely slowing from the cloth pressed against it.

Her voice was soft by my ear. "It's okay. You're gonna be okay. Just relax."

She sat on the ground beside me. Her hand pushed so hard on my forehead, I worried my skull would crush. I loosened her grip on the towel, "Easy. You're not laying tile."

"Not the time for jokes."

My back rested up against a tree as my legs lay straight out in front of me. Katherine sat on the ground beside me, her legs crossed under her. One arm held the cloth to my head, as the other stretched across my body, braced against the ground on my other side. Cloth? What cloth did she have?

I took a closer look. She had pulled her shirt off and sat next to me in her bikini top, forcing my blood to stay in my body. Her porcelain skin contrasted with her green eyes and red hair – this was it. This was my moment. If I didn't take it now, it would never happen.

"Katherine, don't go."

"I'm right here. I'm not goin' anywhere. Everyone's already searching the jungle. They'll find us."

My hand rose to her arm balancing her weight, "No. Don't go."

Katherine's eyes met mine and her understanding of my plea shone through. "You don't know what yer saying."

My hand let go of her arm and rested on her abdomen, the warm flesh intoxicating my senses. "I know exactly what I'm saying. I don't want this life without you."

Dismissively she answered, "I'm a Lapith."

"Second. You're a Lapith Second."

Tentatively she asked, "What am I first?"

"Mine."

She laughed, trying to make a joke of my feelings. "Ya just hit your head. I won't hold you ta anything ya say now."

I wrenched her hand free of my forehead, grabbed her face in both my hands and pulled her lips to mine. She struggled against my lips at first, but I wouldn't let go. I couldn't let go. I kissed her as if my life. . . my existence, depended on it. The warm rusty taste of blood streamed onto our lips.

Katherine yanked away, picked up the cloth that had dropped and pressed it back against my forehead. She wrenched my t-shirt up with her other hand to sop up the blood on our faces.

A long silence hung between us. Would she reject me? Would she decide I wasn't good enough? How could I convince her? Katherine refused to make eye contact with me.

No words came. She'd been quiet for so long that my stomach cinched itself in a knot. Katherine changed hands, applying pressure to my bandage. She whispered, "Have ya heard the story of Lila and Rupert?"

Her voice was so quiet I barely understood the words. "Rupert is my ancestor, the original sire of the Lost Herd. I've not heard of Lila."

"Let me tell ya the other half of the story." Katherine spoke for a long time, long enough that the wound on my head had stopped bleeding. She knew more about our history than I did. When she was done telling the story of Lila and Rupert, more silence hung between us. The day in the tunnel, the spark I felt – it was a chemical reaction. Katherine thought I would see it as trickery or a defense mechanism for Lapiths, which wasn't how I felt at all.

"Interesting. But what does that have to do with you staying with me?"

"Don't cha see? You're not making the best decision. You're throwing away your future for nothing."

Her eyes finally looked into mine, and I was their prisoner. My eyes refused to drop her gaze as my mouth formed the words, "You are my future. The one I want."

"Ya only want it because of the spark."

"No. I only want it because I can't sleep without you invading my dreams. I can't breathe unless I'm close enough to smell your perfume. I can't function if you are out of my sight."

"Yer words mean nothing. They are the sounds of a man trapped under a spell he can't escape."

I pulled her to me and spoke into her ear. "A prisoner dreams of freedom. Life without you is a slow death sentence for me. If you refuse me, I'll die alone. My betrothal is over whether you choose to stay with me or not." Her body went stiff in my arms as my words soaked in.

Unconvinced, her voice broke, "You would break your betrothal even if I leave?"

"I can't help it. Love only happens once. Trying to convince my heart to care for another after it has experienced you would be as useful as teaching a blind dog to hunt. He'd keep searching for something just out of his reach and would be clumsy enough to get himself killed."

"If I take off, you become a blind hunting dog?"

"If you leave, I'll be an empty Centaur."

Katherine brought her face just inches from mine. "If there's one thing I can't stand, it's an empty Centaur." Her lips closed the distance with mine, and I knew I'd never part from her again. The spark I'd felt before ignited. I leaned into her, easing her back to the ground and pressing my weight against her. I heard her breath against my ear and her heart beating against my chest – I would never want another.

Hours passed as the night fully engulfed us. We started back the way we had come. Surprisingly, we didn't pass any of the others looking for Daniel, and none had stumbled upon us. The jungle was alive with sounds. She walked on my right, remaining vigilant and mindful of low hanging branches or thick brush in our way. Twice she stopped to point out roots emerging from the ground for me to avoid.

My injury had to look worse than it felt. As fast as I healed, there was little pain at all now, and happiness filled my heart, my body conscious of her every touch.

A shrill voice sounded in front of us, "Daniel?! Is that you?"

Katherine called back, "No, Jess. It's Brent and me. No sign of 'im?"

Jessica was standing some ten feet in front of us, accompanied by a human with an assault rifle. She sounded defeated, "No. It's as if he vanished. You don't think he went back to the states, do you?"

I couldn't figure Daniel out. He was as carefree a spirit as I had ever known, and I wouldn't put it past him. From what little time I'd spent with him, I couldn't imagine he would leave without saying good-bye. Maybe good-byes weren't his thing.

Katherine, clearly full of anger at the suggestion, answered, "If he did, I'll make him wish he were never born." Her voice was laced with enough malice that I believed her. "We need to get Brent to a doctor. He's going to need stitches."

"Maybe we can get a two-for-one rate." We froze looking in all directions. That was Daniel's voice, I was sure of it.

Jessica shouted, "Daniel? Daniel, is that you?"

"It ain't the stinkin' Easter Bunny."

CHAPTER 27

Daniel – Jungle Outside of Cancún, Mexico

Jessica shrieked, "Where are you?" My heart skipped at the sound of her. It didn't matter how angry I was – she was here. She was looking for me. She hadn't left.

I tried to answer, but my words wouldn't come out. I felt like I would lose consciousness again, succumb to the darkness. I took the machete still clutched in my hand and started tapping it against the trunk of a tree. Tap. . . tap. . . tap.

Loud and shrill I heard her again, "Daniel!" She sounded close. Foliage gave way under feet running away from me. I kept tapping, less intense than before, but still loud enough to scare away every animal in an eight mile radius. Her voice echoed off to my left, "Daniel. Daniel, we're here!"

I was face planted into the ground. Strong hands rolled me over onto my back then lifted my head. Water was poured into my mouth. I looked up expecting to see Jessica's angelic face staring back at me. I spit out the water when my eyes focused on a man with bronze-skin, dark hair, and a stubbly chin. "Drink, Señor."

I did as I was told. I had finished several small gulps when the man eased my head back onto the ground. I was sure I'd heard Jessica's voice. Was my mind playing tricks on me? Maybe it wasn't her at all. Maybe subconsciously I knew she wouldn't come, so my mind tricked me into hearing the man's voice sound like Jessica's.

The man took my hand and caressed it. I wrenched it away unable to make sense of his action. His accent was replaced by Jessica's voice. "You're going to be fine. I promise." I looked to my side and there she sat. I thought it was Jessica but couldn't be sure. Was my mind clear enough to tell fantasy from reality?

"He went to get a stretcher to get you back to the house. Can you drink some more water?"

Her voice was so beautiful. She kept caressing my hand again. Then her words from earlier came to my mind. "*He's just a diversion.*"

Jessica's grip on my hand tightened. Her voice sounded sad, "Is that what this is about? That's why you ran off into the jungle?"

Confused at first, I'd forgotten she could read my thoughts. I tried to form words, but nothing would come out. She lifted my head and put water to my lips again. She scooted around so my head was cradled in her lap. I looked up into her beautiful face. Tears were streaming down her cheeks. Jessica's voice was soft, almost remorseful. "Drink."

Why was she crying? Her words played in my mind again: "*He's just a diversion.*"

She answered my thoughts, "My life is too complicated for you, Daniel."

Her words hung in the air. The stab of her words went straight to my heart. I closed my eyes, so I couldn't see her mouth form the words. If I could have shut my ears, I would have.

"I can't stay on the run forever. My family has got to be furious with me by now. When they find me, and they will – my freedom, my decisions, they won't be mine any longer."

I couldn't look at her. I wouldn't. I tried to listen to the birds in the trees, hoping for the sound of insects – any noise that would drown out her words. Her hands went to my face, the gentleness of her touch intoxicating. Why did she have to be the one to find me?

"You weren't just a diversion. You were my life preserver. I'm sorry I hurt you."

The moon was up straight overhead and the illumination made it easy to see. Where was the man with the stretcher? I couldn't ignore her words for much longer. I'd never be good enough for her, and I was too dense to see it before. It was out of my control, and there would be nothing I could ever do to change it. I'm just a half-breed.

"Don't call yourself that."

Dammit. I wish I could keep her out of my head. I'd felt inadequate my whole life. First I was the son my father never wanted, the embarrassment he refused to introduce to his family. Then Cami: good enough to share every event of her life, but not good enough to love me back. Now Jessica: her life was too complicated, and I was too simple.

Her hands stroked my cheek, "If I chose you, your life would be in danger. I can't stand the thought of a world without you, even if it means I can't have you."

A lump formed in my throat. I wouldn't look at her. Was she still reading my thoughts? "*Stop it! Get out of my head.*" Anger spread from my heart, racing through my blood stream and found its way to every remote piece of my body. Words wouldn't form on my lips, so I shouted my thoughts to her, "*Get out of my head. Go away.*"

A muffled sob escaped her. "You think I like it this way? You think I don't wish every day that I could be like you? Don't kid yourself."

Her tears dripped on my face, the salty tears streaming to my mouth. I looked up and her beauty had transformed before my eyes. She was no longer the beautiful, confident, strong woman I'd met at her bar in South Dakota. Her eyes were bloodshot, her face flushed with sadness and soaked like she'd just come out of a rainstorm. The lusciousness of her lips was gone as she pressed them together hard.

Her chuckle was wrapped with a muffled sob, and she wiped the moisture from her face with both hands. "Am I that hideous?"

I nodded. I never lied, not to anyone. Normally I always found a way not to be mean, but she'd hurt me so badly I didn't care. I hoped telling her she was hideous hurt. I hoped it hurt as bad as finding out I was merely a diversion.

"What do you want from me? You knew when we started I couldn't choose you. You told me 'no strings'."

I cleared my throat and motioned for more water. She brought it to my lips, and I took in a large mouthful, drinking it slowly, letting it cool my throat on the way down. My throat was still coarse, and I wasn't sure if the words would even come out. A gravelly whisper answered, "Wasn't looking to be chosen. Looking for someone to care about. Someone who'd care for me."

"I do care about you. Don't you see? I care about you enough to let you live your life. I'm going back to South Dakota. Back to my family. Not because I want that life, but because that's the only way I know my brothers will never find you."

It hurt too much to talk. Her words didn't make sense. Not really. Why would she go back there after we'd gone to such lengths to help her escape?

"Centaurides don't run away, Daniel. Those who try never stay away for long. Their families find them and bring them back. After this stunt we pulled, I am sure my parents have already promised me to a Centaur who will keep me in line." Her body shivered as she spoke.

"So stay hidden. Stay with me. I'll protect you."

"It's not that easy. The only reason I've not been found yet is because I've been with Katherine. I can't ask her to stay with me for the rest of my life."

"She'd do it."

"I know she would, but it's not fair to her. It's not her burden to bear."

I couldn't help but look into her eyes. My mind wouldn't respond. Katherine would stay with Jessica forever. I'd heard her in the tunnel. I knew how much she cared about Jessica.

She'd finally gotten her tears under control and gave me a brave smile. Jessica's voice shook as she spoke, "We've got a few more days. I want to make the most of my time left with you. It'll be my own guilty pleasure I carry in my heart after I return to the life waiting for me."

I couldn't respond – not in words or thoughts. She was serious. She would leave me behind and never look back.

Jessica's lips whispered softly against mine, "For me? Give me a few more days of joy before I go home."

I reached my hands up and pulled her lips hard into mine. My sorrow, my anger, my pain evaporated in that moment, and the longing we two shared enveloped us both. Our lips remained locked for seconds, minutes, maybe an hour. Time lost its meaning – replaced with the knowledge that she was mine. She was convinced we couldn't have forever, but this would be my chance, the only chance I had left to convince her to stay with me. I'd convince her a life on the run with me was better than a day in her old life.

When the humans arrived with a stretcher, I was carried out of the jungle. Jessica walked beside me, her hands holding both of mine, the bright moon in the sky looked like it rested on her shoulder. It didn't matter how exhausted I felt, I refused to let my eyes close. They stayed fixed on her the whole way back to the house.

A doctor was waiting for us when we returned. The wounds on my feet were cleaned and, thankfully, the doctor spoke English. "You'll need to give them time to heal. At least two weeks. The next time you decide to go for a stroll through our jungle, put some shoes on." He snapped his little leather bag closed and walked away without another word. The salve he had put on my feet stung initially, but the relief was like my first drink of cold water – cool and satisfying.

The doctor left and everyone came by to check on me. Beau and Lacey were funny: both decided it was my own way of making sure everyone could have a little more time enjoying the sun and sand. No one was sure who was going to Africa and who was staying with me.

Drake stopped by to tell me they'd be leaving for Centauride in the morning. I'd known their departure was eminent and hoped it wouldn't be the last time I'd see them. I understood the sacrifice he'd made and was prepared to make for Cami. The same old pangs of jealousy stretched from my heart, but for the first time I think he was starting to grow on me.

I didn't know Hannah and Bruce very well, but Hannah brought me a basket of fruit and left it on the bedside table. Bruce said the two of them had half a chance in the daily volleyball tournaments now that I was out of it. When he smiled, he looked just like Beau.

Ben and Bart stopped by. I'd said less than three words to either of them. The only thing I knew about them was they were Cami's brothers. Ben took a seat on the bed next to me while Bart kept his distance a few feet away. Ben leaned in and pulled out a piece of wood and a small knife, "There aren't a lot of options when you're stuck in bed for a couple weeks. I know, I broke my leg when I was a kid – I was laid up for three whole days. Television stinks here. Thought you might need something to keep your mind occupied." I didn't know what to say to either of them and wondered if Cami had forced all of her brothers to say hello.

I'd kept expecting Brent to pop in until I remembered Jessica told me he had banged up his head pretty bad and was holed up in the room next door.

When the last set of visitors appeared at my door, it was all too obvious that Cami had forcibly sent them to see me. It was Gretchen and Cami's dad, Will. I couldn't stand the guy and knew his feelings for me were mutual. His words were stiff, but not overtly hateful, "I've contacted your father through secure channels. He knows you're with my family. He sends his wish for a speedy recovery."

I didn't know what to say. Pops and I had had a big time falling out, and he was the last person I expected to hear from. As I turned over Will's words, I was surprised that I was grateful that Will had contacted him. For all he knew, I'd fallen off a cliff weeks ago. I still had issues with Pops, but maybe if he knew another Centaur family thought I was okay, there'd be a chance he wouldn't be ashamed of me in the future.

I was losing my battle to stay awake. My eyelids were getting heavy when I saw her at the door. I forced myself to sit up a little straighter.

"I'm leaving in the morning, but I wanted to say goodbye. Can I get you anything?"

My eyes went to the ring on her left hand. Just a few weeks ago I would have done anything for her. Who was I kidding? I'd still do anything for her. I understood my own feelings for her much better though. "No. I'm all set."

Cami sat down beside me on the bed. She was different. Maybe going through so much had aged her, matured her or something. She'd always been tough, never wavering in any choice she made. I used to be her voice of reason, talking her off a ledge when she was ready to jump and do something really stupid. Since her mom died, I'd become less important to her, maybe because her life was so full now – I no longer needed to be such a big part of it.

"I think it's stupid for you and Drake to go to the Centaur Council."

"I know you do. Some things are bigger than the sum of their parts."

She was getting philosophical with geometry now? "You remember when you were a kid and your mom couldn't afford to get you new shoes, so she cut the toes out of your sneakers?"

"How could I forget? Paris made fun of me all day."

Paris had been a mean girl in our class. I always thought she was that way because she was jealous of Cami. Paris was my girlfriend in eighth grade. I didn't like her – I never had. I only did it to get back at her for all the mean stuff she was always doing to Cami. I dumped her in front of all of her friends in the lunchroom, then walked around the school for the next week holding Cami's hand.

"I remember you stole money from Pops' wallet to buy me a pair of shoes, too."

"I never told you, and I'm not sure why I'm telling you now – I didn't take money from Pops' wallet."

"Oh?"

"Yeah. He gave it to me. That was the day he told me I'd never be good enough for you." I took her hand. All those times I wanted to tell her I'd always be there for her, but could never get the words out, it was Pops' voice screaming in my head. I used to think, one day I'd prove him wrong.

She shook her head, "Pops is an idiot."

"No. He was right. You were supposed to have a bigger life than I could ever give you. He knew it. I just hate that it's taken me this long to see it."

"You'll always be my best friend."

"Let Drake have that title, too. I'll be here if you ever need me. But any guy who would become a Clydesdale to protect you – well . . . he's earned it."

"This isn't good-bye, Daniel. We're going to be okay. We're all going to be okay."

I brought her hand to my lips. "I know. There's one thing I want to give you – to remember me by." I reached into the drawer by my bed. When we'd flown in I saw them in the window of a store and bought them - a white pair of high-top converse sneakers.

She laughed as I handed them over. Man, I was going to miss hearing that laugh. I missed it already.

"I'll think of you every time I wear them!" Cami leaned in and kissed my forehead. She was letting me go. I hated it, but my heart was finally letting her go, too. I wouldn't trade one day that we'd spent together for anything. Pops was right. She had a bigger life waiting for her.

Cami crossed my room to the doorway, flicked off the light switch and walked away. I lay there in the dark at peace. She loved me as much as I loved her. Deep down I always knew she did – it was me who couldn't see. The love of a friend who would do anything for you is just as important as a lover who will become anything you need him to be. I heard her footsteps walking down the hallway, down the steps and through the front door before I whispered, "Goodbye, Cami."

The meds the doctor had given me were starting to kick in. It was a struggle to keep my eyes open in the dark room. Just before I started to lose consciousness, a freshly-showered, warm body slid in next to mine in the bed. Jessica lay beside me, warm and inviting, just as sleep won the battle.

CHAPTER 28

Drake – Beach Outside of Cancún, Mexico

I took her hand in mine. It was a simple gesture, but her touch had a calming effect on me. Tomorrow we would leave for Centauride. I couldn't help but feel grateful to Bianca and Gage for all they had done for us. My parents had already headed back to the states; surprisingly, it was painful to let them go. I'd spent more time with them the last few days, at least more meaningful time, than I had my entire life up until now.

At my age, I shouldn't need my parents' approval, but it warmed me to receive it anyway. I'd expected Mom to be against our plan, but when I embraced her to bid her farewell, she offered no discouraging words. She only said one word, "Good-bye."

It had nearly brought me to my knees. She was the reason Cami and I had a future, and I had fully expected her to offer up a secluded hideaway or to discourage our trip. She did neither.

If the lack of words from Mom surprised me, it was nothing compared to Dad's goodbye. Our relationship my whole life had been strained. It didn't matter how hard I had tried, what awards I'd won, or any action I had taken, it was never good enough. Mom sat in the taxi while Dad stood there staring at me. He held out his hand. My eyes looked at it, an offer of respect, a salutation of esteem – I'd finally met his expectations, maybe for the first time in my life.

My hand reluctantly took his as his grip wound tight around mine. He looked at Cami standing to my right, then back at me. His voice sounded full of regret, "I've never been more proud, son." His other arm reached over my shoulder and pulled me into an embrace. I stiffened on reflex – Dad didn't hug. Dad let go of me and turned away so I couldn't see his expression. He leaned over to give Cami a kiss on the cheek, turned his back on both of us, and joined my mother in the taxi.

Neither looked at either of us as the taxi drove away. I couldn't find my legs. Both my parents had given us permission to fail. Neither believed we would make it out of Centauride alive, but both gave me the only thing they could – they were at peace with my decision.

The surf pounded in front of me as the good-bye played over and over in my mind. Cami must have known I needed my solitude, and she stayed wordlessly by my side – no words of encouragement or second thoughts about what lay before us. If we died, we'd die together – our last act on this earth trying to save the Lost Herd and the family we had both come to love.

CHAPTER 29

Quinton – Council Enforcer,
Basement of Main House near Cancún, Mexico

We'd missed our opportunity. The whole house was emptying out. They intended to leave. The banging of suitcases, the voices wanting some last minute pictures, and the inevitable questions of, "Did you see my . . ." echoed just outside our walls. Last night would have been our best opportunity for escape. One had been lost in the jungle and most of the house was empty looking for him. No wonder the Lost Herd had stayed hidden for so long. They couldn't navigate an estate's back yard without a search party.

My eyes roamed over my men lying on the cluttered furniture strewn throughout the basement. We were the elite, the protectors of the Centaur Council. Shame for having been captured resonated with us all. None of us understood why we were still alive. We were on a mission – it was kill or be killed. Taking prisoners wasn't an option, so we had no plan in place for becoming prisoners ourselves.

To be dependent on the benevolence of your enemy is a degrading position. For that enemy to show any redeeming qualities did nothing but diminish the good order and discipline my team shared.

The events of that night replayed in my head. I had her in my grasp, squeezing the life out of her just as I had vowed I would to the Chairman. Zandra had promised me I could be a Captain if I returned successful. One minute I was sure I'd be in the Captain's uniform by the following day, the next minute I was locked up in the basement like a mutt.

I still couldn't understand how it had happened. Had someone followed me from the beach? Who would dare interfere with an enforcer carrying out the will of the Chairman? Worse yet, why were these Centaurs so defiant in staying here? Were they too dense to understand more of us would come?

We'd been down here for days. I wondered where the reinforcements were. I had phoned my commander right before the raid. He had our last known location and should have been here the next day when we didn't check in. The first night we rested and healed, expecting our brothers to open the door and set us free by morning.

When the door opened the following morning, I recognized the Centaur immediately: Gage Richardson. He had no ties to the Lost Herd, and initially I'd believed him to be one of our rescuers. Gage was one of Zeus's Centaurs. He came from excellent stock.

Gage had been identified as an officer recruit for our ranks. He couldn't possibly understand the life he was giving up by aiding the Lost Herd. The invitation had already been sent – it waited for him at his home in South Carolina. What would he think when he arrived home to find out he'd been invited into the enforcer ranks? There is no greater honor to represent one's family than as an enforcer protecting the Council.

Selection had been done in secret. I was the only one among my team to know he'd been invited. If I told him in front of my men, I couldn't be sure what their reaction would be. His selection to join our ranks would not go over well as they would view him as a traitor. If I could quietly tip him off, would he set us free? He would have to; Gage would have no other choice. His presence alone, here, with *them,* brought shame upon his family.

The first morning he brought food and water to us, I tried to strike up a conversation, tried to win his trust – which had backfired horribly. He ignored me, provided the food for my men and me, and then left without a word, locking the door behind him. My men were trained observers; they mistook my actions. Seeing me try to befriend a captor, they began to question my loyalty to the Council. None voiced their concerns to me, but I could see it in their expressions.

That was the only time Gage had entered our room. For every meal a different Lost Herd member brought us food and drink. They must have been on some sort of rotation, and it didn't take long to figure out we were outnumbered. Each time the door opened, I looked quickly into the Centaur's face, and each time I was disappointed not to find Gage Richardson.

By accepting the food, it felt like we were accepting favors from the enemy, but we needed our strength. Our brothers would free us soon, and we couldn't afford to be weak when that happened. I'd ordered my men to eat the food; I watched as their scowls for me grew with each meal.

I couldn't allow them to question my orders. Not here, not anywhere.

My men told me the stories of seeing Drake Nash on the beach. The rumors from South Dakota had not been exaggerated – he was a true Centaur Warrior. Drake Nash was not my target that night; I was to kill Camille Chiron. That was the promise I had made to the Chairman.

I expected her to be hiding, allowing her family to sacrifice themselves for her when we stormed the beach, so I was not at all surprised to find her cowering in the jungle.

At first, when I found her, I couldn't believe my luck. I didn't need to confirm who she was: she looked like a female version of Cameron.

His blood disgusted me as much as his sister's, but I was not permitted to kill him. It didn't make sense that Ms. Zandra would choose him as her successor. They were both of the Lost Herd. Zeus will pass judgment, and my only hope is that he is merciful on those who followed orders like the soldiers we have been trained to be.

I remembered the night the chairman had summoned my squad. The chairman rarely singled out anyone, but she chose me that night. I had just finished my evening physical training regimen when she summoned me. She was deceptively small, but no one doubted her authority. My men and I had been told to report to the Chairman's residence for a special security detail. We had flown immediately to her estate in Florida, offering our lives as protection if required, unaware of what the threat might be.

Rumors had surfaced that she might appoint an enforcer to take her place. Her son, Angelo, was the only remaining relative for her to pass her position onto. My commander told me he believed she had summoned the additional protection in the event Angelo took the news badly. I had met Angelo on several occasions – he could not lead the Council. My commander's theory made sense.

Rumors were running rampant. Heads of families that made up the Council believed they, too, might take over her position. Calling a special session put all potential successors on high alert. After arriving at her estate and reporting for duty, I did not expect her words when she told me, "Cameron is my grandson, my rightful heir."

It was not my place to question the Chairman. I had been trusted with information she had not readily shared with the rest of the Centaurs in the world. She had called a special council meeting where many believed she would name her successor – no one would be expecting a grandson. "Escort him to his quarters and see that he is provided round-the-clock security until we leave for Centauride."

Ms. Zandra's property was already a fortress. There was only one way onto her island in the swamp, but I did as I was told. It was the dirty-blood grandson who let slip why he required protection.

His voice was condescending when he said, "I don't need your protection. I'm just letting you walk me to my room to keep Grandma happy."

"Of course, sir." It was not my place to have an opinion on whether he needed protection. It was merely my position to follow the orders I had been given.

"I mean, people wouldn't really kill me because of who my father is, right?"

Confused I could only answer, "I couldn't say, sir."

"William Strayer. My father is William Strayer. I've spent less than four hours with him my whole life."

Taken aback, I didn't understand how he was the chairman's grandson if his father wasn't Angelo. I'd never heard the name, but sensed this young man felt compelled to talk to me. Part of being a good warrior was knowing when to fight, but it was just as important to know when to listen. "I'm not familiar with his crimes, sir."

"This Lost Herd business is being blown out of proportion then, eh?"

I paused in mid-stride but caught myself so the lad didn't notice. Lost Herd? They were still alive? It couldn't be; they had been extinct generations ago – at the decree of Zeus himself.

When I couldn't formulate a response, he continued, "That's what I thought. If it was such a big deal why aren't his other sons in danger? I met them in South Dakota."

The kid wasn't making sense. Either Angelo or Angela had to be Cameron's parent. Each would only have a set of twins. How could he have brothers? There were never triplets born of the Chiron line. My curiosity was piqued, but I couldn't let on that I was digging for information. "Your brothers, you say? How many brothers do you have?"

"Five. Well, half-brothers. I've got a twin sister, too, but she's still in South Dakota."

A twin sister? Cameron was Angela's son? Only a daughter of Chiron birthed a son and daughter. But Angela had been killed when I was just a boy, or she had gone missing and everyone believed she was murdered. Half-brothers? Was he mistaken? Half-siblings were only something humans had. A Centaur could not have more than one wife. I corrected myself almost as soon as the ridiculous thought occurred – a Centaur who was not subject to Zeus's rules could have more than one wife.

Anger started at slow boil under the surface of my skin. The Chairman ordered me and my men to ignore Zeus's law. It was my duty to murder Cameron. If his words were true, why would she claim him as her grandson? He should already be dead to her. I could kill him now. What would the repercussions be? I couldn't be punished for disobeying Miss Zandra if I was following Zeus's decree.

The stories I had heard about the Chairman must have been true because she appeared directly in front of me as soon as I had decided to end Cameron's life. She waved Cameron into the house as she looked into me with stony resolve. "No harm will come to you for killing his sister or any member of the Lost Herd. You will not lay a hand on Cameron."

"Chairman, it is our duty. We have an oath to Zeus."

"You swore an oath to me, too. Do you remember?"

"Yes, ma'am. I only worry that the Chairman's feelings for this Centaur may be clouding her judgment." I cringed. Questioning a Centauride in her position was the quickest way to a twenty year sentence in a room without windows. I felt my heart rate pick up speed. I awaited her order for me to turn myself in. I should have kept my mouth shut. Dad would be humiliated with me. He had taught me better.

The Chairman answered my thoughts, "Yes, Quinton, your father did bring you up better than that. I trust you will not make the same mistake twice?"

"No, my lady."

"Good. I have a proposition for you. If you are successful in killing Camille Chiron, I will see to it myself that you wear Captain's bars."

The shuffle of a food tray outside the door brought me back to the present. I had failed Zandra. I would not fail her a second time. My stomach grumbled. Food would be delivered soon. Motioning for my men to come closer, I spoke quietly but quickly. "This is it. We are enforcers. We take down the next to walk through the door. We need to get word to the Council. One of us gets out. Understand?"

A resounding, "Yes, sir," answered me as their posture straightened.

"Biggs, you're the fastest among us. When the door opens, you make a run for the stairs. We'll take him by surprise. The rest of us will stay here and take out as many as we're able." My eyes searched the faces of my men for an ounce of fear. There was none.

"The rest of you: we won't be captured again. It's a fight to the death – yours or the traitors'. Understand? We take out this family or we die trying."

CHAPTER 30

Camille – Bungalow Outside of Cancún, Mexico

Our backpacks were packed. I looked around the little house we'd shared for the last five days. A necklace I had made out of seashells we'd collected lay by itself on the coffee table. I picked it up, smoothing my fingers over the little grooves.

Drake's voice echoed through the open window. "Plane's thirty minutes out. You ready?"

I gripped the necklace, as if that action could somehow steady my voice, "Yeah, just finishing up."

No. I wasn't ready. I would never be ready. I didn't fear my grandmother. Zandra was evil and she could only rule out of fear for so long. Others would have to have their doubts. She needed to pass her position on to someone: her only choices were Angelo, Cameron or me.

I didn't know Cameron, and I hated Angelo. Cameron was also part of the Lost Herd, so if she passed her position to him, it would be easier to convince others on the Centaur Council to rally together. Zeus's reason for his death decree was that we were dangerous, we possessed powers other Centaur families didn't. I had first-hand experience of this one – Phineas had ordered his daughter Violet to plant false memories in my head.

It would be much easier to convince the others if this skill had somehow been bred out of our bloodline – but that wasn't the case. I'd never tried to do it myself – truthfully I didn't know if I could. The idea that this was possible had terrible implications for Centaurs in all families. I wouldn't lie to them and tell them it was no longer a possibility, but all of the Lost Herd had been killed except Rupert. The Lost Herd had paid dearly for the mistake of one Centauride. The debt should have been paid in full when all of Rupert's family was killed.

Something Katherine had told me on the beach made me wish I had asked more questions. She said all Lapiths in her family were sworn to protect the Lost Herd. It was Lila's promise to Athena. If I couldn't make the Centaur Council agree to rail against Zeus, how could we contact Lila's family to have them protect mine? Did all of them take this oath as seriously as she did?

Maybe there was still time to assemble a plan B. I grabbed my backpack and slung it over my shoulder. If we were unsuccessful at Centauride, I wanted Katherine to rally her family. Worried for Gage and Bianca, I told myself they had no ties to the Lost Herd; no matter what happened to Drake and me, they'd be set free. When I said my goodbyes to the others, I'd ask Katherine to work out a strategy with Will. He seemed to know who all the members of our family were; between the two of them, they could figure out how to save as many as possible.

My feet were steady on the path to the main house. I would keep my good-byes short and discreetly pull Katherine and Will together. When I emerged from the bungalow's path, the view didn't make sense. Was everyone departing today? I assumed our departures would be staggered.

If Will had several private planes arrive at the same time, wouldn't that look suspicious?

Bianca heard the questions in my head, "*We have company. Gage just turned over the job of watching the enforcers to the security detail we hired. They'll be set free this time tomorrow after we're all gone.*"

"*Company? Shouldn't they wait a day or two before they leave? Won't people at the airport notice multiple planes? Is everyone leaving to get a head start before the enforcers are set free?*"

"*Not company to the airport. Company to Centauride.*"

"*What? No way! They can't come with us. What if the Centaur Council won't listen? They need to be in hiding. All of them.*"

Lacey "overheard" the conversation between Bianca and me. She stepped forward and placed her hand on my arm. "There is no other way, Cami."

Lacey saw the future. She was the one who had alerted Daniel and Beau that I needed their help before Phineas kidnapped me. I trusted her visions, but this was too dangerous for all the others. "There are lots of other ways. There are too many of us. We can't all march into the Centaur Council."

She cleared her throat, looked to Gretchen and Hannah, then back to me. "We married into your family. We have as much to lose as you do. There is strength in numbers. We tried to decide who should accompany you, to give you the best odds. But there was no way any of us wanted to be safely hidden away when you would be fighting for our family."

I looked around the group, collecting my thoughts before I told them no.

Gretchen stepped forward. "I see the future. I am able to see outcomes you can't. If you fail, it's a death sentence for my five sons and the Centaur I've loved for three decades. You need me, and I need you to be successful."

I couldn't argue with Gretchen. She had every reason in the world to hate me, but she had been nothing but kind to me since I stumbled into her life.

Will stood behind Gretchen and wrapped an arm around her. "You can't ask me to stay behind if you and Gretchen could be in danger. I'm sworn to protect her, and it is my doing that has you in the situation you face now." Gretchen leaned back into my father's protective grasp. The worry in her eyes and his love for her shone brightly.

Beau confessed, "Lacey knew what she was marrying into. She did it without reservation. She chose our family over her life – we will both be there to protect you."

Hannah, who I'd spent almost no time with, stood where she was. Her eyes fixed on me, concentrating, almost looking through me. Her gaze made me uncomfortable; I wondered if she was upset that most of the family wanted to accompany Drake and me. My body began to rise, ever so gently being hoisted into the air with invisible hands. Looking below me, I was hovering two feet off the ground – suspended and unable to gain any kind of footing. She smiled widely, "I can protect you in ways the others cannot." My body went from two feet above the sand to being suspended ten feet in the air.

I knew some Centaurides could move objects, I was able to do that myself, but I'd never considered it possible to suspend another Centauride. Hannah was significantly more powerful than I had realized.

I laughed at the thought of an enforcer trying to kill me if he couldn't reach me, sailing just out of his reach. Hannah laughed with me then gently brought me back to my feet. It was the same feeling as the first time I rode a Ferris Wheel, "That was amazing!"

Ben and Bart were off by themselves, but I heard Ben's words in my mind. "*We don't have as much to lose as our brothers do. You have to let us come. We can't sit back while the rest of our family is in danger.*"

I'd spent little time with Ben or Bart but understood their reasoning. I wanted to argue that someone had to remain behind, to help the others if we were unsuccessful. Katherine couldn't read my thoughts but somehow she must have sensed what I was thinking. "I've phoned Mom. She knows what we're doing. She's working out a plan for my family to protect the others now." Her eyes darted to Will, then back to me, "Your dad gave me some names. Mom's going to make contact with others in the Lost Herd today. She'll see that our family keeps Lila's pledge."

I nodded. "So you and Brent are going back to South Dakota then?" I breathed a sigh of relief that at least one of my brothers would be safe.

"No. You are my charge. I go where you go until you no longer need me."

My eyes instinctively went to Brent. His eyes wouldn't meet mine. I didn't want to be responsible for anything happening to either of them, "You don't have to do that, Katherine."

Katherine bit her lip, as if unsure how to say what was on her mind. Her eyes darted to Brent then pulled away to find mine. "I do. More than just Lila's pledge, I'm not ready to leave you," she paused then added, "or Brent." Blush spread brightly on her cheeks. I waited for the collection of gasps from around the group, but none came.

Brent was betrothed to a Centauride I hadn't met. No one had mentioned his plan to back out of the betrothal, or if they had, I hadn't been included. Not that I rated a vote – but I would have been all for it. Katherine looked around at all the eyes watching her and added, "I'll be able to keep you safe, all of you," her eyes rested on Brent.

Will wrung his hands together. His thoughts were hidden from all of us. He made no move toward Brent or Katherine who seemed to purposely avert his eyes. Will's voice sounded hollow, maybe a little disappointed, "This is your choice, son?"

Brent turned toward Will, his voice unsteady, "It is." He shuffled the few feet to Katherine's side. His arm stiffly wrapped itself around Katherine.

Will remained quiet. I didn't know what to expect. If his bloodline was his concern, Bruce and Beau were already married to full-blooded Centaurides. From what I understood, this was better than most families where it was considered lucky if two sons were able to carry on a bloodline. I wanted to come to Katherine and Brent's defense, but I couldn't if I didn't know what Will's issue was. I sensed how Katherine and Brent felt for each other – I had from the first night in the tunnel, and I wasn't convinced it had much to do with her being a Lapith.

Gretchen's soft voice carried out over the breeze. "We only want you to be happy, Brent. If Katherine makes you happy, then we're thrilled for you both."

Drake took my hand, "It's time. The pilots are waiting." He brought my hand to his lips, "We need to go."

I looked around the group. I couldn't argue with any of them. It wasn't just my fight – all of us shared this war. I wondered about Daniel and Jessica. If Katherine came with me, Jessica would be exposed. What would happen to her? If they stayed here, maybe the distance would be too far and her mother wouldn't be able to find her. Daniel liked Jessica, but they had no chance together if she were taken back to South Dakota. Despite Daniel's Centaur blood, he wasn't fully healed from his injuries yesterday, even if he were – he shouldn't be involved.

A scuffle sounded from inside the house. All eyes turned toward the near empty house as a Centaur blur ran past us. Ben and Bart shot after the enforcer who had just escaped. Drake took my arm and pulled me behind him waiting for whoever would emerge from the door next.

The enforcers were free. Their eyes wild. Our next fight wouldn't be in South Africa, it would be right here in our Caribbean paradise. Drake pushed me back as light peppered his skin. Even in the brightness of daylight, he seemed brighter than the sun. Mere seconds passed before he transformed, those few seconds was enough time that one of the enforcers was on his back with a knife against Drake's throat. I concentrated on the blade, using my mind to pull it from the enforcer's hand. The dagger landed at Drake's feet.

Brent ran full-speed toward Drake, leaped into the air and tackled the enforcer clinging to Drake's back. The two struggled on the ground, the enforcer on top getting the better of Brent. I looked in all directions for a weapon I could throw to Brent but came up empty. I lunged forward, grabbed the Centaurs ears and yanked with every ounce of strength I owned. I felt his flesh rip from his head before his wail sounded. That second was all the advantage Brent needed: he squeezed the life out of the Centaur.

Ben and Bart were back and had subdued a stocky enforcer. Another moved in on them after they had bound the first one's hands and feet. The three moved so fast that I was unable to see who had the upper hand. I saw a vine from a tree and launched it toward Bart's feet. Bart had swiped it off the ground and didn't hesitate wrapping it around the enforcer's neck.

It had been the most underwhelming attack I'd ever seen. The enforcers, despite their advanced combat training were outnumbered and quickly subdued. The Centaurs from my family tried to tie them up, much the same as they had the night of my wedding, but something was different this time. The enforcers who were still conscious knew they had no chance and just kept fighting: punching, kicking, throwing sand, bouncing off Centaurs as if they were pin balls.

Each had to be knocked out, and I was saddened when I saw the one Brent had killed leave his body and gallop off to the pasture. I hated being responsible for his death, but I could live with the guilt because no one from my family was joining him. One final enforcer remained standing, fully surrounded by Drake, Will, Brent, Gage, Ben, Bart, Beau and Bruce.

This was it. I knew what I needed to do, this moment was mine. "Stop!!" All eyes looked at me. The final standing enforcer spat blood onto the sand and wiped a cut over his eyebrow with the sleeve of his shirt. "What is your name?" I asked.

The only answer I received was a glare and a second wiping of his brow. I didn't need an answer; I didn't care who he was. "It doesn't matter. My name is Camille. I am the daughter of Chiron and daughter to the Lost Herd. This is my family." I waived my arm gesturing to the Centaurs who surrounded him. "I want you to deliver a message to the Centaur Council, to the heads of all the families, and to the Chairman: we are on our way."

The enforcer's eyes grew larger and he made no effort to stop the blood oozing down his face and off his chin. "We will no longer live in the shadows. We will peacefully take our place among the herds, or we will take our place by force, but know that all Centaurs will unite again – those who stand against us will fall."

I looked at the bodies lying unconscious on the ground. My feet walked confidently toward the enforcer, "Take a good look at these Centaurs. Commit the image of their beaten and bloodied bodies to memory, and then share that image with every Centauride you meet. Let them know this is the fate that awaits their husbands, nephews, uncles, sons and grandsons if they choose to hunt the Lost Herd."

The color in the enforcer's face drained. He was excellent at hiding his thoughts, but I felt his fear. Drake stood closest to the enforcer, standing ready to knock him unconscious with the others. I looked at Drake, a tower of strength prepared to do whatever I asked of him. I smiled, "Let him go free. He has a message to deliver."

FROM THE AUTHOR

I hope you enjoyed *Centaur Rivalry*! I would love for you to write a review on Amazon. It doesn't have to be long, just let others know what you thought of the story. Here is the link: www.amazon.com/review/create-review?ie=UTF8&asin=B00CKU148K

I am an independent author, which means I do not have an agent, a publicist, or a publishing company backing me up. I DEPEND on word-of-mouth advertising. If you enjoyed *Centaur Rivalry*, it would mean the world to me for you to recommend it to a friend (or ten friends!). If you recommend it to someone who tells you they do not have time to read, let them know it is also available as an audiobook!

If you would like to chat with me, here are the best places to find me:

Amazon author page: www.amazon.com/author/nancystraight

Facebook: www.facebook.com/nancystraight.author

My blog: www.nancystraight.com

Twitter: www.twitter.com/NancyStraight

Goodreads: www.goodreads.com/NancyStraight

Email: nancystraight@gmail.com

I read and respond to every message I receive. (Sometimes a day or two late, but I do respond to everyone who reaches out to me). I hope to hear from you!

If you wish to receive free promotional items, notification of book signing events, and upcoming book releases, you can join my subscriber's list here: http://eepurl.com/bDtmDL

Happy Reading,

Nancy

ACKNOWLEDGEMENTS

Centaur Rivalry would not have been possible without the support of several incredible people. Linda Brant, my aunt, has painstakingly edited and polished *Centaur Rivalry.*

Rebecca Ufkes, Charles Young, Melissa Balentine, and Christie Rich volunteered to be Beta Readers – their feedback was invaluable.

The beautiful cover was designed by Amber McNemar at eTHINK Graphic Solutions.

I wish there were a way to single out each of the independent authors out there who have helped and inspired me along the way, but a thank-you to each one would be a book in itself. A few that I cannot leave out of this section are Shelly Crane, Rachel Higginson, Charlotte Abel, Amy Bartol, Christie Rich and Shannon Dermott – each one has been an incredible inspiration to me, and I highly recommend all of their books!

Book bloggers are the unsung heroes for independent authors. There have been many that I feel indebted to. Three book bloggers deserve a special place on this page, because each one has been a true advocate for me and someone I consider a dear friend:

Heather at: www.supagurlbooks.blogspot.com/

Maghon at: www.magluvsya03.wordpress.com/

Jessica at: www.justabooklover.blogspot.com/

My husband, Toby, has been supportive of my every adventure. Thanks for all the nights you made dinner and did homework so that I could follow my dream! Alex and Zack, thank you both for all the humor you insert into my every day. There is no luckier Mom on the planet.

I love you all!

www.ingramcontent.com/pod-product-compliance
Lightning Source LLC
Chambersburg PA
CBHW070637310726
48982CB00001B/309
9780692798614